UNSEEN

UNSEEN

MARI JUNGSTEDT

Translated from the Swedish by Tiina Nunnally

ST. MARTIN'S MINOTAUR

NEW YORK

This is a work of fiction. All of the characters, organizations, and events portrayed in this novel are either products of the author's imagination or are used fictitiously.

www.minotaubooks.com

Library of Congress Cataloging-in-Publication Data

Jungstedt, Mari, 1962–
    [Den du inte ser. English]
    Unseen / Mari Jungstedt.—1st St. Martin's Minotaur ed.
        p. cm.
    ISBN-13: 978-0-312-35157-1
    ISBN-10: 0-312-35157-7
    I. Title.

PT9877.2.U64D46 2006
839.73'8—dc22

                                                2006005453

First Edition: September 2006

10 9 8 7 6 5 4 3 2 1

To my mother, Kerstin Jungstedt, who taught me
to see the positive in myself and life

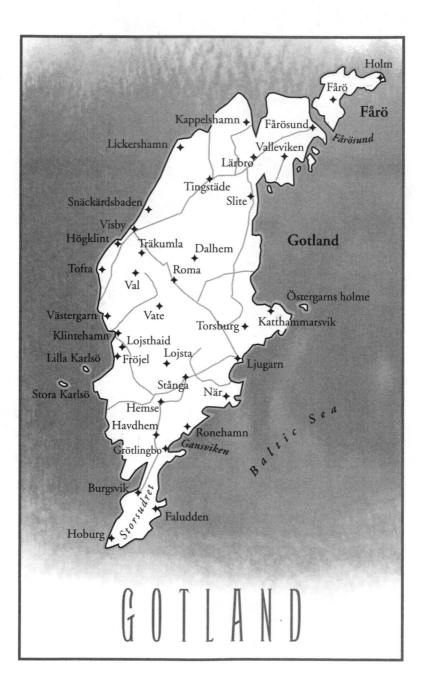

Holm

Fårö

Fårö

Fårösund

Kappelshamn   Fårösund

Lickershamn   Valleviken

Lärbro

Tingstäde

Snäckärdsbaden   Slite

Visby

Högklint   Träkumla   Dalhem   **Gotland**

Tofta   Roma

Val

Östergarns holme

Västergarn   Vate

Torsburg   Katthammarsvik

Klintehamn   Lojsthaid

Lilla Karlsö   Fröjel   Lojsta

Ljugarn

Stora Karlsö   Stånga   När

Hemse

Havdhem

Ronehamn

Grötlingbo   Gansviken

Burgsvik   Baltic Sea

Storsudret

Hoburg   Faludden

GOTLAND

UNSEEN

MONDAY, JUNE 4

The evening was turning out better than expected. Of course she had been a little nervous earlier, because it had been a long time since they had all seen each other, but now her anxiety had eased. After an extra-strong welcome drink, white wine with the appetizer, several glasses of red with the entrée, and port with dessert, everyone at the table was in a lively mood. Kristian told another joke about his boss, and the hoots of laughter echoed off the walls in the old limestone house.

Outside the window, fields of grain were swaying, and the poppies were still a few weeks from blooming in the meadows. Beyond the fields, the sea could be glimpsed in the last glow of twilight.

Over Whitsuntide, Helena and Per had taken a few days off and driven to the cabin on Gotland. They usually got together with Helena's childhood friends on one evening during the holiday. This year, the second day of Whitsun was the only time that was good for everybody, so that's when they had agreed to meet.

It was unusually cold for the time of year, around fifty degrees. The wind was blowing hard, howling and whistling in the treetops.

Helena laughed loudly at Per when he started singing the Gotland song, a satirical ballad she had taught him, about the field mice from the mainland who chased Gotland girls on their summer vacation.

Around the table, they all raised their voices for the chorus. Helena's best girlfriend, Emma, was there with her husband, Olle, along with the neighbors Eva and Rikard, and Beata with her new husband, John Dunmar, who came from the States and was the new member of the group. Kristian was the only one who was still single. A handsome guy but an eternal bachelor, it seemed. To this day he hadn't ever lived with a woman, even though he was thirty-five. Helena had wondered over the years how that could be.

The candles were burning in cast-iron candlesticks in the bay windows; the log fire crackled in the open fireplace. Spencer, Helena's dog, lay on a fur rug on the stone floor, licking his paws. He gave an audible sigh and curled up in the warm glow of the candles and fireplace.

Helena went out to the kitchen to uncork a couple more bottles of wine.

She loved this sparsely furnished cabin, where she had stayed every summer since she was a child. Actually, she and Per needed to be alone. Have some time to talk and be together without cell phones, computers, or alarm clocks, after a stressful and hectic spring. Still, dinner with her old friends wasn't a bad idea, Helena thought, realizing how much she had missed them.

She was awakened from her reverie when somebody ran a finger down her spine.

"How's it going?" Kristian's voice was low and disarming behind her.

"Fine," she replied, turning around with a laugh that was slightly forced.

"How are you doing, anyway, you and Per?" He gave her nose a little pinch. "Does he still make you happy? Or what?"

"Well, sure. If a girl can't have you, she has to take the next best thing," she said, and walked ahead of him out of the kitchen.

"Okay, it's time to dance," piped Beata, who seemed to be in high spirits. She leaped up from the table and started rummaging through the CDs. One of the few modern touches in the cabin was the stereo, an absolute must for Per before he could even imagine spending more than twenty-four hours in the house.

Soon the voice of Håkan Hellström could be heard from the speakers. Per followed Beata's example and began whirling around with her. The others also got to their feet and danced so the floorboards shook.

Afterward nobody could remember when exactly everything went wrong.

Suddenly Per tore Helena out of Kristian's arms, and they disappeared out to the veranda. Inside the house the dancing continued.

After a while the porch door opened. Helena came rushing in with her hands in front of her face and dashed into the bathroom. Her upper lip was bleeding. In an instant the party atmosphere was replaced by a bewildered gloom.

John shut off the music. Silence descended on the room. Except for the barking of the dog, who stood outside the bathroom door and snarled at anyone who came close until Helena opened the door a crack and let him in.

Kristian went out to talk with Per, and the others followed.

The blow came so fast that Kristian didn't have time to react. Per landed a direct hit on the bridge of his nose.

Rikard and John grabbed hold of Per before he had a chance to do any more damage. They dragged him from the veranda and onto the lawn, wet with evening dew. The wind had died down, and a gray mist hovered all around them. Emma and Beata looked after Helena. Eva helped Kristian wipe off the blood and put on an ice pack to reduce the swelling as much as possible. Olle called for cabs. The party was definitely over.

TUESDAY, JUNE 5

When Helena opened her eyes at six thirty the next morning, she had a splitting headache. She always woke up especially early when she was hungover. Now she lay in bed stretched out on her back with her arms pressed tightly to her sides—at attention, but lying down rather than standing. As if during the night she had avoided moving for fear of coming into bodily contact with Per, only four inches away from her in the bed. She looked at him. He was asleep, taking calm, deep breaths and completely wrapped up in the quilt. Only the dark curls of his hair stuck out.

It was quiet in the house, except for Spencer's light snoring from the floor. The dog hadn't noticed yet that she was awake. Helena's body was tense, and she felt sick. She stared up at the white ceiling, and it took a few seconds before she remembered what had happened the night before.

No, she thought, *no, no, no.* Per's jealousy had erupted many times before. It had gotten better over the past year—she had to admit that—but now this setback. Like doing a gigantic belly flop. Pain burned inside her when she realized the extent of what had happened, not only between her and Per but also with her friends. And the party. It had all started out so well.

After dinner they had danced. It was true that Kristian's hand had slid a bit too far down her back when their bodies pressed against each other during a slow song. She had thought about moving his hand away but was too drunk to really care.

Without warning she had been torn out of her trance. Per took a firm grip on her arm and brusquely led her out to the veranda. She was so flabbergasted that she couldn't pull herself together enough to protest. Outside he showered her with accusations. Then she flew into a rage, screaming back at him, spitting and hissing. He shook her. She hit, scratched, and bit him. The whole thing ended with him giving her a resounding slap, and she dashed into the bathroom.

In shock she stood there in front of the mirror, staring at her face, fixed in a silent grimace. She held one hand over her half-open mouth, her fingertips trembling against her upper lip, which was already swollen. He had never hit her before.

Through the door she could hear the others talking. Subdued yet agitated voices. She listened to them calming Per down, calming Kristian down, calling for a taxi.

Emma and Olle stayed till the end. They didn't leave until Per was asleep and Helena was almost asleep, too.

In spite of everything, they were now lying here in the same bed.

As he lay there next to her, she didn't understand how things could have gone so wrong. She wondered what today would be like. How were they going to smooth this over? The jealous quarrel, the actual coming to blows. They were behaving like immature brats who couldn't even manage to drink a little wine and have some fun with their friends. It was hardly worth it. The shame lay like a heavy stone in her belly.

Cautiously she climbed out of bed, afraid that Per would wake up. She slipped out to the bathroom, peed, and inspected her wan face in the mirror. Looked for visible signs of the abuse from the night before, without finding any. The swelling had already gone down. *Maybe he didn't hit me that hard after all,* she thought. As if that were any consolation. She went out to the kitchen and drank half a can of Coke. Then she returned to the bathroom and brushed her teeth.

The floor felt cool under her bare feet as she walked between rooms. Spencer followed her like a shadow. She got dressed and went out into the hall and put on her running shoes, to the dog's undisguised delight.

The morning air washed over her, cold and liberating, when she opened the door.

———

She took the path down toward the sea. Spencer trotted along beside her with tail held high, darting out into the grass alongside the gravel path, pissing here and there. At regular intervals he would turn around and look up at her. The shiny black retriever was a good watchdog and Helena's constant companion. She breathed deeply, filling her lungs, and her eyes teared up from the morning chill.

The instant she climbed over the dune and out onto the beach, she was enveloped in a grayish-white fog. It lay like a carpet of spun sugar all around her. The dog quickly vanished into the silent softness. No horizon was visible. What little she could see of the water was steel gray and almost completely still. It was remarkably quiet. Only a lone seagull screeched far out over the sea. She decided to walk the entire length of the beach and back, even though visibility was poor. *As long as I follow the waterline it should be all right,* she thought.

Her headache began to subside, and she tried to collect her muddled thoughts. After last night's fiasco, she didn't know what to do.

Despite everything, she believed that Per was the one she wanted to live with. She was sure that he loved her. She was going to turn thirty-five next month and knew that he was expecting an answer, a decision. For a long time he had been wanting to set a wedding date, so she could stop taking the pill. Lately, when they made love, he would often say afterward that he wished he had made her pregnant. She felt uncomfortable every time.

Yet she had never felt so secure, so loved. Maybe that was all she could expect; maybe it was time to make up her mind. She hadn't had much luck with her love life in the past. She had never been truly in love and didn't know whether she was this time, either. Maybe she wasn't capable of it.

Helena's thoughts were interrupted by the dog barking. It sounded like a hunting bark, as if he had caught the scent of one of those small rabbits that were everywhere on Gotland.

"Spencer! Come here!" she commanded.

He came trotting obediently over to her with his nose to the ground.

She squatted down to pet him. She tried to look out to sea but could barely make out the water anymore. On clear days you could see from here the outlines of the cliffs in all their detail on both islands, Big and Little Karlsö. That was hard to imagine right now.

Helena shivered. Spring was normally cold on Gotland, but it was unusual for the chilly weather to last into June. The cold, damp air penetrated through one layer after another. She was wearing a T-shirt, a sweatshirt, and a jacket, but it didn't help. She turned around and started heading back the way she had come. *I hope Per's up so we can talk,* she thought.

She was feeling better after the walk, starting to think that maybe everything hadn't been ruined after all. She would call around to her friends today, and soon it would all be forgotten and they could continue on as usual. His jealousy wasn't really so bad. Besides, she was the one who had started clawing and scratching.

When Helena reached their end of the beach, the fog was even thicker. White, white, white, everywhere she turned. She realized that she hadn't seen Spencer in quite a while. All she could see clearly was her sneakers, half sunk into the sand. She called out several times. Waited. He didn't come. How strange.

She took a few steps back, straining to see through the fog.

"Spencer! Here, boy!"

No reaction. Damn dog. This wasn't like him.

Something was wrong. She stopped and listened. All she could hear was the lapping of the waves. A ripple of fear ran down her spine.

Suddenly the silence was broken. A short bark, and then a whimper that died out. Spencer.

What was going on?

She stood utterly still and tried to fight back the panic that was surging in her chest. The fog surrounded her. It was like being in a silent vacuum. She yelled straight out into the fog.

"Spencer! Here, boy!"

Then she sensed a movement behind her and realized that someone was standing very close. She turned around.

"Is anyone there?" she whispered.

There was a relaxed mood inside the regional newsroom in the big headquarters of Swedish National Television. The morning meeting was over.

Reporters were sitting here and there with cups of coffee in front of them. One held a phone to his ear; another stared at his computer screen; a couple were talking in low voices with their heads together. A few cameramen were leafing listlessly through the evening papers, then the morning ones.

Everywhere were stacks of paper, discarded newspapers, half-empty plastic coffee cups, telephones, computers, and baskets full of faxes, files, and folders.

At the news desk, which was the focal point of the newsroom, only the editor, Max Grenfors, could be found this early in the morning.

Nobody knows how good they have it here, he thought as he typed in the day's agenda on the computer. A certain energy and enthusiasm ought to be expected after the long weekend, instead of this dull apathy. It was bad enough that the reporters hadn't come up with any ideas of their own at the morning meeting on this dreary Tuesday, but they had also grumbled about the jobs that needed to be done. Grenfors thought that most reporters lacked the spirit and drive that he himself had possessed as a reporter before he was promoted to the editor's desk.

Max Grenfors had just turned fifty, but he did what he could. By now his hair was salt-and-pepper, but he had it regularly dyed by one of the city's most talented hairdressers. He kept in shape with long, lonely workouts at the company gym. For lunch he preferred cottage cheese or yogurt at his computer instead of high-fat meals in the noisy TV lunchroom with his equally noisy colleagues.

As editor it was his job to decide on the content of the broadcast: which stories to run and how much airtime to give them. He liked to get involved in how a story was shaped, which often annoyed the reporters. That didn't bother him, as long as he had the final say.

Maybe it was the long, cold winter, followed by the wet, windy spring with a chill that never seemed to let up, that had made weariness hover like a musty wool blanket over the newsroom. The summer warmth they were all longing for seemed far away.

Grenfors assigned titles to the stories he was going to air and arranged them in order for the broadcast. The day's top story was the catastrophic finances of the Academic Hospital in Uppsala, followed by the strike at the Österåker Prison, the night's shooting drama in Södertälje, and then Elsa the cat. Two twelve-year-old boys had rescued her from certain death in the recycling room of an apartment building in Alby. A real human interest story, the editor thought contentedly, forgetting his bad mood for a moment. Anything with children acting as heroes, and animals, always drew viewers.

Out of the corner of his eye he noticed the anchorman enter the newsroom. It was time for a run-through and the same old discussion about which guest would be invited to the studio that evening—a discussion that could develop into a dispute, or a royal squabble if he let it.

He discovered the dog first. Erik Andersson, sixty-three years old and living on a disability pension, was from Eksta in the island's interior. He was visiting his sister in Fröjel. He and his sister took long walks by the sea in all kinds of weather, even on a foggy day like this.

Today his sister had decided not to come along. She had a cold and a bad cough and wanted to stay indoors.

Erik had his mind set on a walk. Together they ate a lunch of fish soup and lingonberry bread, which he had baked himself. Afterward he climbed into his rubber boots, pulled on his parka, and went out.

The morning's blanket of fog had lifted. Above the fields and meadows on both sides of the narrow gravel path, it was quite clear. The air felt cold and damp. He straightened his cap and decided to walk down to the water. The gravel made a familiar crunching sound under his feet. The black sheep he passed looked up from their grazing as he walked by. Three crows sat in a row on the old half-rotten gate down by the last patch of woods before the beach. They lifted off in unison with an offended cawing as he approached.

Just as he was about to refasten the rusty latch after him, his eye was caught by something odd at the edge of the ditch. It looked like part of an animal. He went closer to the ditch and bent down to look. It was a paw, and it was bloody. Too big to be from a rabbit. Could it be a fox? No, it was black underneath the blood.

Erik moved his gaze along the bloody trail. A little farther off he saw a big black dog. It was lying on its side with its eyes wide open. Its head was twisted at a funny angle, and its fur was completely drenched in blood. The tail looked strangely thick and shiny in the midst of the butchery. When he got closer he could see that its throat had been cut and the head was almost severed from the rest of the dog's body.

He felt sick and had to sit down on a rock. He was breathing hard, holding his hand to his mouth. His heart was pounding. It was horribly quiet. After a while he got up with an effort and looked around. What had happened here? Erik Andersson had scarcely finished the thought when he caught sight of her. The dead woman lay half covered by pine boughs and branches. She was naked. Her body was covered by big bloody wounds, like stab wounds. Dark locks of hair fell over her forehead, and her lips had lost all color. Her mouth was half open, and when he ventured closer he discovered that a piece of cloth had been stuffed between her lips.

The call came into Visby police headquarters at 1:02 P.M. Thirty-five minutes later, two police cars with sirens screaming pulled into Svea Johansson's yard in Fröjel. It took another five minutes before the medics arrived to take care of the old man, who was rocking back and forth on a chair in the kitchen. His older sister pointed out the wooded area where her brother had made the discovery.

Detective Superintendent Anders Knutas and his colleague Detective Inspector Karin Jacobsson hurried on foot toward the patch of woods. They were followed closely by crime scene technician Erik Sohlman and four other officers with dogs.

On the path, before it reached the beach, lay the slaughtered dog in a ditch. Its throat had been cut, and one front paw was missing. The ground all around was spattered with blood.

Sohlman bent over the dog. "Hacked to death," he observed. "The injuries seem to have been caused by a sharp-edged weapon, presumably an axe."

Karin Jacobsson shuddered. She was a big animal lover.

A short distance away they found the mutilated body of the woman. They studied the corpse in silence. The only sound came from the waves breaking on the beach.

She lay there naked under a tree in the grove. The body was covered with blood, through which patches of skin could be seen, shining white. Deep stab wounds were visible on her neck, breast, and stomach. Her eyes were wide open, her lips dry and cracked. It looked as if she were yawning. A tight feeling of nausea settled in Knutas's stomach. He bent over to look more closely.

The perpetrator had shoved a piece of striped cloth between her lips. It looked like a pair of panties.

Without a word Knutas pulled his cell phone from his inside pocket and called the forensic medicine division in Solna. He needed a medical examiner to fly over from the mainland as quickly as possible.

The first report on the wire service was typed in at 4:07 P.M. Information was scanty.

VISBY (TT)

A woman was found dead on a beach on the west coast of Gotland. According to a statement from the police, she was murdered. The police will not yet say how she was killed. All roads in the vicinity have been blocked off. A man is being interviewed by the police.

It took two minutes before Max Grenfors noticed the message on his screen.

He picked up the telephone and called the duty officer at the Gotland police department. He didn't learn much more, except that the police could confirm that a woman, born in 1966, had been found murdered on the beach near Gustavs, the Baptist summer camp, in Fröjel Parish on the west coast of Gotland. The woman had been identified as a resident of Stockholm. Her boyfriend was being interviewed by the police. The area was being searched with dogs, while the police were busy going door to door in the vicinity, looking for possible witnesses.

At the same moment, the direct line belonging to reporter Johan Berg rang. He was among those who had worked the longest in the newsroom. He had started in television ten years ago, and it was by chance that he became a crime reporter right from the start. On his first day on the job, a prostitute was found murdered at Hammarby Harbor. Johan was the only reporter in the newsroom at the time, so he was given the assignment, and that night it was the top story. Because of that, he had continued as a crime reporter. He still thought it was the most exciting area of journalism.

When the phone rang, he was engrossed in his story about the strike at Österåker Prison, polishing up the wording on his computer screen. The piece was due to be edited soon, and everything had to be ready before he and the editor could start working to put together video footage, the script for the anchorman, and sound bites. Preoccupied, he picked up the phone.

"Johan Berg, Regional News."

"They've found a woman murdered on Gotland," rasped a voice in his ear. "She was butchered, apparently with an axe, and she had a pair of panties stuffed in her mouth. A real lunatic is on the loose."

The man on the phone was one of Johan's best sources, a retired police officer who lived in Nynäshamn. After an operation for throat cancer, he had to breathe through a tube sticking out of his throat.

"What the hell did you say?"

"She was found today on a beach in Fröjel, on the west coast."

"How sure are you about this?" asked Johan, feeling his pulse quicken.

"A hundred percent sure."

"What else do you know?"

"She was originally from Gotland but moved to the mainland a long time ago. To Stockholm. She was just over on the island to spend a few days with her boyfriend. He's being interrogated right now."

"Who found her?"

"Someone who happened to come past. An old fellow they've taken to the hospital. He's probably suffering from shock. That's all I know. You'll have to check it out yourself."

"Thanks. I owe you a couple of beers," said Johan as he got up from his chair and then put down the receiver.

The relaxed mood in the newsroom was replaced by feverish activity. Johan reported what he knew to the editor, who quickly decided that Johan and a cameraman should take the first plane to Gotland. Someone else could put together the Österåker story. Right now it was a matter of getting out there and being first on the scene.

Actually Max Grenfors was obligated to inform the managing editor at the big central desk, who was in charge of the news reports for the whole TV station, but that could wait. *We'll just get a little head start,* he thought as he barked out orders. He moved down the top story on the priority list for the broadcast. Who cared about the finances of the Academic Hospital now?

Johan outlined what he knew to a female colleague, who hastily put together a script for the anchorman based on the existing information. She also prepared a telephone interview with the duty officer at the Visby police department, who was able to confirm that a woman had been found dead and that the police suspected murder.

It took only a few minutes before all the editors from the largest news programs at the state-owned TV station were swarming around the desk in the Regional News office.

"Why are you sending a reporter to Gotland? Is there something special about this murder?" asked the managing editor from the central desk.

Like the others, he had read only the wire report, but he had already heard that Regional News was sending a team to Gotland. Four pairs of eyes were staring inquisitively at Grenfors, who realized he had to tell them that the woman had been viciously attacked, probably with an axe, and that her panties had been stuffed in her mouth.

Since it was a slow news day in the world, all the editors reacted strongly. Finally a story that could save the broadcast! Everyone was aware that this was no ordinary murder, and they all began talking excitedly at once.

After some discussion, the managing editor decided that sending one reporter to Gotland was enough. They agreed that they had enough confidence in Johan Berg to make do with him until more details were known.

Johan was told to take along Peter Bylund, the cameraman he liked working with best. They would catch the plane for Visby that departed at 8:15 P.M.

In the cab on his way home, Johan felt a familiar sense of excitement at being in the middle of a story. The fact that a woman had been grotesquely murdered and all the horror associated with such an event took a backseat to his desire to find out what had happened and then file a report. *It's strange how a person reacts,* he thought as the cab drove across Västerbron and he stared out at the water of Riddarfjärden, bracketed by the city hall and Gamla Stan, the Old Town. *You just have to put aside all the usual human emotions and let your professional role take over.*

He thought back to the night in September 1994 when the passenger ferry *Estonia* sank in the Baltic Sea. In the days following that horrible disaster in which over eight hundred people lost their lives, he had rushed around like a madman in the ferry terminal in Värtan talking to family members, the employees of the Estline ship company, the passengers who had survived, the politicians, and the emergency response teams. He went home only to sleep, and then he was back on the job. While he was in the thick of things, he became familiar with all the stories people told him, but as if from a distance. He shut off his own feelings. The reaction came much later. The first bodies recovered and brought home to Sweden were taken in a procession from Arlanda Airport to Riddarholm Church in Gamla Stan for a memorial service before they were transported to their hometowns. When Johan heard a journalist reporting directly from the church on Radio Stockholm, speaking in a deep and somber voice, he broke down. He collapsed on the floor of his apartment, weeping torrents. It was as if all the impressions he had gathered appeared before him at the same time. He pictured bodies floating around inside the ship, people screaming, passengers getting stuck under tables and shelves that were being tossed around, the panic that erupted on board. He felt as if he would go to pieces. He shuddered at the memory.

Back inside his apartment, Johan realized what a mess the place was. He hadn't had time to take care of all the chores lately.

His one-bedroom apartment on Heleneborgsgatan in Södermalm was on the ground floor. From indoors you couldn't tell that the waters of Riddarfjärden were right outside, since his apartment faced the inner courtyard of the building, but that didn't bother him. He was quite happy with the central location, within walking distance of everything the city had to offer in the way of shops and restaurants. The green island of Långholm was also right at his doorstep, with its paths and big slabs of rock, perfect for sunbathing by the water. There was no better place to live.

At the moment his apartment was not in its best state. Dirty dishes were piled up on the kitchen counter, the laundry basket was overflowing, and several old pizza boxes were scattered around the living room floor. The classic bachelor pad. It smelled stuffy, too. Johan realized that he had half an hour to pack, but he had to clean up the worst of it. The phone rang twice while he was racing around the apartment, washing dishes, airing out the rooms, wiping off the table, throwing out the garbage, watering the flowers, and packing. He didn't bother to pick up the phone.

The answering machine clicked on, and he listened to his mother's voice, and to Vanja's. Even though things had been over between them for more than a month, she refused to give up.

It was going to be great to get away.

Far away from there, a solitary man hurries through the woods. His eyes are wild and fixed on the ground. He's carrying a sack on his back. A black garbage bag. His hair is wet and hanging over his forehead. Now there's no going back. Absolutely not. He's agitated, yet at the same time his body is filled with an inner calm. He's on his way to a specific spot. An explicit goal. Now the sea appears. Good. He's almost there. That's where the boathouse is. Gray and rotting. Marked by harsh weather. Storms and rain. Next to it lies a leaky rowboat. It has a hole in the bottom, which he's going to mend someday. First he has to get rid of this baggage. He fumbles for a long time with the rusty lock. The key hasn't been used in years. Finally it turns, and with a click the lock opens. At first he considers burying the contents of the sack. But why should he do that? No one ever comes here. Besides, he's not completely ready to give up these things. He wants to keep them here. Accessible, so he can come back to look at them. Smell them. In the boathouse there's an old kitchen bench with a compartment under the seat. He opens the seat. Inside are some old newspapers. A phone book. He empties the contents of the sack. Closes the seat. Now he's happy.

Visby police headquarters is located right inside the ancient stone wall surrounding the town. It's an uncommonly ugly building. A long rectangle with light-blue metal siding, it looks more like a fish cannery somewhere in Siberia than a police department in this beautiful medieval city. The building is called "the Blue Mound" by the locals.

Inside one of the interrogation rooms, Per Bergdal was leaning over the table with his face in his hands. The ashtray in front of him was full of cigarette butts, even though he didn't usually smoke. His hair was standing on end, he was unshaven, and he smelled of old, sour wine.

He hadn't seemed very surprised when the police knocked on the door. His girlfriend was missing, after all. They decided at once to bring him in for questioning.

Now he was sitting here, holding a cigarette with trembling fingers. Hungover and miserable. Apparently also in shock.

Although it's actually impossible to say whether that's the case, thought Detective Superintendent Knutas as he sat down on the other side of the table. Regardless, Bergdal's girlfriend had been found murdered, he had no alibi, and he had visible scratches on his neck, arms, and face.

Karin Jacobsson sat down on a chair next to Knutas. Silent but alert.

Bergdal raised his head and looked out the only window in the room. A hard rain was pelting the windowpane. The wind had picked up, and on the other side of Norra Hansegatan, over by the parking lot, sections of the stone wall near Österport could be seen. A red Volvo drove past. For Bergdal, it seemed so far away that it might as well have been on the moon.

Anders Knutas adjusted the tape recorder on the table, cleared his throat, and pressed the record button.

"Interview with Per Bergdal, the boyfriend of murder victim Helena Hillerström," he said in an authoritative voice. "The time is four ten on the fifth of June. The interview is being conducted by Detective Superintendent Anders Knutas, and the witness is Detective Inspector Karin Jacobsson."

He cast a somber look at Bergdal, who was slumped forward, staring down at the table. "When did you discover that Helena was missing?"

"I woke up just before ten. She wasn't in bed. I got up, but she wasn't in the house, either. So I thought she must have gone out with the dog. She usually takes the first walk with Spencer in the morning. I'm a sound sleeper, so I didn't notice when she left."

"What did you do?"

"I lit a fire in the woodstove and made breakfast. Then I sat down and drank my coffee and read yesterday's paper."

"Didn't you wonder where she was?"

"When the eleven o'clock news came on the radio, I started thinking it was strange that she hadn't come back yet. I went out on the porch.

You can see all the way to the water from our house, but today there was a thick fog, so I could see only a few yards. Then I got dressed and went out to look for her. I walked down to the beach and called, but I couldn't find her or Spencer."

"How long did you look for her?"

"I must have been out there at least an hour. Then I thought that maybe she'd returned to the cabin in the meantime, so I hurried back. The house was still empty," he said, and his voice faded out. He hid his face in his hands.

Anders Knutas and Karin Jacobsson waited in silence.

"Are you ready to continue?" asked Knutas.

"I just can't believe she's dead," Bergdal whispered.

"What happened when you got back to the house?"

"It was still empty, so I thought maybe she'd gone to visit some friends of ours nearby. I called them, but she wasn't there, either."

"What are their names?"

"Their last name is Larsson. Eva and Rikard, her husband. Eva's an old friend Helena has known since childhood. They live year-round in a house a short distance from ours."

"Did they have any idea where she might have gone?"

"No."

"Who answered the phone?"

"Eva did."

"Was her husband home, too?"

"No, they own a farm, so I guess he was out working."

Bergdal lit yet another cigarette, coughed, and then took a long drag.

"What did you do next?"

"I lay down on the bed and thought about various places she might have gone. Then it occurred to me that she might have fallen and hurt herself. Maybe she couldn't get up. So I went out looking for her again."

"Where?"

"Down at the beach. The fog had lifted a little. I saw her footsteps in the sand. I also searched in the woods, but I didn't find her. Then I went back home."

His face crumpled. He started crying, quietly, without moving. The tears poured out, mixing with snot, but he didn't notice. Karin didn't really know what to do. She decided not to disturb him. He took a couple of gulps of water and regained his composure.

Knutas continued the interview. "How did you get those marks on your neck?"

"What? Oh, these?" Embarrassed, Bergdal touched his hands to his throat.

"Yes, those. They look like scratches," said Knutas.

"Well, you see, we had a party last night. We had invited some friends over. Helena's friends, actually. We ate dinner and partied and had a good time. Everyone drank a little too much. I have a problem with jealousy. Well, sometimes I get really jealous, and that's what happened last night. One of the guys was coming on to Helena when they were dancing."

"In what way?"

"He was grabbing her, a little too much . . . several times. I was drunk, and it made me see red, to be quite honest. I pulled Helena outdoors in back and told her what I thought of it all. She got mad as hell. I guess she'd drunk too much, too. She screamed and flew at me, and that's when I got these scratch marks."

"Then what happened?"

"I hit her. I gave her a slap, and then she ran into the bathroom and locked the door. I've never hit her before," he assured them, giving Knutas a pleading look. "Then Kristian came out to talk to me. He's the one she was dancing with, and I slugged him, too. He didn't have a chance to strike back, because the others intervened. Then everything calmed down, and they all went home."

"What did you do next?"

"Helena's best friend, Emma, and her husband, Olle, were still there. Olle made sure that I got into bed, and he must have stayed until I fell asleep. I don't remember anything else until I woke up this morning."

"Why didn't you tell us about all this right from the start?"

"I don't know."

"Who was at the party?"

"Mostly Helena's childhood friends. Emma and Olle Winarve, as I mentioned, and our neighbors Eva and Rikard Larsson. Helena has known them for a long time. A friend named Beata and her husband, John, the Dunmars. They've been living in the States, so I've never met them before. And the guy named Kristian, who made me so mad. He's single, and Helena has known him a long time, too. I think they were really into each other for a while."

"What do you mean by 'into each other'?"

"Well, I think they might have slept together a few times. Helena denied it, but I have a feeling I'm right."

"Do you think that might be your jealousy talking?"

"No, I don't think so."

"How long have you and Helena been together?"

"Six years."

"That's quite a long time. How old are you?"

"Thirty-eight."

"Why haven't you gotten married or had kids?"

"I've wanted to for a long time. Helena was more reluctant. She started her studies rather late, and she wanted to work some more before we had a family. We were thinking of getting married, though. We talked about it."

"Were you unsure about the relationship? Since you were so jealous?"

"No. I don't know. It was getting better and better. It's been a long time since I got so mad. Yesterday it all just exploded."

"Do you know whether she'd had a falling-out with anyone here on the island? Anyone who disliked her?"

"No, she was the sort of person that everyone liked."

"Do you know whether she's ever received any threats?"

"No."

"Were you friends with anyone else here on Gotland, other than the people who were at the party?"

"Just with some of Helena's relatives. Her father's sister, who lives in Alva, and a few cousins in Hemse. Otherwise we usually kept mostly to ourselves. We came here to relax, you know . . . and to get away from all the stress back home . . . and then something like this has to happen."

He could hardly speak.

Knutas could see that there was no reason to continue for the time being, and he stopped the interview.

When Anders Knutas had concluded his interview with Per Bergdal, he went to his office for a few minutes to think and reflect. He sat down heavily in his old desk chair, which was worn shiny. It was made of oak and had been with him all these years. It had a high back, and the seat was covered in soft leather. Gently he spun around, rocking the chair a bit as he leaned against the back. The chair seemed to have become molded to his body over the years. He did his best thinking while sitting in that old chair.

Knutas, who was the head of criminal investigations in Visby, was always careful to set aside time like this. It was especially important whenever there was a lot of drama surrounding him. Like today. His long experience with the police had taught him to pay attention to every impression at the beginning of an investigation. Otherwise it was easy, in all the fervor, to overlook things that might turn out to be important or even crucial to solving the case. He started filling his pipe.

In his mind he went back over the impressions he had brought back from the murder scene. The bloody body. The panties in the mouth. The slaughtered dog. What did the macabre scene tell him? It was difficult to say whether the murder been planned or not, but there was no doubt that it had been committed in extreme rage.

The medical examiner had arrived by plane from Stockholm in the afternoon. He was already out at the site. Knutas decided to go out to the murder scene the next day, when things should be significantly calmer.

He was interrupted by a knock at the door.

Karin Jacobsson stuck her head in. "Everyone's here now. Are you coming?"

"Of course," said Knutas, and stood up.

There were twelve police detectives in Visby. At the moment most of them were out at the site in Fröjel, working to gather statements from witnesses and secure any evidence at the crime scene. Knutas and his closest colleagues were meeting with the prosecuting attorney, Birger Smittenberg, to go over what should be divulged to the media and what they should hold back for the time being. They were all sitting around the worn pine table in the conference room, which was right across from Knutas's office. The room had glass walls facing the corridor, so it was possible to see everyone who went past, but at the moment the thin yellow cotton drapes were drawn.

Knutas sat down at the head of the table and looked attentively at his colleagues. He liked this group. Karin Jacobsson was his closest associate and best sounding board, a smart, short, thirty-seven-year-old woman with brown eyes who lived alone. Next to her sat Thomas Wittberg, ten years younger and a very capable detective, especially with regard to his interrogation techniques. Somehow he always managed to get more out of the people they interviewed than anyone else. Lars Norrby, divorced, had two sons who lived with him. Almost six foot six, he was a pleasant man with a very proper appearance, perfect for dealing with the press. Erik Sohlman, the technician of the group, was energetic and temperamental, close to being hot-tempered. Birger Smittenberg, the hardened chief prosecutor of the Gotland district court, was originally from Stockholm. He had married a singer from Gotland, having fallen in love with both her and the island, and had now lived here for twenty-five years. Knutas had always thought they received excellent cooperation from him.

"Just a brief discussion right now," said Knutas as he started the hastily organized meeting. "We're putting all our efforts into the homicide investigation, but at the same time, unfortunately, we have to deal with the press. They've already started calling, both from here, the local media, and from the mainland. It's incredible how fast news like this travels." He shook his head. "I always wonder how that happens. At any rate, we're not going to divulge the victim's identity, even though the press will find it out sooner or later. We'll tell them that all indications point to homicide, but we won't give them any details. We say nothing about the dog, the panties, or the hacking wounds. We say nothing about a possible murder weapon. We reveal nothing about any leads. This is probably going to make the reporters call all sorts of people here at the department, trying to get more information. Refer everyone to me or Lars. Nobody is to say anything. Nothing at all. Okay?"

A murmur of agreement was heard.

"I'll send out an internal memo with instructions after this meeting," said Norrby. "A basic ground rule will be in force: Keep the reporters at a distance. They're going to pounce on you, both in town and here. Don't tell them a thing."

"By the way, I'd like us to meet in my office right after the press conference to compare notes," Knutas continued. "Make sure you get something to eat to tide you over. We're going to have to work all night. I've also contacted the National Criminal Police. They're sending down a few men tomorrow. This is all going to take a lot of time and resources if we don't catch the killer quickly."

Even though it was horrible that such a grisly murder had been committed, he felt a fluttering of excitement in his stomach. He recognized that tingling sensation. A kind of anticipation at being able to seize hold of something solid. What should he call it? Taking pleasure in his work? It was a paradox that he couldn't explain, not even to himself.

Maybe it was his form of motivation.

It was still light out when the plane landed at Visby Airport just after 9:00 P.M. The cab ride into town went fast, since the airport was less than two miles north of Visby.

"That's some thick wall!"

Peter had never been to Gotland before.

"It was built in the thirteenth century," Johan told him. "It's more than two miles long, and one of Europe's best preserved ring walls. You can see how many towers it has. Soon we'll be driving through Norderport, the north gate, to get to our hotel. There are several archways. The big ones are named for the points of the compass: Österport, Söderport, and Norderport. There has never been a Västerport, because to the west is the sea and Visby Harbor."

He pointed out the window.

"That's St. Mary's Cathedral. It's also from the thirteenth century."
Its three black towers loomed against the sky.

Luckily they had been served dinner on the plane. They stopped at
the hotel just long enough to drop their suitcases and then headed
straight for police headquarters, where the press conference was going
to be held at 10:00 P.M.

In the cab Johan scribbled out a report from what he had learned so
far. They would edit the piece at the local television offices, which still
existed even though the Gotland editorial operation of Swedish TV
had been shut down six months ago. The old equipment was still there
and at their disposal, for the time being at least.

Inside police headquarters, people were dashing up and down the corridors. The air was vibrating with excitement. Several journalists and
photographers from the local media were already there: Radio Gotland
and the newspapers *Gotlands Tidningar* and *Gotlands Allehanda.*

Johan and Peter briefly greeted their colleagues, and then it was time
to go into the room where the press conference was being held. Detective Superintendent Anders Knutas and Detective Inspector Karin Jacobsson sat down at the head of the table.

"Welcome," said Knutas, clearing his throat. "We've found the body
of a woman on the beach known as Gustavs, in Fröjel Parish. For those
of you who are not from these parts, it's located on the west coast of
Gotland, approximately twenty-five miles south of Visby. The body
was discovered by a passerby today around lunchtime; to be more precise, between 12:30 and 12:45. The victim was born in 1966. She was
originally from Gotland, but her family moved away from the island
and settled in Stockholm fifteen years ago."

Knutas took a drink of water and glanced down at his papers. "The
woman was on Gotland with her boyfriend, spending a few days at the
summer house that her family still owns here on the island," he went
on. "This morning she went out to take her dog for a walk, and at some
point during that walk, she was murdered."

"How was she murdered?" asked the female reporter from Radio Gotland.

"I'm afraid I can't discuss that," said the superintendent.

"What type of weapon was used?"

"I can't comment on the investigation."

"How can you be so sure that she was actually murdered?" asked a reporter from *Gotlands Allehanda.*

"The wounds sustained by the victim can only have been caused by another person. The cause of death has not yet been ascertained, but we assume that the woman's death was homicide."

"Was she subjected to sexual assault?" asked Johan.

"It's too early to comment on that."

"Are there any witnesses?" asked the representative from *Gotlands Tidningar.*

"We're in the process of interviewing a large number of people who live in the area or in some other way had contact with the victim during the final days of her life. The police are very interested in receiving any tips from the public. If anyone saw or heard anything unusual at the site or in the vicinity during the last twenty-four hours, or if anyone thinks he has other information that might be of use in our search for the perpetrator, he should contact the police immediately."

"How do you know that only one person was involved?" asked the local radio person.

"Of course, we don't know that for sure," replied Knutas, a little annoyed.

"She was staying at her summer house with her boyfriend. Is he a suspect?" asked Johan.

"The boyfriend has been questioned by the police. He's suffering from shock and is currently in Visby Hospital. At the present time he is not a suspect. The interview with him will continue tomorrow morning. This afternoon and evening, the canine unit searched the area, and officers have been going door to door to locate any possible witnesses. We will be continuing with these efforts. Now I think that's all we have to tell you at the moment. Are there any further questions before we adjourn?"

The superintendent answered the journalists' questions as best he could. There wasn't much else to say.

Johan Berg from Regional News decided to hold back any mention of the axe wounds on the woman's body or the panties in her mouth. For the time being, he was clearly the only one who knew about them.

When the press conference was over, he went up to Anders Knutas for an individual interview. First Johan asked the obvious questions about what had happened, what the police were doing now, and what evidence they had found. Then he asked quite bluntly, "What conclusions have you drawn from the fact that she suffered multiple wounds, presumably from an axe?"

Anders Knutas gave a start.

"What do you mean?"

"The killer murdered her with an axe or some type of similar weapon, hacking her body multiple times. He also stuffed her panties in her mouth. What does that signify?"

Knutas glanced around self-consciously, looking both left and right, as if hoping for help from his colleagues. The bright glare of the camera shone in his face, blinding him.

"I know from a reliable source that these facts are true," Johan persisted.

"That's not something I can confirm," snapped Knutas, shoving aside the microphone.

"Switch off the camera," Johan told Peter. He took hold of the superintendent's arm and said to him, "I know that it's true. Wouldn't it be better if you confirmed the information?"

Knutas gave Johan a stern look. "I can neither confirm nor deny what you've said, and I advise you to withhold such speculations for the time being. We're dealing with a murderer, and what we need to concentrate on right now is catching him as soon as possible and nothing else," he bellowed. "And I expect you to respect that."

His voice was sharp as an awl, and it was easy to see what he thought of journalists as he turned on his heel and strode off down the corridor.

For Johan and Peter, Knutas's reaction was sufficient confirmation that their information was accurate. The question was how much of it they should make public.

Johan called Max Grenfors from the cab on the way to the TV offices where the story was going to be edited. Even though he thought Grenfors was a slave driver of an editor, Johan trusted his journalistic judgment. After a brief discussion, they decided not to divulge the information about the victim's panties being stuffed in her mouth, out of respect for her family. On the other hand, they did choose to report that the murder weapon was most likely an axe.

In the late-night news broadcast, Swedish TV was the first to report how the murder had been committed. The feature story began with images of police headquarters, then a map showing the scene of the crime. Next, Johan appeared on the screen.

"Here at police headquarters in Visby, a press conference was held a short time ago. The police confirm that a woman was murdered, but they are being quite reticent about the circumstances surrounding the death. The police will not yet say how the woman was killed. According to information provided this evening to Regional News from a very reliable source, she was killed with what is believed to be an axe. Multiple wounds were sustained on various parts of the body. It is not yet known whether she was subjected to sexual assault, but the woman was naked when she was found. Her clothes are still missing. The body will be sent to the forensic medicine division in Solna for autopsy. In spite of an intensive search of the area with dogs, which continued all afternoon and evening, at this time the police have no clues as to the killer's identity."

This was followed by a brief interview with a pale and resolute-looking Knutas, before the story concluded with what little was known about the murdered woman.

It turned out to be a long workday for the Visby police. The light June night facilitated their work down at the beach area. They kept on knocking on doors until late in the evening. At the same time, those who had been dinner guests at the home of Helena Hillerström on the previous evening were brought in to be interviewed. Except for Kristian Nordström, who had flown to Copenhagen to visit his parents. The police had contacted him, and he was supposed to fly back to Visby early Thursday.

By the time the most important interviews had been conducted, it was close to one in the morning. Earlier that evening Knutas had called home and told his wife, Lina, that he would be late. As usual, she was very understanding and asked him if she should wait up with a cup of tea for him. Reluctantly he had declined her offer. He didn't know how late he would be.

Now, as he walked home through the streets of Visby, he regretted his decision. It would have been pleasant to sit down for a while and talk about his impressions of the day. It always did him good to share his thoughts with his wife. She would often come up with a new way of looking at things because she was not part of the investigative work. Many times she had turned his thoughts to new avenues that helped him to solve a case. Knutas felt a twinge of warmth in his heart. He loved her above all else. Except for their children, of course. Their twins, a boy and a girl. Petra and Nils. This summer they would be twelve.

When he got home, he looked in on them. They still shared a room, but in the fall they would each have their own. He was in the process of remodeling the study into a bedroom. The study would be moved down to the basement. They used it so seldom, anyway.

The children were sound asleep, breathing calmly. He left the door to their room slightly ajar and went to his own.

Lina lay stretched out across the whole double bed with her arms above her head. *Look how much room she takes,* he thought. She always did everything with the greatest enthusiasm. Whether she was sleeping, eating, working, laughing, or making love, she did it with such zest. She truly threw herself into life. No matter what she did, she did it properly. If she was baking, she never made do with just one batch. No, she had to make two hundred cinnamon rolls. When she did any major grocery shopping, she gave the impression that a war was on the way, and she always cooked too much food, so the freezer was full of leftovers. That was one of the things he loved about her, her sensual vitality. Right now she was sleeping heavily, wearing a long orange T-shirt decorated with a big flower. Her hair was ruffled, her cheeks rosy. Her arms were sprinkled with freckles. She was the most beautiful woman he had ever known.

Her profession was perfectly suited to her personality. She was a midwife. How many children had she helped come into the world? Lina worked part-time in the childbirth center at Visby Hospital, and she loved it. She was used to unanticipated events and having things not turn out the way you expected, and that made her very patient. Many times she would stay with an expectant mother because she didn't have the heart to leave even though her shift was over, or else out of sheer curiosity. If she had been working for hours with a birth, she didn't want to let it go before everything was resolved. Sometimes this could irritate her colleagues. Lina didn't care. She was strong-willed and the most wonderful woman he had ever met.

Cautiously he closed the door again and went downstairs to the kitchen, where he poured himself a glass of milk and dug into a package of cookies. He took out a handful and sat down at the kitchen table. He often found it difficult to sleep after an eventful day. He petted the cat, who jumped up on the table and lovingly brushed against him. *She's more like a dog,* he thought. Faithful and always in need of company. She also loved to play fetch. He threw a foam-rubber ball a few times. She ran off and got it, then brought it back to his feet. *What a funny thing you are,* thought Knutas, and went off to bed. Contrary to custom, he fell asleep at once.

WEDNESDAY, JUNE 6

Johan Berg was awakened by the merry tune from his cell phone that stubbornly kept on playing. At first he had no idea where he was. The melody stopped. He stretched and saw pastel flowers on the wallpaper. There wasn't a sound. None of the noisy traffic that he was used to hearing outside his window. *Oh, that's right.*

The beach hotel in Visby. The murder. His eyes fell on the digital alarm clock next to the bed. It was five thirty in the morning. Then the tune from his cell phone started up again. With a groan he climbed out of bed to answer it.

It was the editor of the morning news. "Hi. Did I wake you? Sorry to call so early. But of course we'd like to have a fresh spot this morning. If you can't come up with anything new, maybe we could do a phone interview?"

"Sure," said Johan wearily. "Not that I know anything more than I did at midnight, but I can always call the duty officer."

"Great. How much time do you need? Shall we say in an hour?"

"That'll work. I'll get back to you later."

After a quick breakfast, he emerged onto the cobblestone street outside the hotel to head over to the TV offices. It had rained during the night; here and there puddles of water glistened. The air held a scent of the sea.

The cramped editorial office of the Regional News division, which still existed, was located next to the Radio Gotland building in the center of town. It made Johan mad to think that the local team had been laid off when Swedish TV had to cut costs. Their huge deficit had to be turned around, and this had been done partially at the expense of

regional coverage. With the reorganization, the responsibility for covering Gotland had been shifted from the Norrköping newsroom to
Stockholm. The new management at Swedish TV headquarters felt
that the Gotlanders had more in common with the citizens of Stockholm than with Norrköping. Johan basically agreed with this, but it
was a shame that they had laid off the local reporters and cameramen,
the people who were truly close to their viewers. At the same time, he
was happy to be here. He had always felt a great fondness for Gotland.

A skinny old man was in the process of putting up Swedish flags
outside the hotel. *Oh, that's right, today is National Commemoration
Day,* thought Johan. The sixth of June.

It looked as if it was going to be a beautiful day for the celebration.
The sun was caressing the facades of the medieval buildings, and there
was no wind. The town was practically deserted. It should take him
only a few minutes to reach the TV offices. Right now he was wishing
it was a longer walk.

He decided to allow himself a slight detour, even though he really
didn't have time. Only a few yards away he saw the northern section
of the ring wall extending beyond the buildings. There was a break in
the wall on this side of the old Gunpowder Tower, which originally
had been a defensive stronghold. Johan enjoyed the view until he
turned onto Rostockergränd. He walked past the low stone buildings
with their budding rose vines and the planking that protected the gardens inside. Many of the buildings had windows that were only a foot
or two above the ground. The street doors were so low that anyone
taller than five feet had to duck his head to go in.

A radio was blaring from the open window of a bakery, and he
breathed in the fragrance of freshly baked bread. A black cat was sitting on the curving stairs outside a building, watching him as he
walked past.

He pulled his cell phone out of his pocket and called the duty officer.

"Good morning. It's Johan Berg from Regional News, Swedish TV.
Any new developments during the night with the murder of the woman
in Fröjel?"

"Yes, the prosecuting attorney has decided to arrest the boyfriend, under suspicion of murder."

"No shit. On what grounds?"

"I'm not at liberty to say. You'll have to take that up with the head of the investigation, Anders Knutas."

"Is he there now?"

"No, he should be in around eight, but then there's a meeting scheduled."

"Where's the boyfriend?"

"He's still in the hospital. He's going to be picked up sometime this morning and taken into custody."

"Who's the prosecuting attorney?"

"Chief Prosecutor Birger Smittenberg."

"When did he decide to arrest him?"

"At four o'clock this morning. Otherwise we couldn't hold him any longer."

"Do you know whether Anders Knutas will be out at the crime scene today?"

"I can't say. You'll have to take it up with him."

"Okay, thanks."

Johan dashed for the TV offices.

The logos of both Radio Gotland and Swedish TV adorned the facade of the radio building. The blue-and-white awnings above the windows were looking rather the worse for wear in the morning sunlight. Several cars belonging to local radio were parked in the lot in the courtyard. He noticed that one space was reserved for Regional News. It stood empty and gaping, as if it were mocking him. In the past the local TV van was parked there, but, of course, that didn't exist anymore, either. Johan was ashamed to think about how badly Regional News had been covering the island lately. Most often the only news from here dealt with tourism, oil spills, and the traffic.

He went in and put together a story running just over a minute for the morning program. He could handle the simpler types of editing himself. When he was ready, he sent the story by e-mail on the new computer system. In a few minutes they would be able to open the file and watch it in Stockholm. He was also interviewed on the phone by Madeleine Haga, one of the reporters he liked best at Swedish TV.

The morning news had gotten what they wanted. Now it was past seven, and Johan thought it was worth giving Knutas another try. The superintendent himself answered.

"I heard the boyfriend was arrested last night," said Johan. "Why?"

"I'm not at liberty to say."

"Surely you can tell me something?"

"No."

"Will you be out at the crime scene today?"

"Yes, for a while this morning. I'm going out there around ten."

"How long will you be there?"

"A few hours, I would think."

"Could I do a short interview with you out there?"

"I suppose that's all right."

"Good, then that's agreed. Thanks. See you there."

When Knutas switched off his cell phone, he thought to himself that this time he was going to be prepared for the interview. No unpleasant questions were going to throw him off balance.

The room was almost completely dark when he woke up. The shades were pulled down, but a little of the white night still managed to seep through. Rain was pelting the windowpanes. His body was sore, and his tongue stuck to the roof of his mouth. With an effort he got out of bed. Outside he could hear the sea rolling in. He turned on the faucet to get a drink. The cold water gushed out and hit the porcelain bottom of the sink before he managed to hold out the glass. He drank the water in big gulps, then stuck his feet into his wooden clogs and went outside. With precision he made the stream of urine strike the hole in the stone wall surrounding the house, the spot he was always trying to hit. The fresh nighttime chill felt wonderful on his bare skin. He wasn't cold, even though he was wearing only pajama bottoms.

He had dreamed about her. About how he had followed her along the beach. About her fear when he stood right behind her in the fog. He had been so focused. Totally focused. When she turned around, his hatred had exploded like red fireworks inside his head, and he took pleasure in the terror he could see in her eyes before he struck. When she collapsed to the ground, he felt like a conqueror. He kept on hacking. Even though he realized that he had done something terrible, something irrevocable, he had never felt so good.

The dog had interrupted his elation. It turned out that the animal wasn't dead, even though the first blow had landed right on its head. When he was done with her and was dragging the body into the grove, he heard a whimpering. The fact that the fucking dog was still alive filled him with rage.

Normally Anders Knutas stayed at the police station whenever anything dramatic happened, in order to gather his forces around him like a spider in his web. Nothing like this murder had ever occurred before on Gotland, though, and he wanted to go over the crime scene one more time, in peace and quiet. Right now he was in Fröjel, standing on the steps of the summer house that belonged to the Hillerström family. He was dressed in blue jeans and polo shirt, as usual, with soft walking shoes on his feet. He had left his jacket in the car. It was a cloudless day, and the air was clear and fresh. Between the trees he could see glimpses of the shimmering water. *So this is where she started out yesterday morning,* he thought.

He decided to follow the route they assumed Helena Hillerström had taken.

Just beyond the yard surrounding the house, a narrow gravel path led down toward the water, a few hundred yards away. Several police vehicles were parked near the shore.

Crime scene tape fluttered in the wind. He stayed outside of it so as not to disturb the work of the techs. It took him only a few minutes to reach the beach. He climbed over a sand dune and he was there.

Today the sea was choppy. The waves were breaking and foaming. Flocks of seagulls flapped over the crests, screeching. The islands Big and Little Karlsö looked exotic out there, sticking up from the sea. The rock formations were clearly visible, at least on Little Karlsö. Big Karlsö lurked behind the smaller island, flatter and farther away.

He looked out across the beach. It wasn't long, half a mile at most, with fine, light-colored sand. A short distance from the water's edge, grass and reeds grew on the dunes. Perfect for sunbathers seeking a haven in the summertime, since it was often windy on the beach itself.

Knutas glanced at his watch. Nine thirty.

He strolled along the edge of the water, outside the area that had been cordoned off. She had walked along the shoreline with her dog. Not suspecting a thing. It had been foggy yesterday morning, so the killer wouldn't have had any trouble keeping out of sight. Sohlman had reported finding several tracks from shoes down on the beach. They had secured the shoe prints left by Helena; the others found at the crime scene must belong to the killer. Bloodstains and marks on the ground revealed that she had been murdered on the beach and then dragged into the grove of trees. The crime techs were working intently inside the restricted area. Everything of interest that they found in connection with the crime scene would be sent to SCL—the Swedish Crime Laboratory—in Linköping for analysis.

He came to the end of the beach without noticing anything special and started back. All indications were that the murderer had killed the dog first. Of course, that had to be the case. It had been a good watchdog, so naturally he was forced to kill it. If the dog didn't know him, that is. Otherwise it was a whole different story. The perpetrator could have been an acquaintance of the victim. That was most often the case with a murder. Knutas had a strong feeling that the boyfriend wasn't guilty. That was his personal theory, and for the time being he was keeping it to himself. One of the people at the party seemed most likely. Kristian Nordström?

He was the only one Knutas hadn't yet talked to. The interview was scheduled for the following day.

Knutas didn't believe it was a coincidence that Helena Hillerström had been murdered, that she just happened to come upon a killer carrying an axe on this calm stretch of beach several weeks before the start of the tourist season. The murder had the mark of rage, which was often associated with revenge. That didn't necessarily mean that it had to do with Helena. It could be revenge on women in general.

By this time Knutas had returned to the place where he started his stroll on the beach, without being any the wiser.

There were almost no cars on the road. It was past nine o'clock, and Johan and Peter were on their way south. On both sides of the road, the landscape stretched out flat in the glow of the morning sun. On the right side, they occasionally caught a glimpse of the sea, while on the left, cultivated fields alternated with meadows.

Herds of livestock were grazing in the green meadows. Johan wondered why the sheep on Gotland were black while almost all the cattle were white. On the mainland it was exactly the opposite: white sheep and black or brown cows.

They passed the Tofta artillery range and Tofta Church with its wood-covered tower before they slowed down through the little village of Västergarn and drove past the larger town of Klintehamn.

After several miles they came to Fröjel's white-plastered church, which stood by the road. From here they could see the water much more clearly. A few brown horses were trotting around in a yard. The fields of grain took on still more shades of green. Down near a strip of woods close to the sea, they caught sight of police cars and tape cordoning off the area. They parked next to the other vehicles.

Knutas was engaged in a conversation with a female colleague. He glanced up as they approached. He would give them an interview in fifteen minutes, he explained, and they were not allowed to go inside the restricted area.

An area that looked to be several hundred square yards had been blocked off. Johan gazed out at the strip of woods, the sand dunes, and the sea. So it was in this beautiful, idyllic spot that the bestial murder had occurred. He wondered how it happened, and whether the woman who was killed had enough time to be scared.

They walked down to the beach. Inside the restricted area, a couple of police officers, most likely technicians, were walking around and staring at the ground. Now and then they would pick up something and then put it inside a plastic bag.

Was it the boyfriend who had sneaked up on her and murdered her so viciously? thought Johan. He had been arrested, after all. At the same time, experience told him that occasionally the prosecuting attorney would arrest individuals on quite flimsy grounds.

His thoughts were abruptly interrupted by Peter.

"Hey, could you move over?" he shouted, hidden behind the camera, concentrating on his shot and with his eye at the viewfinder. He had attached the big TV camera to a tripod, and Johan was standing in the way of the shot he was considering, panning across the beach.

It was eleven o'clock. The editor of the noon news was prepared to make do with the morning's material, so they didn't need to worry about that.

"I think we should drop by and see the sister of the old man who found the body," said Johan as they got into the car. "Her name is Svea Johansson, and she lives nearby. We can try to get an interview with her."

"Sure," replied Peter, who was usually quite cooperative.

Svea Johansson opened the door after they knocked four times. The fragrance of newly baked cinnamon rolls greeted them.

"Yes? And who might you be?" she asked bluntly with a lilting Gotland accent, peering up at them.

They had never seen such a tiny old lady before. Her hair was white and pulled back into a bun. Her face had a rosy hue and delicate little wrinkles, and there was flour on the tip of her nose. She was wearing a striped cotton apron. *She can't be more than four foot seven,* thought Johan, fascinated. He introduced himself and Peter.

"Ah, well, come in then," said Svea, letting them into the cramped, dark hallway. "I'm in the middle of baking rolls, so you'll have to come sit in the kitchen."

They sat down on the kitchen bench, and in an instant two coffee cups were set on the table before them.

"You'll have a little coffee, won't you?" murmured the old woman without waiting for them to reply. "You're in luck, because the first batch of rolls will be done soon."

"That would be great," they said in unison.

Johan looked out at the yard and realized that this was going to take some time.

"We were wondering if you could tell us about your brother finding the dead woman," said Johan.

"Of course I can," she replied as she took a pan of cinnamon rolls out of the oven. "It made him very upset, the poor thing. He's still in the hospital. They wanted to keep him another day. I talked to him this morning, and he was sounding quite cheerful."

"How did he happen to find her?"

"Well, we were supposed to go out for a walk. That's what we usually do every day, but yesterday I didn't want to go along. No, I didn't. Because I had a sore throat and a terrible cough. Today I'm feeling much better," she explained, pinching the skin of her wrinkled neck.

"Well, anyway, he came over around eleven, as usual. We had a little lunch together, the way we always do. Then he went out alone. I stayed here and did some needlework. It didn't take long before he was back, pounding on the door even though it was open. He was very upset and babbling something about a dead woman and a dead dog and that he had to call the police."

Johan gave a start. "A dead dog? Can you tell us more about that?"

"Yes, apparently there was a dog that was killed. The head had been cut off, and it was quite horrible," she lamented, shaking her head.

Johan and Peter exchanged glances. This was something new.

"Did the dog belong to the woman?" asked Johan.

"Yes, apparently she went everywhere with that dog. That's what the police said when they were here."

Half an hour later Johan and Peter left the farm. By then they had Svea Johansson's account on videotape.

Emma Winarve was hot and sweaty. She had a disgusting taste in her mouth and a knot of fear in her stomach. The nightmare still had a grip on her. She and Helena were walking on the beach together, as they had done so many times before. Helena walked on a short distance ahead. Emma called to her to wait but received no reply. Then she picked up her pace and called Helena again. Her friend still did not turn around. Emma tried to run but made no headway. Her feet lifted off the ground in slow motion, and even though she tried as hard as she could, she didn't get any closer. She never caught up with Helena, and she woke up with a shout.

Angrily she kicked off Olle's blanket, which had slipped onto her side of the bed on top of her own, making her much too hot. She felt like crying, but she shook off the feeling and instead got out of bed. Sunlight was filtering through the thin cotton curtains, and it lit up the big, airy bedroom.

She had stayed home from work even though there were only two days left until the end of the school year and she had a lot to do. She didn't want to leave her pupils in the lurch, but she just couldn't bear to see them at the moment. From home she would try to take care of all the last-minute preparations before school closed for the summer. The principal understood. The shock. The grief. Emma and Helena. Helena and Emma. They had been the best of friends.

Mechanically she went through her usual morning routine. The shower water sprayed against her warm body, but it didn't feel refreshing. Her skin was a thick shell, far away from all that was inside her. The contact between her exterior and interior had been broken.

Olle had taken the children to school before he went to work. He offered to stay home, but Emma had firmly declined this suggestion; she wanted to be alone. She pulled on a pair of jeans and a sweater and went out to the kitchen in her bare feet. She frequently went barefoot in the house, even in winter. After a cup of strong coffee and a couple of pieces of toast, she began feeling a little better, but the sense of unreality swirled inside her. How could this have happened? Her best friend murdered on the beach, where they had played in the sand with buckets and shovels; where they had held horse races when they were horse-crazy twelve-year-olds; where they had walked as teenagers, discussing their problems; and where they had ridden motorbikes and gotten drunk for the first time. She had even lost her virginity on that beach.

Her thoughts were interrupted by the ringing of the telephone. It was Detective Superintendent Knutas.

"I'm sorry to disturb you, but it would be good if we could have a little talk as soon as possible. I also wanted to tell you that Per Bergdal was arrested this morning. Would it be all right if I come out to see you after lunch?"

Emma felt chilled. Per, arrested? That couldn't be possible. *The police must know everything about the fight,* she thought.

"Why was he arrested?"

"There are several reasons, which I can tell you about when we meet."

Shocked and confused as she was, she didn't want any police officer in the middle of her private hell. It would be better to meet on neutral ground.

"Could we meet at the police station? Around two o'clock?"

"That would be fine. As I said, I'm sorry I have to disturb you, but it's important," Knutas repeated.

"That's okay," she said in a toneless voice.

Knutas took a gulp of coffee from the china mug decorated with the emblem of the local AIK soccer team, a present from his brother. It infuriated his colleague Erik Sohlman, who had been a fan of the arch-rival Djurgården team since birth.

He glanced at the clock on the wall. Quarter to twelve. His stomach growled. He hadn't gotten enough sleep, and he always had to compensate for that by eating. Soon it would finally be time for lunch.

The investigative team had gathered to go over what had been uncovered so far. The prosecuting attorney was also present.

The room was hot and stuffy. Wittberg opened the window facing the police station parking lot. Rays of sunlight played tag among the light green foliage of the trees. The Swedish flag flapped and fluttered in the wind. A truck filled with bellowing high school graduates wearing white student caps drove past over on Birkagatan. It was the end of the school year and a national holiday, and here they sat indoors, talking about what was probably the worst murder ever to occur on Gotland.

"We're here to sum up the situation," Knutas began. "Helena Hillerström was murdered sometime between 8:30 A.M. and 12:30 P.M. yesterday. The shoe tracks, the blood, and the dragging marks down from the beach indicate that the murder was committed near Gustavs, the Baptist summer camp. Which means that the body was not transported there from somewhere else. The preliminary report from the medical examiner says that she died from extensive trauma to the head. The nature of the head wounds indicates that they're the result of blows from a sharp-edged weapon, presumably an axe. The body was also subjected to numerous blows from the axe. In addition, the perpetrator stuffed her panties into her mouth. Helena Hillerström was found naked. We don't know yet whether she was raped or not. There are no outward signs of sexual assault, nor were any of the blows directed at her sexual organs. The body is being taken to the forensic medicine lab in Solna. It will take a few days before we have a preliminary autopsy report. The panties were sent to SCL for analysis. No trace of semen was found on the body or the panties, at least not any that the techs could discover. We'll have to wait and see what the results of the analysis are. Her other clothing has not been found."

"What about the murder weapon?" asked Wittberg.

"That's gone, too," interjected Sohlman. "We've searched the area where the body was found. Nothing special turned up except for a few cigarette butts that have also been sent to SCL. We've interviewed witnesses in the vicinity, but no one saw anything, no one heard anything.

The only real clues we have so far are the shoe prints. The same prints show up both on the beach and in the forest grove. A running shoe of unknown manufacture, size 11$\frac{1}{2}$. They had to belong to the perpetrator."

Sohlman stood up. With some difficulty he unrolled a map and fastened it to the wall. It was a map of the beach at Gustavs and the surrounding area. Sohlman wiped the sweat from his brow with a handkerchief and pointed out the scene of the crime.

"This is where the body was found. The tracks show that the victim walked in this direction along the shore. Then she must have turned around and walked back the same way. At the other end of the beach, meaning where she started out, the grass has been trampled down. It looks as if that's where he stood waiting for her. He may have known which way she would walk and then intercepted her before she could reach the road. There are no tire tracks, so the killer must have been on foot. He most likely murdered her there. The bloodstains on the ground indicate as much. Then he dragged the body over to the grove."

"What about the dog?" asked Karin Jacobsson.

"It must have been disposed of first. According to the boyfriend, it was an alert and excellent watchdog, who always kept close to Helena, ready to protect her. The dog was struck on the head and the neck with an axe. The head was practically severed. One paw was also chopped off. We can only wonder why."

The others stirred uneasily. Jacobsson grimaced.

"How many people knew she was here on the island?" asked Norrby.

"About thirty or so, if I've counted correctly," said Jacobsson as she leafed through her notes. "Her family, her work colleagues and a couple of friends in Stockholm, her friend Emma Winarve, the closest neighbors, and the people who were at the party, of course."

"What leads you to believe that it could be the boyfriend?" Wittberg asked, turning to the prosecuting attorney.

"A fight erupted between him and Helena at the party, and it ended with him slapping her," replied Smittenberg. "He was jealous. She was apparently dancing with an old school friend, Kristian Nordström. In Bergdal's view, Kristian was groping Helena, and she let him do it. He pulled Helena outside, they started fighting, and he slapped her. He in turn was scratched and bitten by Helena. The fight lasted only a couple of minutes. Then Nordström came out to talk to Bergdal, and he got punched, too. The other friends intervened, so it never turned into a real fistfight. They say that everything was calm when they left the house. Bergdal was asleep, and Helena had also gone to bed and was even lying next to him. The most serious strikes against him are that he was the last one to see her alive and the fact that they had a fight on the night preceding the murder. I view that as sufficient grounds for arrest, as things now stand. On the other hand, in order to charge him with a crime, I need something more. If you don't come up with any new evidence, such as some sort of forensic proof, we'll have to let him go. You've got two days."

"What do we know about Helena?" asked Jacobsson. "What was her life like?"

Knutas glanced down at his notebook. "Helena seems to have led an ordinary life. She was born on July 5, 1966, so she was thirty-four years old. She would have been thirty-five next month. Born and raised on Gotland. Her whole family moved to Stockholm in 1986, when Helena was twenty. They kept the summer cabin near Fröjel, and they came to stay here several times a year. They used to spend every summer here. She was educated in computer science at Stockholm University, and she has worked for a computer company for the past three years. She had lots of friends. Before Bergdal, she seems not to have had any long-term love relationships. Never married or engaged. According to Bergdal, she once had something going with this Kristian who was at the party. That might also be complete nonsense. The boyfriend suffers from jealousy, as you know. None of the friends has been able to confirm that the story was true, and surely at least one of them ought to know something about it. We haven't been able to interview Nordström yet because he flew to Copenhagen the day after the party. That's where his parents live. I've talked to him on the phone, and he's flying back here tomorrow."

"Does Helena Hillerström have any kind of record?" asked Wittberg.

"No. The question now is how we should proceed. We'll conduct more interviews with the people who were at the party. Above all, I want to talk to Kristian Nordström. Someone needs to go over to Stockholm and interview Helena's family, colleagues, friends, and other people she knew. We should do that as soon as possible. We need to keep working with an open mind. It's not at all certain that Bergdal is the killer. If he's not the one, then we don't know whether the murderer is on the island or whether he followed her here from the mainland. Or whether it's someone she didn't even know, someone she met by chance."

"I'd be happy to go to Stockholm," said Jacobsson. "We need to talk to the people she knew as quickly as possible. I can leave this afternoon."

"Take someone with you. There's a lot to be done in Stockholm, and plenty of people to interview. I'm sure you'll have the assistance of the National Criminal Police over there, but I think two of you should go."

"I'll go," said Wittberg.

Jacobsson gave him a grateful smile. "All right, that's decided, then. By the way, we're waiting to hear back from SCL. In the meantime, we need to map out Helena's circle of acquaintances here on the island. Who did she spend time with when she was here? Aside from her best friend. We need to do another round of interviews with the neighbors. I'll conduct a more intensive interview with Emma Winarve. What did Helena do on the days preceding the murder? Conversations on her cell phone? E-mail messages? The boyfriend says that they switched off their cell phones as soon as they got off the ferry. How do we go about searching for her clothes? We need to expand the area around the crime scene, both in terms of searching the area and talking to the neighbors. Those are what I see as the most pressing matters right now. Any comments?" Knutas concluded.

No one had any objections, and so the tasks were divided up.

After a late lunch, Johan and Peter went to the police station to do a supplemental interview with the superintendent. They wanted to have the new information about the dog confirmed before the story for the evening news was edited.

Pulling open the glass door to the criminal department, Johan collided with a woman. She had shoulder-length sand-colored hair and dark eyes that glared at them. She said a curt hello and then walked away down the corridor with her bag over her shoulder—tall and attractive, wearing washed-out jeans and cowboy boots.

"Who was that?" asked Johan even before greeting Knutas.

"A friend of the murder victim," replied the inspector briefly. "Come in."

Knutas sat down heavily behind his desk and said wearily, "So, what is it you want now? I'm very busy."

Johan dropped into one of the visitors' chairs. He chose to get right to the point.

"Why haven't you said anything about the dog?"

Knutas's expression didn't change. "What dog?"

"The killer chopped off the head of the girl's dog. It was found right near the body."

Red patches appeared on Knutas's neck. "I can't confirm that."

"What conclusions have you come to, based on this information?"

"Since I can neither confirm nor deny what you've said, I can't offer any conclusions, either."

"We've now heard from two different sources that she was killed with an axe. That part has already come out, and it's in all the newspapers. Wouldn't it be just as well for you to confirm it?"

"It doesn't matter how many sources you have, I'm not saying anything regarding the investigation. You'll just have to accept that," said Knutas, controlling his impatience.

"In any case, I need to do another interview."

"Sure, but I'm not going to say any more than I already have. As far as the police are concerned, we're not ready to divulge anything else at the moment. So far, the suspect has not been charged, and the prosecuting attorney has not submitted a request for indictment to the district court. For that reason, with regard to the investigation, we cannot confirm what you've said about the dog. It's possible that the murderer is still on the loose, and if so, it's important that sensitive information does not get out. I hope that you'll show enough sense not to report anything about this but to wait until we know more," said Knutas, giving them a stern look.

After the interview, which had been quite tiresome for both parties, Johan and Peter hurried back to the office. They worked for a couple of hours, putting together three evening stories that differed enough from each other to satisfy the various editors at TV headquarters. Heaven forbid the news programs were too much alike.

After consulting with Grenfors, they decided to report on the dead dog and include the interview with Svea Johansson. The information was considered relevant because it revealed something about the personality of the murderer. It was also deemed to be of interest for the viewers to hear what the sister of the man who found the body had to say.

Grenfors was happy that they had managed to get an interview with the sister, who without hesitation had granted permission for the story to be broadcast on TV. When Johan warned her about the widespread impact of television, she merely said that this was how it happened, and there was no reason why people shouldn't know what had taken place. *The old woman should have been a journalist,* thought Johan.

When they were ready in the newsroom, he called Knutas and explained that they were going to air the interview with Svea Johansson and that she had told them about the dog. He knew how important it was not to get on the wrong side of the police. That would make it more difficult for him to obtain any information in the future. Knutas did not get angry; he just seemed resigned. As compensation, Johan promised to say in his report that the police would be grateful to receive any tips from the public.

They walked home in the mild early summer evening. Peter suggested taking a walk and having a bite to eat at an outdoor café instead of going straight back to the hotel.

Johan knew Gotland well. He had spent numerous summers on the island, mostly on bicycle vacations when that was a big fad back in the eighties and practically everybody had to go bicycling on Gotland in the summertime—families, school classes, teenagers, and couples newly in love. He wondered why it wasn't popular anymore. The island was still just as well suited to bike riding, with its flat terrain, the flower-filled roadsides, and the long sandy shores along the roads.

They walked down to Strandgatan and continued through an opening in the wall and out to Almedalen, a big open square with park benches, fountains, grassy spaces, and a stage that had been constructed for the politicians who usually gave speeches there during the week traditionally devoted to politics in July. In the summertime the park was filled with sunbathing tourists and families with children.

Right now it was deserted. Johan and Peter walked through the park and then made a circuit of the harbor, where the wind was blowing in from the sea. The harbor was almost empty of boats. Most of the outdoor cafés and restaurants were still closed. In two or three weeks they would be nearly full every evening.

The town took on quite a different look when it wasn't overflowing with hordes of tourists. Johan and Peter climbed up Kyrktrappan to see the picturesque buildings on Klinten. Visby was spread out before them, with a maze of houses, old ruins, and narrow lanes all compressed inside the ring wall, and the sea in the background.

Twilight had settled over the town as they walked down Rackarbacken and past the cathedral. Inside, the choir was practicing. The lovely tones of a Swedish hymn came floating out through the wooden door.

Late that evening, as they walked back to the hotel, they agreed to try to get an interview with Helena Hillerström's friend the next day.

THURSDAY, JUNE 7

The house stood in an older residential neighborhood in Roma, in the center of Gotland, right next to Roma School and the sports field. It was surrounded by houses with well-established gardens. The whole area breathed an idyllic calm. Johan had already ferreted out the name of the friend of Helena's they had met in the corridor of the police station, and he had called her up. At first she was very hesitant to submit to an interview, but Johan was good at persuading people, and after a short conversation she had reluctantly agreed to meet with him and Peter.

They parked outside the overgrown lilac hedge; its lavender and white blossoms were just starting to open. The garden was impressive, with large expanses of lawn and flower beds with all sorts of flowers that Johan couldn't name. Black clouds were building in the north. It would undoubtedly rain before lunchtime.

Emma Winarve opened the door, dressed in a white T-shirt and soft gray pants. She was barefoot. Her hair was wet and hung loose. *How beautiful she is,* thought Johan before he managed to collect himself. It took him a few seconds too long. She was starting to look puzzled.

"Hi. Johan Berg from Regional News, Swedish TV. This is Peter Bylund, my cameraman. How nice of you to see us."

"Hi. Emma Winarve," she said, shaking hands with them. "Come in."

She showed them into the living room. It had a dark hardwood floor, white plastered walls, and big windows looking out on the garden. There wasn't much furniture. Along one wall stood two grayish-blue sofas facing each other. They sat down on one of them. Emma sat on the other and looked at them. Pale, with a red nose.

"I don't know that there's much I can say."

"We want to hear about your relationship with Helena," said Johan. "How well did you know her?"

"She was my best friend, although we haven't spent much time together over the past few years," she said in her soft Gotland accent. "We went through all the school years together, and we've known each other since kindergarten. After the ninth grade we ended up in different classrooms, but that didn't stop us from spending just as much time with each other as before. During that period we lived in the same row-house neighborhood in Visby, on Rutegatan near the Ericsson company. Or rather, Flextronics nowadays."

"Did you still spend time together when you got older?"

"Helena's family moved to Stockholm about a year after high school. That was the summer she turned twenty, by the way. I remember because she had a big party here on Gotland for her twentieth birthday. They moved to Danderyd. But we still kept in touch and called each other several times a week, and I used to go to Stockholm to visit her. She always came back here in the summer. They still had their summer house near Gustavs."

"What was Helena like as a person?"

"She was almost always happy. Lively, you might say. Extremely extroverted. It was always easy for her to meet new people. She was an optimist. She saw the bright side of everything."

Emma stood up hastily and left the room. She came back at once with a glass of water and a roll of paper towels.

"What about Helena's boyfriend?" asked Johan.

"Per? He's really great. Sweet, considerate, and he adored Helena. I'm positive that he's not guilty."

"How long have they been together?"

Emma took a gulp of water. *She's amazing*, thought Johan.

"It must be almost six years now, because they started seeing each other the same summer that I got married."

"So things were good between them?" Johan went on, at the same time that he felt a touch of disappointment when she mentioned her marriage. Of course she was married. Big house and a sandbox and little tricycles in the yard. *You idiot,* he told himself. *Stop thinking about her as your next conquest!*

"Yes, I think so. Of course, now and then she would get tired of him, and she'd wonder whether she was really in love. I guess most people feel that way after they've lived together for a long time. But I think she had made up her mind that he was the one. I know that several times she said that if she ever had children, it would be with Per. He made her feel secure."

"Could we ask you a few questions in front of the camera? We'll only use the parts that you think are okay."

"I don't know. I don't know what I'm supposed to say."

"How about if we give it a try? If you think it's too uncomfortable, then we can stop."

"All right."

Peter brought in his camera. He didn't bother with a tripod or extra lighting. The situation was touchy enough as it was. Johan moved over to sit on the sofa next to Emma. He could smell the scent of her newly washed hair.

The interview went well. Emma talked about Helena and their friendship, about her own fear and about how her life had been shaken as a consequence of the murder.

"Let me give you my card in case you happen to think of anything else you want to say, or if you just want to call me about something," said Johan before they left.

"Thank you."

She put his card on a chest of drawers without looking at it.

When they reached the stretch of gravel outside the house, Johan took a deep breath.

"What a woman," he groaned, and turned around to look at Peter, who was walking right behind him with the camera on his shoulder.

"The prettiest one I've seen in a long time," his colleague agreed. "What a charming accent. And those eyes. And what a body. I'm a goner."

"You, too? Too bad she's married and has kids."

"That's just my luck," said Peter with a grin. "We need some shots of the outside, too. Give me a few minutes." He disappeared around the corner of the house.

The parking lot outside Obs supermarket in the Östercentrum shopping center was almost empty. *In a couple of weeks it'll be nearly impossible to move,* thought Knutas as he sat at the desk in his office. He had talked to his wife on the phone. With the greatest enthusiasm she had described bringing a pair of twins into the world that day. She waxed poetic, since she herself was the mother of twins. Her positive attitude rubbed off on him, but it only lasted a little while. The warmth he had felt during their conversation was quickly replaced by a nagging uneasiness over Helena Hillerström's murder.

Up until now, Gotland had been relatively murder free. Since 1950 only twenty murders had been committed on the island, and ten of them occurred during the nineties. The increase disturbed him. Almost all the murders had to do with internal disputes, usually within a family. Jealousy and drunken fights, for the most part. Two murder cases remained unsolved. One involved an elderly woman who was killed with a cane in her own home in Fröjel in 1954, and one at the Visby Hotel in December 1996, when a female night clerk was murdered, presumably in connection with a break-in. That killing had taken place during Knutas's time as head of the criminal department. In spite of the fact that the NCP were brought in at an early stage and three of their detectives stayed in Gotland for six months after the murder, they never managed to crack the case.

It still rankled inside him, like a thorn, but he tried not to think too much about it. The hotel murder had already given him enough sleepless nights.

He pulled out his pipe and carefully began filling it.

And now this. *But this is something completely different,* he thought. A young woman killed in a bestial way and with her panties stuffed in her mouth.

Two inspectors from the NCP had arrived in the morning, and that's when they had their first meeting. The jovial Detective Superintendent Martin Kihlgård, convivial and loud, seemed almost a little too hearty. Previously Knutas had only heard people talk about him, and he knew that the man was quite competent. Even so, he didn't really feel comfortable with him. No doubt things would get better with time. Kihlgård's assistant, Detective Inspector Björn Hansson, made a more formal and precise impression, and that suited Knutas better.

Helena Hillerström's body had been sent to the forensic medicine division in Solna, but first the medical team had examined the body at the scene. He was grateful for that. Experience told him that the chance of solving this murder increased significantly if the body was examined at the scene of the crime itself by the ME. In addition, a large area had been immediately cordoned off after the body was found. That was something else he had learned over the years. The bigger the area that was off limits, the better.

One problem was the lack of witnesses. No one had seen or heard anything. There were no buildings in close proximity to the beach. The only houses in the area stood some distance up the slope.

No murder weapon had been found, and no other clues of major significance. The only concrete evidence they had was several cigarette butts, which could just as well have been discarded there at some previous time, and a couple of shoe prints. The only thing they thought they knew about the killer was that he had big feet.

Everyone who had been at the party, except for Kristian Nordström, had now been interviewed. Nothing useful had come out. Knutas was almost positive that Per Bergdal was innocent. He had conducted enough interrogations in his years with the police that he could depend on his gut feeling. There was something straightforward and sincere about Bergdal's manner of responding. By all accounts the scratches had been made by Helena, and the ME had found bruises on Helena's cheek and behind her ear, indicating that she had been struck before she died. On the other hand, they knew that there had been a fight. The fact that Bergdal had not immediately admitted as much might be understandable. Now they needed to find something new, and quickly.

Knutas turned halfway around in his chair and looked out the window. It was a dreary gray day. This early summer season hadn't been worth much so far. Yesterday's sunshine had been a welcome change, but now the clouds were back.

Karin Jacobsson and Thomas Wittberg were now in place in Stockholm. Jacobsson had called him earlier in the day. They were very busy interviewing people who knew Helena Hillerström, and they would most likely have to stay a few more days. Knutas missed Karin whenever she wasn't at the station. Of course, he was on good terms with the others in the group, but there was something special between him and Karin. They had found it easy to talk to each other from her very first day with the Visby police, after she had spent several years as a trainee in Stockholm. It wasn't long before he had the utmost confidence in her. In the beginning, when they were getting to know each other, Knutas thought for a short time that he was in love with Karin, but it was just then that he met his future wife and fell instantly in love with her.

Karin Jacobsson did not have a boyfriend, as far as Knutas knew. Even though they worked so closely together, she rarely talked about her personal life.

It was three o'clock in the afternoon by the time Johan and Peter finished editing and sent off the interview with Emma Winarve. It took ten minutes for Grenfors to call. He praised them for the story, which was going to be shown on all the news programs that evening. Even so, Grenfors, who was never completely satisfied, wanted them to talk to the neighbors in the area as well. The murder had occurred right in their own backyard, after all, he said.

"But we've already been out there and talked to the old lady in Fröjel," Johan objected. His voice crackled with displeasure.

Peter was sitting in an armchair, watching him.

"Channel Four had the neighbors on their noon broadcast," the editor pointed out.

"And so we have to include them, too?" said Johan, annoyed.

"You have to admit that it's good to talk to anyone who happens to live in the neighborhood of a murder scene."

"Sure, but I don't know if we can make it in time for the evening news."

"Try," Grenfors urged him. "If nothing else, we can use it for later programs."

"Sure thing."

They left immediately, driving down toward Klintehamn once again, and then in the direction of Fröjel. It was still only two days since the murder. Johan thought it felt like a lot more time had passed. *It's actually incredible how much a person can get done,* he thought.

They stopped at the first farm after the turnoff to Gustavs, a red house and a barn with a chicken coop. The hens were scratching the dirt inside a pen, cackling merrily. A dog came running up to them, wagging its tail. Obviously not much of a watchdog.

They rang the bell. A woman opened the door at once. She had curly blond hair and an alert expression on her face.

"Yes?" She gave them an inquisitive look.

A long-haired cat rubbed affectionately against their legs. They could hear children's voices inside the house.

Johan introduced Peter and himself. "We're out talking to people who live around here. Because of the murder, you know. Did you know the woman who was killed?"

"No, I can't say that I did. Of course we knew who the family was, but we didn't spend any time with them."

"What do you think about what happened?"

"It's terrible that something like that could happen here. I certainly hope they catch the person who did it as quickly as possible. It's so upsetting. I can't stop thinking about it. And the children, well, I'm keeping a close eye on them. We have five."

The woman called to her children, then closed the front door and sat down on the single bench on the porch. She pulled out a can of snuff, pinched off a piece, and stuck it under her lip. She held out the can to Johan and Peter, but both of them declined the offer.

"There's one thing I happened to think about last night. The police were here earlier, asking about things. They talked mostly to my husband. Last night when I couldn't sleep, it popped into my head."

"What was that?" asked Johan.

"I have a hard time sleeping, so I lie awake a lot at night. Last Monday night I heard a car turn down our street outside. There are never any cars going past here at night, so I thought it was odd. I got up to see where it went, but when I looked out, I couldn't see anything. As if it had been swallowed up by the earth. And it's strange because the road continues down toward the sea. I just had to go out and have a look. When I opened the front door, I heard it again. Then it went past our house. The street curves just outside here, so I never managed to see what kind of car it was."

"Did you notice anything else?"

"I noticed the sound. The engine sounded . . . what should I say . . . it sounded older somehow. It didn't sound like a new car."

"Could it have been one of your neighbors?"

"No, I asked all the neighbors today, just because I thought it was strange that someone was out driving past here in the middle of the night. But no one had been out, and besides, I know what all my neighbors' cars sound like."

"How many of you live around here?"

"Well, there's us and the veterinarian who lives on the next farm. Then there's the Jonsson family, who are farmers and own the fields you see all around here. They have a big farm on the left side of the road a little farther down, past the veterinarian. And then there's a family with children, the Larssons, closest to the water on the right-hand side."

"Do you know what time it was when you heard the car?"

"I think it must have been around three."

"Have you told the police about this?"

"Yes, I called them this morning. I went over there to be interviewed earlier today."

"I see," said Johan. "Could we ask you a few questions on camera?"

After a little coaxing, the woman agreed. The rest of the people who lived in the area firmly declined.

Yet Johan reluctantly had to admit that Grenfors had been right. It was a good idea to go out and interview the neighbors.

Once again they sat in the newsroom and spliced together a two-minute story that was sent over to Stockholm five minutes before the main news broadcast, to their editor's great satisfaction.

Kristian Nordström arrived at the police station at precisely five o'clock in the afternoon, as agreed. *He looks good,* Knutas observed as they shook hands. He had decided to hold the interview in his office, with Detective Inspector Lars Norrby present.

"Would you like some coffee?" asked Norrby.

"Yes, please. With milk. I came straight from the airport, and the coffee on the plane tasted like cat piss."

He brushed his hair back from his forehead and leaned back in his chair, crossing one leg of his elegant trousers over the other. He smiled a bit tensely at the superintendent, who got out a tape recorder and placed it on the desk in front of them.

"Do we really need that?"

"Unfortunately, it's necessary," said Knutas. "I hope it doesn't bother you too much."

"Well, it's just a little distracting."

"Try to pretend it's not there. As I said on the phone, this is a purely routine interview. We've talked to everyone who was at the party except you. That's why you're here."

"I see."

Norrby returned with the coffee, and then they could begin the interview.

"What were you doing on June fourth, meaning on the second day of Whitsun?"

"As you already know, I was having dinner with my old friend Helena

Hillerström and her boyfriend, Per Bergdal. Helena and I have known each other for many years. We went to school together."

"Did you come alone?"

"Yes."

"Tell us about the evening."

"At first it was very pleasant. We had dinner and drank a lot of good wine. It had been a year since the whole gang had seen each other. After dinner we started dancing. No one had to go to work the next day, so I think everybody was really planning to party."

"How did the fight start between you and Per Bergdal?"

Kristian laughed nervously and stroked his short, neatly trimmed beard, which actually wasn't much more than a stubble. "Yes, well, that was really stupid. I don't know what got into him. He acted like some kind of damned Neanderthal. It started with me dancing with Helena, the way I usually do. Suddenly Per came rushing over like some sort of tornado and yanked her away from me. I hardly had time to react. Then I saw them going out through the balcony doors. Out onto the veranda in back, I mean. I didn't pay much attention. I started dancing with Beata instead. After a while Helena came racing back inside. She was sobbing and ran into the bathroom. And she didn't come out. I didn't see her again that evening."

You never saw her again at all, thought Knutas, but he didn't say anything except "Then what happened?"

"I went out to talk to Per, but no sooner did I walk through the door than I got punched right in the face. Fucking idiot," he muttered half to himself, shaking his head.

"Didn't you strike back?"

"I'm sure I would have if the others hadn't come out and separated us. After that the party was over, of course. He certainly succeeded in wrecking the whole thing."

"Where did you go afterward?"

"I shared a cab with Beata and John. They live in Visby, and I live in Brissund."

"So they got out of the cab and you continued on home by yourself?"

"Yes."

"Do you live alone?"

"Yes."

"Do you have a girlfriend?"

"No."

"Why not?"

His reaction to the question surprised them. Kristian Nordström turned bright red in the face.

"What the hell business is that of yours?"

"Everything is our business," replied Knutas calmly. "At least for as long as this murder investigation is going on. Answer the question."

"I don't have an answer."

"Are you gay?"

The color of Nordström's face got even redder, if that was possible. "No."

"Come on," coaxed Knutas. "You're a good-looking guy. I'm sure you're aware of that yourself. You seem to have a good job, you're single, and you're in your prime. Have you ever had any long-term relationships?"

"What the hell is this? What's the point of all these questions? Are you psychologists?"

"No, we're police officers. And we want to know the answer."

"I've never been married or engaged, and I've never lived with anyone, either. My job requires me to travel two hundred and fifty days a year. So maybe it's not inconceivable that this has something to do with the matter," said Nordström sarcastically. "If you want to know whether I'm sexually active, the answer is yes. You can have sex in lots of different ways, and I don't need anything else in my life right now."

He started to get up from his chair. "Is that enough, or is there something else you want to know? How about which positions I like best?"

Both Norrby and Knutas were surprised at his vehement reaction.

"Take it easy. And sit down," Knutas urged him.

Nordström sat down again and wiped the sweat from his forehead with a handkerchief. *This guy's the sensitive type,* thought Knutas. He would have to proceed more cautiously.

"How was your relationship with Helena Hillerström?"

"Good. We were good friends. We've known each other since middle school."

"Was there ever anything between you besides just friendship?"

"No. There never was."

"Did you have other feelings for her, feelings that went beyond mere friendship?"

"Obviously I thought she was pretty. Everyone did. Well, you've seen her yourself."

"Nothing ever happened between the two of you?"

"No."

"Why not, do you think?"

"No clue. It just never happened."

"According to Per Bergdal, you and Helena had something going, as he put it. For a while a long time ago."

"Bullshit."

"Where do you think he got that idea?"

"No clue. He's so damn jealous. He imagines all sorts of things."

They didn't get much more out of Kristian Nordström during that first interview. He was allowed to go home, with the promise to inform them if he had plans to leave the island.

Afterward the two officers had a cup of coffee together to sum up their impressions.

"We need to keep an eye on this guy," said Knutas.

"Yes, he seems like he's walking on pins and needles. An incredibly hotheaded person," agreed Norrby, looking thoughtful. "We should ask more of the people in their circle of friends to corroborate what he said."

Knutas concurred. "I'm going to have someone check up on him right away."

FRIDAY, JUNE 8

In a classroom at the small Kyrck School in Roma, Emma Winarve was getting ready for the final day of school. Outside the window, Roma's wooden church tower loomed against the gray sky. The apple trees were in bloom, and next to the schoolyard Mr. Matton's sheep were hungrily grazing on the early summer grass.

The classroom, which was decorated with birch leaves and lilacs, would soon be filled with sixteen expectant eight-year-olds who had a long summer vacation ahead of them.

She had been gone several days and wanted to be alone for a moment before her pupils came rushing in.

Three unreal days had passed since Helena was murdered. She couldn't comprehend that it had really happened. She had cried and talked, and talked and cried, and talked some more. With Olle, with the friends that she and Helena had in common, with everyone who had been at the party, with Helena's parents and neighbors, and with her colleagues here at school. Per Bergdal was in custody in Visby and was not permitted to speak to anyone.

Emma had been in contact with the police and with the prosecuting attorney. She had begged and pleaded to be allowed to talk to Per, with no results. They refused to budge. He was forbidden to have any sort of contact with the outside world, for reasons associated with the investigation.

Emma was convinced that he was innocent. She wondered what his life would be like after this was all over, vilified by the media as he was. Everyone would have some doubts about him, at least until they found the real murderer. And who could that be? She shuddered at the thought. Was it someone Helena had met by chance? Or someone she knew? Someone she hadn't told Emma about?

Of course, she and Helena knew each other well, and of course, they always told each other everything. At least she thought they did. Or did Helena have secrets that she hadn't shared with Emma? These were the kinds of thoughts that were tormenting her, making her tired and irritable in the midst of her grief. She had quarreled with Olle when she thought he was showing a lack of sympathy. She had screamed loudly at him and then thrown a carton of milk on the floor so that it splattered all over the kitchen—even up on the beams in the ceiling, as she discovered when she cleaned up the next morning.

The whole thing seemed like a nightmare, as if it hadn't really happened. She picked up the remaining half-withered potted plants that stood on the windowsill. *I'll take them home and try to revive them,* she thought.

She cast a glance at the clock. Almost nine. It was time for her to open the classroom door.

The children greeted her shyly as they poured in and sat down on their benches. Naturally they all knew that the murdered woman was their teacher's best friend. Emma welcomed them and was touched to see the special effort they had made to look nice for the last day of school. Light-colored clothing and newly washed hair. Dresses and newly ironed shirts. Polished shoes and flowers in their hair.

Emma sat down at the piano.

"Are you ready, all of you?" she asked, and her pupils nodded. Then their bright children's voices filled the classroom. *The blossoming time has now arrived,* they sang as Emma played the piano. Everything was in keeping with the traditions for the last day of school. Emma let her thoughts wander as they sang the verses she knew inside and out after all her years of teaching.

Ah yes, summer vacation. For her part, she had no expectations whatsoever. Right now it was just important to try to maintain her composure and not fall apart. She had to take care of her children. Sara and Filip. They had the right to a glorious summer vacation, and they were looking forward to everything the family would be doing together.

Going for walks and swimming, visiting their cousins, taking an excursion out to little Gotska Sandön, and maybe a trip to Stockholm. How was she going to muster the energy for all that? Of course, the sense of shock would diminish. Her grief would seem more distant. But the loss of Helena was so painful. She wasn't going to get rid of that feeling very easily. And how was she supposed to understand what had occurred? Her very best friend had been murdered in a way that happened only in movies, or far away, in some other place.

The date for the funeral had been set. It would be held in Stockholm. Tears rose in her eyes at the thought, but she pushed it aside.

Suddenly she noticed that the children had fallen silent. She had no idea how long she had been playing after the song ended.

As far as Johan was concerned, his time on Gotland was running out. At least this time around. He had spoken with Grenfors about how long it would make sense for him to stay on the island. The police had put a lid on everything having to do with the investigation. No new clues or stories seemed to have emerged. The boyfriend was in custody, and it was likely that he would be indicted. They still didn't know why he was under suspicion. The news frenzy about the murder had waned, now worthy only of a few lines in the news reports. Today was Friday, and Regional News had no broadcasts on the weekends. The national news programs weren't interested in keeping a reporter on site if there were no new developments. They decided that Johan and Peter should return to Stockholm the following morning.

Johan had several free days coming. First he was going to get the cleaning and laundry out of the way, then go visit his mother and spend some time with her. She was still grieving after his father's death. He had died of cancer a year ago. The four brothers did the best they could to look after her, but Johan was the oldest, so it was only natural for him to assume the greatest responsibility. He would try to cheer her up, take her to a movie and maybe go out to eat. Then he was going to relax. Do some reading. Listen to music. On Sunday the Hammarby soccer team was playing AIK at Råsunda. His buddy Andreas had gotten them tickets.

He needed to go over to the newsroom to pack up his things, but first he decided to take a walk through town. A light, silent drizzle was making the streets wet. He didn't bother with an umbrella. He turned his face up toward the sky, closed his eyes, and let the drops run down his cheeks. He had always liked rain. It made him feel calm. It had rained when his father was buried, and he remembered that the rain made everything feel better, more dignified and peaceful in some way.

On Hästgatan he saw her through the big glass window of the café on the other side of the street. She was sitting alone at a window table, leafing through a magazine. In front of her stood a tall glass containing what looked like a caffe latte.

Johan stopped, feeling indecisive. He had some time to himself before he had to meet Peter at the newsroom. Without knowing how he was going to approach her or what he would say, he decided to go in.

The café was almost deserted. He was struck by the trendy interior: nice high ceilings; straight-legged bar stools at the bar; shiny coffee machines. Baguettes were piled next to Italian cheeses and sausages. Enormous chocolate muffins were heaped on trays. A luscious-looking girl stood behind the cash register with her hair attractively arranged in a loose knot. Just like any other Italian café.

How incredible to find this kind of place in little Visby, he thought. Ever since the college had opened on the island a few years back, new businesses had sprung up, and the town had acquired a new life during the off-season.

Emma was sitting at the far end of the café. As Johan approached, she glanced up.

"Hi," he said, thinking how ridiculous his smile must look. What was it about this woman that had such an effect on him? She peered at him inquisitively. Good Lord, she didn't even recognize him! In the next instant her expression changed and she pushed her hair back from her face.

"Oh, hi. It's you from the TV station. Johan, right?"

"Exactly. Johan Berg, from Regional News. May I join you?"

"Sure." She put away her magazine.

"I'll just get some coffee. Would you like anything?" he asked.

"No, thanks. I'm fine."

Johan ordered a double espresso. While he waited at the counter, he couldn't help looking at her. Her hair was straight and thick, hanging loose. She wore a denim jacket over a white T-shirt. Washed-out jeans again today. Prominent eyebrows and big dark eyes. She lit a cigarette and turned to look at him. He could feel himself blushing. Damn it all.

He paid for his coffee and sat down across from her. "I didn't think I'd see you again."

"No, I guess not." She gave him a searching glance and took a drag on her cigarette.

"How are you?" he asked, feeling like an idiot.

"Not so good. But at least now summer vacation has started. I'm a teacher," she explained. "Today was the last day of school, and this afternoon the school is giving a party for the children and their parents. I didn't feel up to going. I'm just not feeling well. Because of Helena's murder and all. I still can't believe it's true. I think about her all the time." She took another drag on her cigarette.

Johan felt the same attraction to her that he had felt before. What he most wanted to do was to take her in his arms, to hug and comfort her. He repressed the impulse.

"It's so hard to understand," she went on. "That it really happened."

She gazed absentmindedly at her cigarette, which she waved toward the ashtray, dropping tiny flakes of ash in it. "Mostly I think about who might have done it. And then I feel so furious. That someone has taken her away from me. That she no longer exists. Then I feel ashamed for having such selfish thoughts. And the police don't seem to know what they're doing. I don't understand how they can keep Per Bergdal in custody."

"Why not?"

"He loved Helena more than anything. I think they were even planning to get married. It's probably just because of the fight that the police think he's the murderer. Sure, it was unpleasant, but that doesn't necessarily mean that he killed her."

"What fight?"

"It was at the party, the night before Helena was found dead. Some of us went to Helena and Per's house for dinner."

"What happened?"

"Per got jealous when Helena danced with one of the guys, Kristian. He slapped Helena hard enough to draw blood, and then he punched Kristian, too. It was so stupid. They hadn't done anything. They were just dancing like everyone else."

"And this happened on the night before the murder?"

"Yes, didn't you know about it?"

"No, I had no idea," murmured Johan.

So that's the reason, he thought. Here was the explanation for why Bergdal had been arrested.

"It's so horrible . . . so unreal." She hid her face in her hands.

He reached his hand across the table and patted her clumsily on the arm. Emma's shoulders were shaking. Her sobs came in big, ragged gasps. Cautiously Johan sat down next to her on the sofa and handed her a paper napkin. She blew her nose loudly and leaned her head on his shoulder. Johan put his arms around her to offer some comfort.

"I don't know what I'm going to do," she whimpered. "I just want to get away from here."

After she had calmed down, he walked her out to her car, which she had parked on a side street. He walked a few paces behind her, with his eyes fixed on her slumped shoulders. When they reached her car, they stood there a moment as she rummaged through her purse to find the car keys. Just as she said, "See you," and bent down to unlock the car door, he took her arm. Very lightly. As if it were a question. She turned around and looked at him. He stroked her cheek, and then she leaned forward. Ever so slightly, just enough that he dared kiss her. A cautious kiss that lasted only a second before she pushed him away.

"I'm sorry," he said in a low voice.

"That's okay. No need to apologize."

She climbed into the car and turned the key in the ignition. Bewildered, Johan stood in the rain, staring at her through the car window. Then she swung the car out into the street and drove off. His lips were still burning from the kiss, and he was staring foolishly down the street.

Slurp, shluuump. Rubber boots, sizes 2½ and 3½, sloshed through the muddy field. Matilda and Johanna loved the sound when the mud tried to hold on to their boots and pull them off. Here and there the sheep had created mini lakes that they were stomping and splashing around in. The rain was pouring down, and the rosy faces of the girls were lit up with delight. They pressed their feet firmly down in the muck and then pulled them back up. Swuuup, swuuump. From a distance two little figures in rain gear could be seen out in the field. As they were playing, the girls had wandered quite a ways from home. They weren't actually allowed to go this far, but their mother hadn't noticed. She was sitting and nursing their baby brother, immersed in a discussion about infidelity on Oprah.

"Look at this," shouted Matilda, who was older and the more adventurous of the two.

She had caught sight of something under a bush at the edge of the field and was using all her strength to lift up the object. It was an axe. She held it out toward her sister.

"What's that?" asked Johanna, her eyes wide.

"An axe, dummy," said Matilda. "Let's show it to Mamma."

Since the axe was stained with what looked like blood and the girls had found it near the murder scene, their mother immediately called the police.

Knutas was one of the first to hear about the find. He jogged through the corridors of the police station and down the stairs to the tech department. Today all sorts of things were happening. The preliminary autopsy report had arrived in the morning, and it showed, as they thought, that Helena Hillerström had died from an axe blow to the head, but she had not been raped. On the other hand, she did have skin scrapings belonging to Bergdal under her fingernails, which was not particularly surprising, since they already knew about the fight. He had also spoken to SCL and learned that the panties had no trace of semen.

When Knutas came huffing and puffing through the glass door, Erik Sohlman had just received the axe in a paper bag.

"Hi, there," he greeted Knutas.

"Did it just get here?" Knutas leaned over the bag.

"Yup," said Sohlman as he pulled on a pair of thin latex gloves. "Let's have a look."

He switched on a couple more fluorescent lights that hung over the white examination table and carefully opened the bag, which had been sealed with a label that said: "Found 2001-06-06 at approx. 3:30 P.M. in a field at Lindarve Farm, Fröjel. The find was made by Matilda and Johanna Laurell of Lindarve Farm, Fröjel. Tel: 0498-515-776."

Sohlman began photographing the axe. Cautiously he turned it this way and that so he could capture it from various angles. When he was done, he straddled a stool next to the examination table.

"Now let's see if we can find anything interesting," he said, pushing his glasses higher on the bridge of his nose. "See this on the blade?"

Anders Knutas studied the heavy blade of the axe. He could clearly see dark spots on it. "Is that blood?"

"It looks like it. We'll send it to SCL for DNA analysis. The worst part is that they always take so damn long. It may be several weeks before we get an answer," muttered Sohlman.

He took out a magnifying glass and turned his attention to studying the handle of the axe. "We're in luck. Since the handle is both painted and varnished, there's a greater chance that there will be fingerprints."

After a moment he gave a whistle. "Look at this."

Knutas almost stumbled as he stood up from his chair. "What is it?"

"Here, on the handle. Do you see it?"

Knutas took the magnifying glass that Sohlman handed to him. The print of a finger appeared on the handle. He turned the magnifying glass, and suddenly he could see several fingerprints.

"They seem to be from at least two different people," said Sohlman. "Can you see that they're two different sizes? One small and one big. That means we're going to need prints from the two little girls who found the axe, so we can make comparisons. It must have been protected in some way. Otherwise the rain would have destroyed the prints."

"Do you think this could be the murder weapon?"

"Absolutely. The size and type correspond to the wounds."

Sohlman pulled out a box of soot powder, which he brushed onto the axe handle. He took out two tubes, mixing their contents into a plastic paste, which he spread on the handle, using a little plastic spatula.

"Now we have to let it harden. It'll take ten minutes."

"Okay," said Knutas, controlling his eagerness. "In the meantime I'll go get Bergdal's prints."

They had their answer forty-five minutes later. The fingerprint on the handle of the axe turned out to belong to Per Bergdal.

So that's how it's going to be after all, Knutas observed, disappointed. Bergdal had apparently murdered his girlfriend on the beach. They couldn't be entirely sure until the results from the DNA analysis of the blood came in, but if the blood on the axe was Helena's, there could be no doubt. The boyfriend was the perpetrator. *Maybe I'm getting old,* he thought. *My judgment is starting to slip.*

He gathered the other members of the investigative team in his office to report on the results.

"Goddamn, that's great," said Norrby.

"This calls for a celebration," exclaimed Sohlman. "Let's go out on the town for a mandatory beer. I'll buy the first round."

Everyone got up, chattering happily.

Anders Knutas immediately notified the county police commissioner as well as prosecuting attorney Smittenberg. He called Karin Jacobsson and Thomas Wittberg in Stockholm and told them that they could come back home. Per Bergdal would be charged that very evening. The court proceedings for the issuance of an indictment would take place over the weekend.

The news was reported to the newspapers, radio, and TV, and the case was regarded as closed. Gotland could breathe a sigh of relief.

MONDAY, JUNE 11

Johan's week would turn out to be tougher than he thought. As soon as he set foot in the newsroom on Monday morning, he was summoned to Grenfors's office.

"Great job you did on Gotland."

"Thanks," said Johan, slightly on guard. He always had a feeling that the editors wanted something special from him whenever they started off the conversation by praising him.

"I assume nothing else is going to happen over there. After all, the boyfriend seems to be guilty," Grenfors went on.

"Could be."

"The thing is, now we're in the shit here."

"Is that so? Seems I've heard this before, haven't I?" Johan said dryly.

Grenfors ignored his tone of voice. "We had to scrap the feature story that was supposed to run on Friday. We don't have any new ideas. You talked before about putting together something on the gangster war in Stockholm. Do you think you'd have time to do it now?"

Johan understood the problem, so he didn't want to be unreasonable, even though he'd been hoping for at least one calm day after the Gotland trip. Emma Winarve had haunted his mind all weekend, making it hard for him to sleep. He couldn't understand what had gotten into him. A married woman and the mother of young children, from Gotland, and he hardly knew her. It was ridiculous. He looked at Grenfors.

"Well, I guess so. I have a lot of material already on tape from before. I don't think there's time to do a full-length story, but I could probably put together seven or eight minutes."

Grenfors looked relieved. "Good. Then that's what we'll do. I knew I could count on you."

When Johan returned to his cubicle in the editorial office, he started going through his material. The shooting in Vårberg, when a man with a criminal record was killed right on the street with three shots to the head. An execution, pure and simple. Two months earlier the victim had been involved in the murder of a pizza maker in Högdalen, who was shot to death while sitting in his car in a parking lot. The pizza maker in turn was in debt, big time, to the unknown owner of a restaurant in Stockholm's underworld, which everybody knew had connections to the Russian mafia. In addition, he was an accomplice in the murder of a gym owner in Farsta, who was shot to death at the Täby racetrack several years before. And so it continued. Shootings, armed robberies, and even murder had become common fare in Stockholm. The news desk had stopped reporting all the incidents of armed robbery. They occurred so often that they no longer qualified as news on the broadcast. Most of the murders and serious felonies in Stockholm were committed by a small clique of hardened criminals. That was the angle that Johan was thinking of using for his story.

He had developed a good contact with the girlfriend of one of this year's latest victims. He punched in her phone number. She had promised him an interview.

Now it was time to call in that promise.

FRIDAY, JUNE 15

With long, powerful movements, Knutas covered one yard after another, swimming the breaststroke. He raised his head above the surface for a brief moment to draw in more air and then lowered it back down. In the water he was weightless and timeless. It gave him a different perspective, which made his thoughts clearer.

It was seven in the morning, and he was alone in the seventy-five-foot swimming pool at the Solberg Baths. Almost a week had passed since Per Bergdal was charged. Even though the murder of Helena Hillerström was considered solved, it wouldn't leave him alone. Bergdal was supposed to appear in the Gotland district court on August 15 to be indicted for the murder of his girlfriend. He was still maintaining his innocence, and Knutas was inclined to believe him. Uncertainty was plaguing him like a toothache. He had spoken to SCL in Linköping on the previous day. It turned out that the blood on the axe did come from Helena. So they could establish that the axe was the murder weapon, and it was true that Bergdal's fingerprints had been found on it. Yet Knutas still couldn't shake the feeling that the boyfriend was innocent.

He switched from the breaststroke to the backstroke.

According to Bergdal, the axe belonged to the Hillerström family, and it must have been stolen from the unlocked shed on the property. It had been in their possession for several years, and Per Bergdal had used it to chop wood any number of times. It was no wonder that his prints were found on it.

Knutas expressed his doubts to prosecuting attorney Smittenberg during one of their conversations. The prosecutor was a reasonable man who upheld the principle of maintaining objectivity. He encouraged

Knutas to continue working on trying to uncover the facts. Of course, he had to admit that the technical evidence was convincing, but if new circumstances should come to light supporting Bergdal's story, then he wouldn't stand in the way. Unfortunately, Knutas hadn't had any luck. The fact that Per Bergdal also wore a size 11¹/₂ shoe, which corresponded to the print found at the crime scene, didn't help matters. On the other hand, the police hadn't been able to find a shoe belonging to Bergdal that matched the print. The fact that Helena Hillerström had not been raped or subjected to any other sort of sexual assault perplexed Knutas. The question was: What did the panties in her mouth signify if the murder had no sexual motivation? *Something doesn't fit,* thought Knutas, and he summoned all his energy to swim the last few laps of the pool.

After he had swum his mile, he was happy. He spent some time in the sauna, then took a cold shower, and he felt like a new man. In the locker room he stood in front of the full-length mirror in that ruthless lighting and critically examined his body. His gut had definitely gotten bigger lately, and his arm muscles were no longer worth showing off. Maybe he should start lifting weights. There was a small gym at police headquarters. He ran his hand through his hair. It was streaked with gray, but at least it was still thick and shiny.

Back at headquarters he ate a breakfast of fresh cheese rolls and coffee in his office.

Karin Jacobsson and Thomas Wittberg had returned from Stockholm and submitted a detailed report on the interviews they had conducted. They had found nothing remarkable about Helena Hillerström's life.

She took judo classes several times a week at a Friskis & Svettis gym, and she was known as something of a workout addict among her friends. In addition, she had developed a great interest in dogs over the past several years. She often went to dog training classes with her smooth-coated retriever named Spencer, who almost never left her side when she wasn't at work. They had all attested to the fact that the animal was a superb watchdog.

The meeting with Helena's parents hadn't yielded much. Both parents were still so shocked that they had a hard time talking. The mother had been taken to the emergency room of the psychiatric ward at Danderyd Hospital, where she had been kept under observation for a couple of days. When Wittberg and Jacobsson met the parents, Helena's mother had just returned home. She gave only brief answers to their questions. The father couldn't think of anything unusual in Helena's life. No jealous old boyfriends, no threats, or anything else that might be of interest to the homicide investigators.

Helena's siblings, friends, and work colleagues had all presented the same picture of her. A stable, career-oriented woman. Smart and socially talented. She had plenty of friends but didn't easily allow anyone to get too close. The person who seemed to be closest to her was Emma Winarve, in spite of the fact that they lived far away from each other.

Per Bergdal's parents were, of course, in despair over the fact that their son was accused of murder. Most of the people who knew him and who had been interviewed by the police were certain that he was innocent. The only one who seemed convinced that Bergdal was the killer was Kristian Nordström. *Ah yes, Nordström,* thought Knutas. There was something sneaky about him. Knutas couldn't really put his finger on it, but it was there. He was also positive that Nordström hadn't told them everything.

Knutas devoted the morning to dealing with a pile of paperwork. For several hours he pushed aside all thoughts of Helena Hillerström's murder. His office was quite large, although looking the worse for wear. The paint around the windows had begun to peel in several places, and the wallpaper had yellowed over the years. The wall behind him was hidden by rows of orange, green, and yellow ring binders. Near the window facing the parking lot, four visitor's chairs were grouped around a table, intended for small meetings. Several brochures about the community police substations lay on the table. Over the years he hadn't devoted much attention to sprucing up his office, and it showed.

A photograph on his desk bore witness to the fact that he had a life outside of police headquarters. Lina and the children, laughing in the sand at Tofta beach. A single flowering plant stood on the windowsill, a hardy white geranium that he talked to and watered practically every day. Karin Jacobsson had given it to him as a birthday present several years ago. He was in the habit of saying good morning to the plant and asking it how it was doing, but he kept that habit private.

He went out to lunch by himself. It was liberating to get outdoors. The height of summer was almost upon them. The approach of the summer season could also be seen in town. More and more restaurants were opening, tourists were streaming in, and there was more life and commotion in the evenings in Visby. Many school groups and conference participants came to Gotland at this time of year.

After lunch he shut himself up in his office with a cup of coffee. He didn't feel like talking to any of his colleagues, and on this Friday everything was calm at police headquarters. He leafed through the documents from the Hillerström investigation and studied the photographs.

He was interrupted by a discreet knock on the door. Karin stuck her head in. She gave him a big smile, displaying the gap between her front teeth.

"Are you still here? It's Friday, for God's sake, and it's past five. I have to stop at the state liquor store. Do you need anything?"

"I'll go with you," he said, and got up from his chair.

A good dinner with a bottle of red wine would undoubtedly put him in a better mood.

The inn was packed. The Monk's Cellar was still popular. The rustic inn with its medieval archways had been in business for more than thirty years now, and it was practically an institution in Visby. In the winter, only the smaller bar and part of the restaurant were open. Then it could get crowded on weekend evenings. During the high season "the Monk" was transformed into a pleasure palace with several restaurant sections, bars, and dance floors, as well as a stage for live performances. On this Friday evening, several of the smaller bars were already open: the salsa bar, the vinyl bar, and the little intimate beer bar. All of them were full to the bursting point.

Frida Lindh and a group of women friends were sitting at a round table in the middle of the vinyl bar. They had positioned themselves so that they had a full view of the room, and they were also quite visible themselves.

There was a great deal of noise and commotion. From the loudspeakers, "Riders on the Storm" by the Doors was blaring at top volume. People were drinking beer from big tankards and doing shots. At one table several young guys were playing backgammon.

Frida was feeling pleasantly tipsy. She was wearing a tight-fitting top and a short black skirt made of a clinging fabric. She felt attractive and sexy and full of energy.

It was great to be out with her newfound girlfriends. She had moved to Gotland with her family only a year ago, and at the time she didn't know anyone in Visby, but through her children's daycare center and her job in a beauty salon, she had met lots of women who had become good friends, and she had grown quite fond of them. They had already made it a tradition to try to go out and have fun several times a month. This was the third time, and everyone at the table was in a great mood. Frida enjoyed the interested looks from various men in the bar, lapping up their attention. She laughed loudly at a joke, and out of the corner of her eye she noticed a newcomer. A tall medium-blond man had sat down at the bar. Dark eyebrows, thick hair, broad shoulders, wearing a polo shirt. He reminded her of someone who did a lot of sailing.

The man was alone. He glanced around the room, and their eyes met. *A real cutie,* she thought. He took a gulp of his beer and then fixed his eyes on her again, holding them there a little longer and smiling. Frida blushed and felt heat wash over her. She was having a hard time concentrating on what the others at the table were saying.

Her friends liked to talk about all sorts of subjects, from books and movies to recipes. Right now they were all engrossed in a conversation about how little their husbands helped out at home. Each of them had the same opinion about her husband's lack of imagination and insight when it came to realizing that the kids couldn't go to daycare wearing grubby shirts, or that the dirty clothes were actually overflowing in the laundry basket. Frida listened with half an ear, sipped her wine, and now and then looked over at the man at the bar. When the conversation around the table started focusing on how poorly the daycare center was operating and how big the classes were, she completely lost interest. She decided to go to the ladies' room so that she could walk past the newcomer at close range.

On her way back he tapped her on the shoulder and asked if he might buy her a drink. She happily said yes and sat down next to him at the bar.

"What's your name?" he asked.

"Frida. And you?"

"Henrik."

"You're not from around here, are you?"

"Is it that obvious?" he said with a smile. "I live in Stockholm."

"Are you here on vacation?"

"No. I own several restaurants with my father, and we're thinking about opening a place in Visby. We're scouting out the territory a bit."

He had almost unnaturally green eyes that gleamed at her in the dim light.

"That's great. Have you been to Gotland before?"

"This is my first time. Pappa comes here often. He's thinking of opening an inn with good Swedish food and live music in the evenings. For people who want to eat well and enjoy a little entertainment without having to go to a club. And not just a summertime inn, but one that's open all year round. What do you think of that idea?"

"Oh, I think that sounds wonderful. It's not really as dead around here in the wintertime as many people think."

By now her girlfriends had discovered what was going on. They eyed the pair sitting at the bar. Their expressions were by turns inquisitive, gleeful, and envious.

Frida straightened her skirt and sipped the wine that had been placed on the bar in front of her. She stole a glance at the man next to her. He had a cleft in his chin and looked even better close up.

"And what do you do?" he asked.

"I'm a hairdresser."

Involuntarily he ran his hand through his hair. "Here in town?"

"Yes, at a salon over at Östercentrum. It's called the Hairline. Drop by if you ever need a haircut."

"Thanks. I'll keep that in mind. I notice you don't have a Gotland accent."

"No, I moved here about a year ago. How long are you staying?"

She had quickly changed the subject to avoid having to explain why she had moved here or to mention her husband and children and all that. Frida was aware of her power to attract men. She liked to flirt, and she wanted to keep this tasty morsel interested. At least for a little while. Just because it was fun.

"I don't know. It depends on how things go," he said. "Maybe a week. If we find a place I'll probably be here most of the summer."

"I see. How nice. I hope you find something."

She sipped her wine again. What an exciting man.

He looked around the room, and when he turned his head, she was positive: He was wearing a hairpiece. *I wonder why,* she thought. *Maybe he has really thin hair.* He didn't look particularly old. About her own age. *There are plenty of people who lose their hair early on. Good Lord, guys should be able to look good, too.* Her thoughts were interrupted when he asked a question.

"What are you thinking about?"

"Oh, it's nothing." She could feel the color rising in her face.

"How sweet you are," he said, squeezing her knee.

"Do you think so?" she said foolishly and removed his hand.

After about an hour her girlfriends called to her, and she decided to go back to their table. Henrik was leaving, anyway. He had asked for her phone number. That's when she decided to break the spell. She told him that she was married and that it wouldn't be a good idea for him to call.

Around one o'clock the bar closed, and the group of women broke up. They said good-bye outside with hugs and reassurances that they'd get together again soon. Frida was the only one who lived in the section of town called Södervärn, about three-quarters of a mile south of the ring wall. She got on her bike and pedaled off alone in that direction.

When she went through Söderport, a cold wind greeted her. It was always windier outside the wall. *How nice that it's still so light out, at least,* she thought. She kept on pedaling, but her foot slipped on the pedal and she scraped her leg so that it started to bleed. It stung.

Shit. She realized she was drunker than she thought. But she kept on going, wanting to get home as fast as possible now.

She turned left at the parking lot and rode past the Gutavallen sports center. She crossed the street and headed up the long, steep slope near the water tower. Halfway up the hill she had to stop and get off her bike. She was too worn out.

On the left side of the road was the cemetery. The headstones were lined up as if for some sort of dreary parade inside the low stone wall. Even though she was practically numb from all the alcohol, she felt a sense of uneasiness creep over her. Why had she insisted on taking her bike? Stefan had tried to persuade her to take a cab home, especially because of Helena Hillerström's murder less than two weeks ago. She had dismissed the idea by saying it was too expensive. They needed to save their money. Their finances were shaky after buying the house. Besides, the killer had been caught. It turned out to be the boyfriend.

Now she was regretting her decision. Damn, how stupid she was. A cab ride home wouldn't have cost more than a hundred kronor. It would have been worth it.

She was all alone on the road. Not another person in sight. The only sound was her own footsteps in her high-heeled shoes. They were hurting her feet terribly.

The cemetery continued for another hundred yards. She had to walk past it.

When Frida had gone half the distance, she heard footsteps behind her. Heavy and firm. She listened. She had a strong urge to turn around but didn't dare. She picked up her pace.

The footsteps were louder now. She had the distinct feeling that she was being followed. Or was she just imagining things? She tried stopping for a moment. The footsteps stopped. All of a sudden her brain was crystal clear. The road was still climbing uphill, so there was no sense in getting on her bike. On one side of the road was the cemetery. The other side was lined with houses with big shady yards. All the windows were dark.

She walked as fast as she could, no longer feeling the cold. Damn her short skirt and these shoes that hurt her feet.

She considered flinging the bicycle to the ground and trying to head across someone's yard. Instead she started to run. That made the person behind her start running, too. Terrified, she ran as fast as she could. The road leveled out and started sloping downward.

She was just about to jump onto her bike when two strong hands grabbed her by the neck from behind and pressed their fingers into her throat. She couldn't breathe and let go of the bicycle. It fell over with a crash.

SATURDAY, JUNE 16

Stefan Lindh reported his wife missing on Saturday morning. He was awakened at eight o'clock when their youngest child came into the bedroom. Frida's side of the bed was empty. His first thought was that she must be in the bathroom, but it didn't take him long to discover that his wife wasn't in the house at all. He called her girlfriends, but she wasn't with any of them. Then he tried the hospital and the police, with no results. The officer on duty told him to wait a few more hours.

When Frida hadn't come back by lunchtime, he put the kids in the car and drove down to the Monk's Cellar. He drove the same route that he thought Frida would have taken on her bike. By two o'clock in the afternoon, he couldn't wait any longer; he called the police, sick with worry. Knutas was informed, and, considering that a woman had been murdered less than two weeks ago, he decided to call a meeting of the investigative team. While he waited for the others, he phoned the worried husband, who was desperate and begged the police for help. His wife had never disappeared like this before.

"Take it easy," murmured Knutas. "We're going to have a short meeting here at headquarters in a moment, and right after that either I or one of my colleagues will come over to see you. Shall we say in an hour?"

He hung up the phone. The others came in, one by one, and sat down around his little table: Karin Jacobsson, Thomas Wittberg, and Lars Norrby.

"So what we have is a missing woman," Knutas began. "Her name is Frida Lindh, thirty-four years old, married and the mother of three. The family lives in Södervärn, on Apelgatan, to be more precise. She disappeared last night after spending the evening in town with three women friends. They went to the Monk to have dinner and then sat in one of the bars at the inn and drank beer until closing time. According to what her friends told the husband, they said good-bye to each other outside the place. By that time it was a little past 1:00 A.M. Frida is the only one of them who lives south of downtown, so she left the group and headed off alone to bicycle home. No one has seen her since. This is the information we have from her husband. Because Frida Lindh appears to be a conscientious mother to her young children, it doesn't seem right to me that she's missing. Her husband says that she has never disappeared like this before."

"Couldn't she have just gone home with someone?" asked Norrby with a smirk. "Someone who's more exciting than her husband?"

"Of course that's a possibility, but then she should have come back home by now, don't you think? It's almost four thirty, and the woman has three small children, for God's sake."

"You would think so, although in this job you never stop being surprised," said Norrby.

"You don't think that you're overreacting about this?" asked Wittberg, turning to Knutas. "Isn't it a little melodramatic to start sounding all the alarms just because a woman who went out drinking doesn't come straight home?"

Thomas ran one hand through his thick, dark, curly hair and then rubbed it along the stubble that covered his chin and cheeks. In front of him he had placed a bottle of Coca-Cola that was half empty.

"Are you grumpy just because you're hungover? Is that it?" Karin teased him, poking him in the ribs.

"Not at all," said Thomas.

Knutas gave him an annoyed look. "Considering that we recently had the homicide of a woman on our hands, I think we need to give this our immediate attention. We'll start by finding out what her girlfriends have to say. Karin, could you talk to the woman who lives on Bogegatan? The other two live on Tjelvarvägen. You can deal with them," he said, turning to Wittberg and Norrby. "I'll go see the husband. Then we'll meet back here. Shall we say around eight o'clock?"

The chairs scraped the floor as they all got up from the table. Norrby and Wittberg muttered to each other. "Hell, this is stupid. Bringing us in on a weekend for something like this. A woman who's cheating on her husband." They both shook their heads and sighed.

Knutas pretended not to notice.

He was standing up to his waist in the cold water. It was numbingly cold; he was enjoying it. It reminded him of his childhood when he would go swimming with his father and sister near their summer cottage. The first plunge into the sea water that hadn't yet warmed up. How they laughed and shrieked. It was one of the few happy childhood memories he had.

His mother, of course, didn't come along. She never went swimming. She was always busy with something else. Washing dishes, doing the laundry, cooking, making the beds, tidying up. He remembered wondering why all that always took such a long time. There were only four of them in the family, and his father did a lot of the chores at home, too. But somehow she always seemed to have her hands full. She never had any time to spend with them. To play.

If she had any free time, she would do crossword puzzles. Always those damn crosswords. Occasionally he would try to help her. Sit down next to her and give her suggestions for solving the puzzle. Then she would snap that he was ruining all the fun of it. She didn't want anyone to help. And he was pushed away. As usual.

He looked out across the sea. It was gray and motionless. Exactly like the sky. He had an almost spiritual feeling. Everything was calm. As if time and space had stopped. And here he was. By now he was starting to get used to the coldness of the water. He gathered his courage and dove in.

Afterward he sat naked on the lid of the old kitchen bench and spent a long time drying himself off. He felt cleansed. The space in the seat underneath him had been refilled. He exhaled everything that had weighed on him all these years. It seemed as if the more blood he spilled, the more purified he felt.

Södervärn is located about three-quarters of a mile from the ring wall. That part of town consists mostly of single-family homes from the early twentieth century, but here and there are a few recently built houses. The Lindh family lived in one of them. It was a one-story structure with a white-brick facade, a neat driveway, and an American-style mailbox. On the street several little boys were playing with field hockey sticks. They were taking turns shooting the ball toward a goal that had been set up on the sidewalk. Knutas parked his old Mercedes outside the white-painted wooden fence. He noticed little decals in the windows indicating that the house had an alarm system installed by one of the largest security companies. That was quite unusual on Gotland.

He pushed the doorbell and heard it ring inside the house.

Stefan Lindh opened the door almost at once. His eyes were red rimmed and unhappy.

"Where could she be? Have you heard anything?" He asked the questions even before saying hello.

"I think the first thing we should do is sit down and have a talk," said Knutas, and he walked right into the living room and sat down on the sofa with the floral upholstery without taking off either his shoes or his jacket. He pulled out his notebook.

"When did you discover that Frida hadn't come home?"

"This morning around eight o'clock when Svante woke me up. He's our two-year-old."

He sat down on a wicker chair next to the superintendent.

"I took the kids over to my parents' house. I didn't want them to be here at home while I'm so worried. We have two more, a girl who's five and a boy who's four."

"What did you do when you discovered that Frida wasn't in the house?"

"I tried calling her cell phone but didn't get an answer. Then I called around to her girlfriends. No one knew anything. So I alerted the police. A little later I drove over to the Monk's Cellar, taking the same route that she should have taken home, but I didn't see anything."

"Have you talked to her parents or other family members?"

"She's from Stockholm. Her parents and her brothers and sister all live there, but we hardly ever hear from them. They don't have much contact with each other. Frida and her parents, I mean. That's why I haven't talked to them. I didn't call her sister because I didn't want to upset her for no reason."

"Where do your parents live?"

"They live in Slite, on the east side of the island. They came over to pick up the children about an hour ago."

"How long have you lived here?"

"Just about a year. We used to live in Stockholm. Last summer we moved to the island. I was born and raised here, and all of my family is here on Gotland."

"How was Frida when she left home yesterday? I mean, what was her mood like?"

"Same as always. Cheerful, looking forward to the evening. She had really spiffed herself up. She's so happy about making friends with those women. Well, I am, too, of course. It wasn't easy for her to move here in the beginning."

"I understand. You have to excuse me for asking, but how are things between you and Frida? What's your relationship like, I mean?"

Stefan Lindh squirmed a bit. He had one leg crossed over the other. Now he switched legs and blushed slightly.

"Um, well, it's fine. Of course there's a lot of work to do. The three kids take up almost all our time. There isn't much time left over for anything else. Things are about the same for us as for most people, I suppose. No real problems, but we're not exactly floating on cloud nine, either."

"Have you had a fight or any kind of crisis recently?"

"No, just the opposite. I think things have been unusually good between us lately. It was tough when we first moved here, but now Frida seems to be thriving. The kids are doing well. They think the daycare center is fun."

"Has anything out of the ordinary happened lately? Have there been any strange phone conversations, or has your wife met anyone new that she's told you about? Maybe at work?"

"I don't think so," Lindh replied hesitantly, with a frown. "Not that I can recall offhand."

"What kind of work does she do?"

"She's a hairdresser. She works at the salon across from the Obs supermarket at Östercentrum."

"So she must meet lots of different people. Has she mentioned any particular customer lately? Anyone special?"

"No. Of course she talks about plenty of crazy customers, but there hasn't been anyone in particular lately."

"I noticed that you have a security system on your house. Why is that?"

"Frida wanted to have it installed when we moved in. She's afraid of the dark and doesn't feel safe without it. I travel quite a lot for my job, and sometimes I'm gone for several days at a time. Things are much better now that we have the security alarm."

Knutas handed Stefan Lindh his card. "If Frida comes home or contacts you, call me on my direct line. You can also reach me on my cell phone. It's always on."

"What are you going to do now?" asked Lindh.

"We'll start looking," replied Knutas, and stood up.

Knutas took the direct route back to headquarters. The others gradually came in, one after the other. It was past 9:00 P.M. by the time everyone had gathered in Knutas's office. They had all heard approximately the same story: that Frida had met a man and had talked to him for over an hour. None of the girlfriends had ever seen him before. They described him as tall and good-looking, with thick medium-blond hair, about thirty-five. One of the women noticed that he hadn't shaved that day. Frida and the stranger had flirted quite openly, and for a while he had held her hand.

The girlfriends thought she was out of her mind. Married and the mother of three. What would people say? Visby was a small town, and they had seen plenty of familiar faces at the inn.

The others had walked home together because they lived in the same direction, but Frida had bicycled off alone. Even though Frida liked to flirt, they didn't think she would go home with some strange man. They all agreed about that.

Knutas's cell phone rang. During the conversation, which for Knutas's part consisted of solemn grunts and uh-huhs, the superintendent's face took on a grayish hue.

Everyone's eyes were fixed on Knutas when he hung up. The silence in the room was palpable.

"A woman was found dead in the cemetery," he said grimly, and reached for his jacket. "All indications point to murder."

The young man who found the body had been taking his dog for a walk without a leash. When they passed the churchyard, the dog dashed into the cemetery, heading straight for some shrubbery.

When the investigative team arrived, a cluster of people had already gathered at the cemetery. Several police officers were in the process of putting up crime scene tape to prevent the curiosity seekers from coming closer.

One of the officers led the group to the murder scene. The woman's body had been hidden under branches that were arranged to make it seem natural. Knutas looked with horror at the slender figure on the ground. She was naked, lying on her back. Her throat was covered with blood that had run down over her breasts. There were gashes, some several inches long, on her stomach, her thighs, and one of her shoulders. Her arms were at her sides, splotched with dirt. Scratch marks were clearly visible on her legs. Her face was horribly pale. She looked like a wax doll, Knutas thought. As if she had been emptied of blood. Her skin was a yellowish white with no luster at all, her eyes wide open and dull. When Knutas leaned down to look at her head, an ice-cold band began pressing into his forehead. He shut his eyes, then opened them again. A scrap of lacy black fabric was sticking out of the victim's mouth.

"Do you see it?" he asked Jacobsson.

"Yes, I see it." His colleague was holding one hand over her mouth.

Sohlman appeared behind them. "The ME is on his way. He happened to be in Visby for the weekend. Sometimes we're in luck. We
haven't yet confirmed the identity of the victim. She has no purse, no
wallet, or any kind of ID, but it's most likely Frida Lindh. The age and
description match, and a woman's bicycle was found in some bushes
across the road."

"This is too awful," said Knutas. "Just a few hundred yards from
home."

The huge corridor in TV headquarters in the Gärdet district of Stockholm was packed with people. It was the evening of Swedish TV's annual summer party, and all the employees in Stockholm were invited.
More than fifteen hundred guests had arrived, mingling in the enormous studios lining the corridor. They were normally used for taping
entertainment shows and soap operas, but now they had been turned
over to the dancing and partying. The corridor itself had been transformed into a gigantic cocktail lounge in which several different types
of bars had been set up.

Over there the confident meteorologist was snickering with the most
ruthless of the reporters. An anchorman was swaggering around with a
bleary gaze, as if searching incessantly for a smooth-skinned, curva-
ceous intern to sink his teeth into. The cool crowd from the entertainment division was cavorting around on the dance floor, sticking close
together and apparently oblivious to the rest of the people around
them.

Johan and Peter were standing with their colleagues from Regional
News at one of the bars, drinking Mexican screwdrivers: tequila with
sparkling lemonade, lime juice, fresh squeezed limes and lemons, and
plenty of ice.

Johan took a big gulp of his cold drink. He'd been busting his butt
the past few days, working on the report about the gangster war in
Stockholm. It had taken longer than he anticipated, and he'd put in
many late nights all week long. He had finished the report fifteen
minutes before it was broadcast.

The assignment had worn him out, so it was great to relax now and wash away all the hard work of the past week. Even though there had been a lot for him to do, he had still thought about Emma—and cursed himself for doing so. He had no right to approach her and maybe screw up her life, but she had provoked a sense of agitation inside him that wouldn't go away.

Now that the case of the murdered woman had pretty much been solved, there wouldn't be any more trips to Gotland for him. At least not in the near future. It would be just as well to forget about her. That's what he had thought a hundred times over the past week. He knew her phone number by heart and several times had been on the verge of calling, but he stopped himself at the last second. He knew what a mistake that would be. The odds couldn't be worse.

He took another drink and let his gaze slide over the sea of partygoers. A short distance away, he caught sight of Madeleine Haga. She was talking to several reporters from the central desk. Petite, dark, and sweet, wearing black jeans and a glittery lavender top. He decided to go over to her.

"Hi, how's it going?" he asked.

"Good." She smiled up at him. "Just a little tired. I've been editing all day long. I'm in the middle of a big job. How about you?"

"I'm fine. Want to dance?"

Ever since Madeleine started as a reporter on the central desk, he'd been slightly interested in her. She was attractive, in a tough sort of way, with short hair and big brown eyes. It annoyed him that they always seemed to miss each other. They often worked at different hours of the day, and when they finally did run into each other, she always seemed to be busy. Sometimes she didn't even have time to say hello.

At the moment he was enjoying having her right in front of him. She danced rhythmically to the music, her eyes half closed, swaying her hips. Now and then she would give him a long look. They decided to get a beer and sit down somewhere. Somewhere secluded, Johan hoped.

As he picked up two cold bottles of beer from the bar, his cell phone rang. He hesitated about answering it but did anyway. He recognized the raspy voice at once.

"They've found another dead woman on Gotland. In the cemetery in Visby. She was murdered."

"When?" he asked, casting a glance at Madeleine. She was standing with her back to him, already talking to someone else.

"This evening, around nine," rasped his source. "All I know is that she was found murdered and that she couldn't have been there long. And get this: She had a pair of panties in her mouth, too."

"Are you positive?"

"One hundred percent. The police are already talking about a serial killer."

"Do you know how she was murdered?"

"No, but I would guess it's similar to the murder of the broad in Fröjel."

"Okay. Thanks a lot," said Johan.

As far as he was concerned, the party was over.

Emma sat at the kitchen table, slurping up the kefir. Slurping was the word. She lifted the spoon up to her mouth, opened it automatically, tipped in the kefir, and then dropped the spoon down in her bowl. Tiny little specks of kefir splashed onto the round kitchen table. Up to her mouth and down to the bowl, up and down. Over and over again, mechanically, and always at the same pace. She stared down at the bowl without seeing a thing. The children were asleep. Olle had gone out to have a beer with some of his buddies. He was tired of her and the way she kept shunning him. That's what he had told her earlier in the day. It was Saturday evening, and she had no desire to turn on the TV.

Outside a west wind was blowing. She didn't notice the slender birch trees outside the window bending and swaying.

Right now she wasn't noticing anything. For the past week she had gone around wrapped up in her own world. She felt so remote. She held the children, hugged them and kissed them, without really feeling anything at all. She looked at their happy faces and touched their soft arms. She cooked, cleaned up, wiped their noses, packed their book bags, made the beds, folded the laundry, read stories, and kissed them good night, but she wasn't really paying attention. She wasn't there.

She was even less present with Olle. He had tried to talk to her, comfort her, hug her. Everything he said sounded stupid and meaningless and had no effect on her. He had even tried to make love to her. She felt offended and pushed him away. Practically light-years away. How could she be interested in sex right now?

She thought about Helena all the time. The things they had done together. Things Helena used to say. The way she tossed back her hair. Her way of slurping her coffee. How they had grown apart after Helena moved away from the island, in spite of the fact that they kept in contact. She didn't know as much about Helena as she used to. What did her friend think about? What did she feel? How was her relationship with Per? How was it really? In spite of all her speculating, Emma was convinced that he was innocent.

They had argued about that, too, she and Olle. He thought the fingerprints were conclusive evidence, especially considering the fight at the party. The guy was a loose cannon, Olle had snorted, giving her a look of pity when she claimed that Per could never have done anything like that.

As if she didn't have enough problems, that journalist kept haunting her thoughts. Johan.

Emma couldn't understand what had come over her at the café. Those eyes. Lethal. Those hands. Dry and warm. He had kissed her. It was just a fleeting kiss, but that was enough to make her whole body tingle. A feeling from the past. Of what might have been.

She had experienced this before. Until she met Olle, she had gone through a large number of boyfriends. She was always the one who got bored. As soon as things started getting serious and she felt herself growing dependent, she would break up with the guy.

Olle had been a friend, one of the old gang. At first, when he made a few clumsy attempts to ask her out, she was totally uninterested, but then they started dating, and before she knew it, a whole year had passed. It felt comfortable and relaxing to be with him. Just the two of them.

She had grown tired of falling in love. Either waiting by the phone or making the call herself with her heart pounding, meeting at cozy little restaurants, going to bed together, feeling the wet of sex between her legs. *What is he thinking? Am I good enough? Are my breasts too small?*

Then the next phase, with the brief periods of happiness, the demands, the disappointments, and finally the indifference before the whole thing more or less fizzled out.

With Olle she had fun, and she felt secure. Over time she fell deeply in love, and things were good between them for many years. Lately her feelings had cooled. She felt no desire for him anymore. She thought of him more as a friend. Johan had made her feel something else.

Emma turned on the radio, and the soulful tones of Aretha Franklin streamed out. She wanted a cigarette but didn't feel like going outside to stand on the stairs to smoke. Her thoughts went back to Johan. A Stockholm boy who would presumably never make an appearance on the island again. Just as well. Maybe she had been extra susceptible that day because she was so exhausted. Her first day back at school after the murder, and almost her last. She had gone back to work for a couple of days to take care of everything she still needed to do before she could start her summer vacation.

Right now she just wanted some time to herself, an opportunity to regain some sort of balance and collect her thoughts. Luckily the children would be spending a couple of weeks at camp.

She was plagued by a feeling of listlessness. This time of year would normally be so glorious, but she was now a shadow of her former self. She had no energy. Just taking out the trash made her tired.

Emma raised her eyes to look at the clock on the wall. Almost eleven. *Maybe I should put in a load of wash before going to bed. Pull yourself together, goddamn it,* she thought angrily.

With her arms full of dirty laundry, she leaned down to put the clothes in the machine, then abruptly stopped what she was doing. The newscaster on the radio was reporting that a woman had been found murdered in the Visby cemetery.

SUNDAY, JUNE 17

When Johan and Peter climbed out of the cab in front of the Strand Hotel in Visby on Sunday afternoon, they were met by a cold gust. The wind had really begun to pick up. They had even felt the cab sway significantly as they drove in from the airport. Shivering, they dashed inside to the front desk. The fact that they were hungover wasn't helping matters.

They were given the same rooms they had before. *I wonder whether it's a coincidence or if there's something more to it,* Johan thought as he put his card key in the door.

He called Knutas, who explained that they were inundated with journalists and that a press conference would be held at three o'clock that afternoon. He had nothing to say until then.

"You must be able to tell me something," Johan persisted. "Was the woman murdered?"

Knutas's voice was thick with fatigue. "Yes."

"How?"

"I can't tell you anything about how she was murdered."

"What kind of weapon was used?"

"I can't tell you that, either."

"Has she been identified?"

"Yes."

"How old was she?"

"Born in '67, which makes her thirty-four."

"Did she have any sort of previous dealings with the police?"

"No."

"Is she from Visby?"

"Yes. That's enough for now. You'll have to wait until the press conference."

"One last question. Did she go out to a pub that evening?"

"Yes, she was at the Monk's Cellar with some of her girlfriends. They said good-bye to each other outside, and then she bicycled home alone."

"So presumably she was murdered on her way home?"

"That's one conclusion you might draw, yes," said Knutas impatiently. "I don't have any more time right now."

"Thank you. I'll see you at the press conference. 'Bye."

Johan and Peter went over to the cemetery on Peder Hardings Väg to film the crime scene and try to find someone willing to be interviewed. The place where the body had been found was cordoned off, but a short distance from there they found a police officer who was making sure that no one went inside the area. They tried to talk to him, but it quickly became evident that their attempts were in vain. The officer refused to answer any of their questions.

Johan strolled around the cemetery, trying to imagine what had happened, while Peter shot some footage. The woman had been bicycling home from the inn. Was that where she had met the killer? It was less than two weeks ago that Helena Hillerström was murdered. Her boyfriend had been charged, but if Johan's source had understood the situation correctly, the police believed that the same perpetrator was at work here. That meant they were looking for a serial killer, who might strike again at any time. Here on little Gotland. Incredible.

His source was going to try to get more information. Even though the police believed it could be the same perpetrator, he doubted that he would be able to get that confirmed. Two women viciously murdered within a couple of weeks. Right before the tourist season. The police would be very keen to keep any information to themselves.

He was rowing with calm, firm strokes. The oarlocks creaked. They needed to be greased. It had been a long time since he went out in

the boat. Several years. He had repaired the hole in the bottom.
Then he had dragged the boat down to the water. He knew where he
was going. He would head out to the point. That would be a good
spot. He had chosen it carefully. The idea came to him in the night.
He had lain awake, thinking. He wasn't going to make the same
mistake he did before. He had lost control. Been giddy with a sense
of triumph, mixed with fear. Surprised at himself and his power,
the fact that he could actually carry out his plan. He was both proud
and scared. Mostly proud. Now he felt a different sort of tranquil-
ity. He knew what he was capable of. This time they wouldn't find
the murder weapon.

He was lucky the sea was so calm. He had considered bringing
along a fishing rod so he would have an explanation if anyone hap-
pened to see him. But no, it wasn't necessary. Who would care what
he was doing in this boat? He didn't owe anyone an explanation. To
hell with all the people who had no idea what he was up to. To hell
with the rest of the world. Nobody cared, anyway. Or understood. He
was alone. He had always been alone. But now he was strong. The
generous rays of the sun warmed him. He wore only a pair of shorts,
rowing so hard that he was sweating. He looked down at his heaving
chest, hairy and muscular. He could easily deal with this. He felt in-
vincible. He laughed out loud. Only the seagulls heard him.

A tense mood hovered over the conference room of the criminal department at police headquarters. It was noon, and the lead investigators
had gathered prior to the press conference to go over the latest information pertaining to the new homicide. The county police commissioner was present. She was sitting next to Knutas with her lips pressed
tight. Sohlman, Wittberg, Jacobsson, and Norrby were seated on one
side of the table, while on the other sat prosecutor Smittenberg together with Superintendent Martin Kihlgård and Björn Hansson from
the NCP.

"We have a whole new situation now, and it's very serious," Knutas
began. "It seems that we're dealing with one and the same murderer.
For that reason, Helena Hillerström's boyfriend, Per Bergdal, is no

longer under suspicion for killing her. Birger has decided that he can be released from custody immediately."

The prosecutor nodded in agreement.

Knutas continued. "There are strong indications that the same perpetrator is behind both murders. There are similarities pointing in that direction. The women were attacked outdoors, and both had their panties stuffed in their mouths. On the other hand, the killer used different weapons each time, and, as I'm sure you all know, that's extremely unusual for a serial killer. It's the one thing that contradicts the likelihood that it was the same perpetrator. The first victim, Helena Hillerström, was killed with an axe. She died at the first blow to her head. After that the perpetrator delivered ten blows to various parts of her body in what seemed to be a fit of uncontrolled rage. But according to the ME's preliminary evaluation, the second victim, Frida Lindh, died from a wound that severed her carotid artery. After that the murderer delivered a large number of stab wounds to various parts of her body. There are at least ten in this case as well. None of the blows was directed at her sexual organs. The murder weapon was some kind of sharp instrument, presumably a knife. It has not been found. As you know, Helena Hillerström was not sexually assaulted, and there are no indications that the second victim was, either. We won't know for sure until the preliminary autopsy report on Frida Lindh is ready. It'll take a few days. As I mentioned, both victims were found with their panties stuffed in their mouths. No trace of semen was found on the ones belonging to Helena Hillerström. Frida Lindh's are being sent to SCL for analysis. Now let's take a look at a few pictures."

The lights were turned off, and Knutas pressed a button to display the pictures, one after another, on a screen. No one else in the room said a word.

"First we have the pictures of Helena Hillerström, who was killed on June fifth. As you can see, the body was subjected to a brutal assault. No one part of the body was attacked more than any other, and none of the violence was directed at her sexual organs."

A close-up of Helena Hillerström appeared on the screen.

"Fucking hell," muttered Norrby.

"Next we have the second homicide victim," Knutas went on. "Frida Lindh, who was killed early yesterday morning. Ten days after the first murder. Her body was found in the cemetery. Frida Lindh was also naked. In this case, the victim lost a lot more blood, as you can see. She, too, suffered multiple wounds. Again there are no external signs of sexual assault."

"What could the panties in the mouth mean?" asked Wittberg, half to himself. "Why does he do that?"

"It's certainly damn strange," Kihlgård agreed. "Did the murderer know these women? Did he have sexual relations with them? Did they break up with him, and so he wanted revenge? Or is this about a killer who hates women in general?"

Kihlgård fell silent and stuffed a piece of chocolate cookie into his mouth. Little crumbs sprinkled onto his lap.

Knutas was seized with disgust, and he wondered how the man could eat at a time like this. He turned off the projector. "We have to figure out what the connection is between the two victims. If there is one."

He kept on talking in the dark. "This is what we know so far about what the two women had in common: Both of them had strong ties to Stockholm and Gotland. Helena Hillerström was born and raised here, and her family still has a summer house on the island, which she visited at least a couple of times a year. She also has relatives and lots of friends here. Frida Lindh came from Stockholm, but she was married to a man from Gotland. About a year ago, she and her family moved here and settled in Södervärn. According to her husband, they wanted to try living on Gotland because he's from here and his family lives here. We don't yet know whether the two victims knew each other. Both women were in their midthirties. There was only a year's difference in age between them. And they were both attractive. That's about all we know right now.

"What I want us to do is form a work group to map out the lives of the two women, including the people they knew. A second group will be assigned to check on the murderers and assailants who are known in Sweden, concentrating on Stockholm. Do any of them have ties to Gotland? We have the eyes of the whole nation on us at the moment. Not to mention the mass media. As of right now, we're going to put all our efforts into catching this killer before another murder occurs. I've asked for reinforcements from the NCP in Stockholm. We're going to split up into two teams: internal and external. Kihlgård and Hansson will assist us, especially with the interviews and with charting assailants found in police records. A few officers from here will need to go to Stockholm again. The perpetrator could just as well be over there as here on the island."

"It's actually rather likely that the murderer lives in Stockholm," said Wittberg. "Helena Hillerström came to Gotland only a few times a year, and she was here only a few days before he struck. Frida Lindh lived in Stockholm until a year ago. It seems very possible that they met him over there. They might have had an affair with him. Maybe it was still going on. Do we know whether Frida Lindh ever went over to Stockholm? How many times has she been back there since they moved? Maybe she went there to visit relatives and had an affair at the same time."

"In that case, he's smart to kill the women over here. That puts the focus on Gotland, and he can go back to Stockholm in peace and quiet," said Norrby.

"Are we sure that she had never met the man in the bar at the Monk's Cellar before? Maybe she was just pretending she didn't know him for the sake of her girlfriends. What if they already had some sort of relationship going on?" Sohlman suggested.

"He could also be a customer," interjected Jacobsson. "Frida Lindh worked in a beauty salon at Östercentrum, the one that's in the gallery near the Obs supermarket. She could have met him there. It's a really vulnerable type of work. Any lunatic could have been spying on her for days without her knowing it."

"That's a possibility, of course," Knutas conceded. "We haven't yet talked to her colleagues at work. Could you follow up on that at the hairdresser's?"

Jacobsson nodded as she jotted a note on her pad of paper.

"As I see it, this might very well involve a madman who chooses his victims at random," said Kihlgård. "Maybe it was just bad luck for Helena Hillerström that she happened to be on Gotland when he decided to start his killing spree. He caught sight of her somewhere, followed her, and waited for the right opportunity. As simple as that."

"If that's true, it's just too awful," said Jacobsson. "That means that he could strike any woman, at any time."

An uncomfortable tension spread through the room. They were all thinking about their wives, girlfriends, sisters, and female friends. No one was safe.

"We can sit here and speculate forever," Knutas snapped. "Right now we need to deal with the facts." He glanced at his watch. "Okay, we'll stop here for the time being. As you know, the press conference is at three. We'll meet afterward and discuss how to divide up the work. Shall we say five o'clock?"

Karin Jacobsson and Anders Knutas went over to a pizzeria a few blocks from police headquarters. They ate their food quickly and in silence. After almost fifteen years of working together, they understood each other very well. Sometimes they joked about themselves as the hardworking older couple, even though there was a big age difference between them. Karin Jacobsson would be thirty-eight this year, while Anders Knutas was forty-nine. He thought she was charming. He had always thought so. The big gap between her front teeth never prevented her from being quick to laugh. Many times when they worked together, he thought it was her laugh that carried her through. Her male colleagues were not always easy to deal with, especially not when Karin was the newcomer in the group. The fact that she was unusually short, only five foot one, didn't help matters. It made her male colleagues act even more like big brothers toward her. But she had proven herself to be a smart and no-nonsense colleague, and she quickly won their respect.

Karin swallowed the last bite of her pizza. "What are you thinking about?" she asked.

"The man at the inn. Frida Lindh sat and talked to him for over an hour. The question is: Who is he? He ought to come forward when he hears about the murder."

"Did they leave together?"

"No. Apparently he left the restaurant about half an hour before the others did. According to her friends, Frida was alone when she got on her bike to head home."

"What do you think about the idea that both Helena and Frida might have had an affair with the same man? Maybe even the one that Frida met at the Monk?"

"Of course that's always possible. Even though they don't seem to have been raped, the motive could still very well be sexual. The panties indicate as much. But what's so damn strange is the part about the different types of weapons. First an axe, then a knife. I wonder why."

"It's incomprehensible," Jacobsson agreed. "Maybe he's just doing it to mess with our minds."

Knutas leaned back in his chair. "I wonder whether we shouldn't be concentrating on Stockholm, in any case. That's certainly where they might have met the murderer. Then he decides to kill them on Gotland to throw us off the scent. He wants us to be looking over here."

"We still need to check up on Frida's customers," Jacobsson pointed out. "It could be one of them. She hadn't worked here very long—I think only five or six months—and she hadn't lived here more than a year. All her acquaintances were new. Of course the killer could be from Stockholm, but he still had to have spent some time on Gotland to spy on them, to find out where they lived, what their routines were, and where they usually went. I think it all seems very well planned."

"I agree. I actually do think that the murders were premeditated, but we still need to keep all avenues open. It's too easy to get locked into one idea. The whole thing is damned unpleasant," said Knutas, shaking his head. "Do you have time for a quick cup of coffee?"

"Sure, thanks. With milk. No sugar."

"I know." He rolled his eyes. They had had countless cups of coffee together.

Johan didn't care anymore. Even though he knew full well that he shouldn't do it, he was going to call her. Contrary to all expectations, he was back on Gotland, and he had spent too much time thinking about Emma to be able to ignore his desire to call her. His feelings were too strong. He sat on the bed in his hotel room, torturing himself. *It doesn't have to mean anything,* he thought. *We could just talk for a while. That can't be so dangerous.* Soon he would have to leave for the press conference, and after that he'd be working full steam for the rest of the day and night. He knew that.

He picked up the phone and punched in her number.

It rang once, then twice.

Shit, he thought. *To hell with the whole thing. What if her husband answers?* But he didn't hang up the phone.

"Emma Winarve."

A joyous warmth spread through his body when he heard her voice.

"Hi, it's me. Johan Berg. From Regional News. How are you?"

Three seconds of silence. He clenched his teeth so as not to panic.

"I'm okay. Are you here on Gotland?" she asked.

He thought he detected a touch of happy surprise in her voice.

"I've just come back. The second murder, you know. What are you doing right now? Am I disturbing you?"

"Not at all, don't worry. Olle took the children to the swimming pool. How are things with you?"

"I've been thinking about you," he said, and held his breath.

"Really?" she said hesitantly.

He could have bitten his tongue off. *Shit.*

"I've been thinking about you, too," she added.

He could breathe again.

"Could we get together?" he suggested.

"I don't know if I can."

"Just for a short time?"

Now that a hope had been lit, he was his usual self again, persistent and single-minded. "How about later tonight?"

"No, I can't. Maybe tomorrow. I have to go into town anyway."

"Tomorrow would be great."

The room where the press conference was going to be held was full to bursting when Anders Knutas and Karin Jacobsson entered several minutes before it was scheduled to start. This time not only the local media was represented but also the morning papers that covered national news, the evening papers, the TT wire service, Eko radio news, several commercial TV channels, and the state-run Swedish TV. Johan Berg and Peter Bylund from Regional News were there as well.

The air was buzzing with voices. The reporters settled into the rows of chairs, clicking their ballpoint pens and rustling the pages of their notebooks. Some of them were outfitted with radio gear. The guys with their big TV cameras took up strategic positions and adjusted their equipment. Microphones were set up, one after another, along the dais.

The onslaught of journalists had forced the investigative team to change rooms at the last minute. They were now sitting in the big conference hall in a different section of police headquarters. Eva Eriksson, the county governor, had called to say that she would attend.

I wonder what she's doing here? thought Knutas as he made his way through the crowd. Already seated on the dais were Martin Kihlgård and the county police commissioner.

The murmuring in the room ceased as Knutas welcomed everyone. He introduced himself and his colleagues seated next to him and then started off with a brief report about the latest murder. The police were trying to be generous with the amount of information they would share. At the same time, it was important not to release any details that might hamper the investigation. It was a difficult balancing act.

When he was done, he opened the floor to questions.

"Are there any similarities between this homicide and the murder of Helena Hillerström?" one reporter asked.

"Yes, there are certain similarities, but I'm afraid I can't go into any further detail about that now."

"Obviously the same weapon couldn't have been used," said the reporter from one of the local papers, sounding very sure of himself. "But was the same *type* of weapon used this time? Was the latest victim also killed with an axe?"

"No. The latest murder was committed with a sharp instrument."

"You mean a knife?" asked Johan.

"As to what type of sharp instrument, it's too soon to say."

"Are there any witnesses?" wondered the reporter from *Gotlands Tidningar*.

"At this time, it appears that no one saw or heard anything. We're still in the process of interviewing a large number of people."

"Do you suspect that it's the same perpetrator as before?"

"Both yes and no. There are certain things that indicate it might be someone else—for example, the fact that the killer used a different kind of weapon. Other circumstances point to one perpetrator, so at the present time we don't know. Of course we can't rule out that possibility."

"Have you found any connection between the victims, other than that they're both women about the same age?"

"I can't go into that right now, for the sake of the investigation, but I can tell you this much: Both women had ties to Stockholm and to Gotland."

"Could the killer have come over from Stockholm?"

"Certainly."

"Why aren't you looking for him there?"

"We are."

"Where?"

"I can't answer that. I'm sure you'll understand why."

"Are there any similarities in the MO of the killers?" asked Johan.

"I can't comment on that."

There was a great deal of frustration among the reporters, but Knutas was unyielding. The investigative team had decided not to reveal anything about the way in which Frida Lindh was killed. That left the field wide open for speculation.

"Are we dealing with a serial killer here?" asked the woman from Radio Gotland.

"It's much too early to say. We have no idea," said Knutas.

"But you wouldn't rule it out?"

"Of course not."

"What's going to happen to the boyfriend of the first victim?" the reporter from the local radio station continued.

"He's going to be released from custody. He's no longer a suspect."

A murmur spread through the room.

"Why not?" the radio reporter asked.

"I'm afraid I can't comment on that."

"How can you be so sure he's innocent?"

"We can't divulge anything about our reasons for letting him go. The only thing I can tell you is that the boyfriend is no longer suspected of having anything to do with the murder in Fröjel," repeated Knutas, whose face was starting to flush with annoyance.

"That must mean that you think the same person committed both murders," Johan ventured. "The murder of the woman in the cemetery couldn't have been committed by Per Bergdal, since he was being held under arrest in Visby."

"As I've said several times, we can't go into any further details about the circumstances," said Knutas, forcing himself to remain calm.

Johan dropped the matter of the perpetrator.

"What about the murder weapon? Was it found?" he asked instead.

"No."

"What are the police doing now?" asked the reporter from Eko.

"We'll be getting additional reinforcements from the National Criminal Police. We're conducting extensive searches and trying to come up with any points of connection between the two victims."

"Did the victims know each other?" asked another TV reporter.

"No, not according to the information we have now. We're in the process of checking their backgrounds."

Almost an hour later, after all the journalists had finished their individual interviews, Knutas hurried out of the conference room. The governor took his arm.

"Have you got a minute?"

"Of course," he said wearily.

He turned to lead the way to his office and closed the door behind them.

"This is a very serious situation," said Eriksson, who was a vigorous woman of fifty-five or so. Normally she was outgoing and cheerful, but right now there were signs of great anxiety on her face. With a sigh she sank down onto the visitors' sofa in Knutas's office, then took off her glasses and wiped her brow with a handkerchief.

"This is a very serious situation," she repeated. "Here we are in the middle of June. Everyone is hard at work preparing for the tourist season at all the hotels, campgrounds, youth hostels, rental cabins. The reservations are pouring in. For the time being, at any rate. The question is what will happen now. This seems to be a case of a serial killer, and that's not something that will attract tourists. I'm concerned that these two murders will scare people away."

"I know," agreed Knutas, "but there's not much we can do. None of us wants a killer on the loose."

"What are you planning to do now? What resources are you using? I'm sure you realize how important it is that we catch this killer as soon as possible."

"My dear governor," said Knutas, unable to hide his irritation. "We're doing everything we can, especially in view of our limited resources. My entire department, which means the twelve officers that are left in the criminal department after all the cutbacks and reorganizations, are working full-time on the case. I've also called in four investigators from the NCP, and they'll stay on as long as necessary. I've put in a request to borrow a few men from the local police, even though they're already stretched thin. We're about to be deluged by six hundred thousand tourists, and we have to handle it with eighty-three officers for the whole island. Including the island of Fårö. You can figure out for yourself what our capacity is like. There just aren't any other resources to draw on." He gave Eriksson a stern look.

"Oh, I know. I understand. I'm just worried about the consequences. And the employment situation. So many people make their living from tourism."

"You're going to have to give us a little time," said Knutas. "It's scarcely been forty-eight hours since the second homicide was committed. Maybe we'll be able to catch the perpetrator within a few days. Then the whole thing will be over. Let's not rush to think the worst."

"I hope to God you're right," said the governor with a sigh.

"Shit."

Knutas had just taken a bite of a dry sandwich from a vending machine and got a piece stuck in his throat, which led to a lengthy coughing fit. His colleagues, who had all gathered to watch the Sunday evening news in the lunchroom, shushed him.

Knutas felt a throbbing in his temples. The story about the latest homicide had contained far too much information.

"How can they know so much? That part about the knife wound? And the panties?" exclaimed Knutas when he was done coughing.

His face was bright red, both from coughing and from anger.

"How did that happen? How the hell are we supposed to do investigative work under these conditions! Who's been leaking information to the press?"

Everyone exchanged surprised glances. Scattered murmurs of denial were heard. People were shaking their heads. Some decided it was best not to get involved.

Knutas strode back to his office, slamming the door so hard that the windowpane in the upper part of the door rattled. He rummaged around to find Johan Berg's business card. The journalist answered after two rings.

"What the hell do you think you're doing?" thundered Knutas without identifying himself.

"What do you mean?" asked Johan, who knew exactly what this was all about.

"How can you broadcast the sort of information that was just on the news? Don't you realize that it interferes with our work? We're in the middle of hunting for a killer! And what kind of proof do you have? Where did you get that information?"

"I can understand why you're upset." Johan was speaking in his most soothing tone of voice. "But you have to try to see things from our point of view."

"Just what kind of fucking point of view would that be? We're conducting a homicide investigation here!"

"First of all, we would never report any information unless we were a hundred percent sure that it was true. I happen to know that things were exactly the way we described them in the story. Second, we consider it's relevant to report that all indications point to a serial killer at work. The panties in the mouth is the most convincing proof of that, and the information is of such general interest that it had to be made public."

"Who do you think you are, to make that sort of decision? General interest!"

Knutas spat out the words. Johan could just imagine the saliva spattering the receiver.

"Okay, all right," said Knutas. "But the fact that all this information is also being broadcast straight to the murderer—you're not taking that into consideration at all!"

"People have the right to know that a serial killer is on the loose. We're just doing our job. I'm truly sorry if it interferes with your work, but I also have to think about my own work."

"And what tells you that all of those details are true? How do you know for sure?"

"Naturally I can't tell you that, but I have a very reliable source."

"A reliable source, you say. That can only mean someone inside headquarters. One of my closest associates. You have to tell me who it is. Otherwise we're not going to be able to continue working as a team."

Knutas sounded somewhat calmer, but Johan felt his patience running out. "As a police officer, you should know the law well enough to know that you can't ask me that question," he said acidly. "You have no right to investigate our sources. But since I respect your work, I can tell you this much. It's not any of your closest associates or anyone on the investigative team itself. At least not the person who's been giving me the information. That's all I can say. And keep in mind that just because we journalists find out about something, that doesn't mean that we have to make it public immediately. It depends whether it's justified or not. I knew about the panties right after the murder of Helena Hillerström, but it wasn't until now that there was any reason to make it public."

Knutas sighed. "I expect you'll warn me, at least, the next time you're thinking of publicizing sensitive and confidential information. I'd like to avoid having a heart attack."

"Sure, I can do that. I hope you can understand my side of the issue."

"Well, I guess I'll have to. But don't ask me to understand how you journalists think," said Knutas, and he hung up.

It was past eight in the evening, and it wasn't until now that Knutas realized how tired he was. He leaned back in his chair. Who the hell had leaked the information? He trusted his colleagues, but right now he didn't know what to think. Yet he believed what Johan Berg had said, that it wasn't anyone who was part of the investigation.

Even though he had been annoyed by that reporter several times during the investigation, he had a feeling that Johan Berg was serious about his work. Not like certain other journalists who didn't pay any attention to what was said but just continued on, endlessly asking questions about matters that he had told them he couldn't discuss. He got so mad at Johan not because of his manner but because he was so well informed. Reluctantly, Knutas had to acknowledge that he actually could understand the way Johan thought. But how was he finding out so much? Naturally Knutas was quite familiar with how easily information could spread. Something had to be done about it. Was it happening via the police radio? They had to look into how much was being said and what was being said. The Gotland police had little experience when it came to dealing with the press on such a large scale.

Someone knocked on the door.

Jacobsson peeked in. "Malin Backman is here, one of Frida Lindh's friends."

"I'm coming," said Knutas, and got up.

Malin Backman was the only one of the victim's friends he had not yet met. She was one of the two women who lived on Tjelvarvägen.

Wittberg and Norrby had talked to her last night, but that was before they knew that Frida Lindh had been murdered. Now the situation was completely changed, and Knutas wanted to meet with Frida's women friends in person. Malin Backman was also Frida Lindh's colleague at work. The conversations that he had in the morning with her other friends had not produced anything new.

Karin Jacobsson was present during the interview. They went into the conference room.

"Please have a seat," said Knutas.

Malin Backman sat down on the chair across from him. "I'm sorry to be late. My husband has been out of town and didn't come home until this evening. I didn't have anyone to leave the children with."

Knutas made a dismissive gesture. "It's perfectly all right. We appreciate that you took the time to come here. How did you happen to know Frida Lindh?"

"We worked at the same beauty salon."

"How long have you known her?"

"Since she started working there. That must be about six months ago, I think. Yes, that's right, she started right after Christmas. In early January."

"How well did you know her?"

"Quite well. We saw each other every day at work, and we also used to go out together once in a while."

"Did you notice anything different about her lately?"

"No, she was just the same as always. Very lively and cheerful."

"She didn't talk about anything special that had happened? Any customer who was unpleasant?"

"No, I don't think so."

"Do you know whether anyone had been acting strangely toward her or threatening her?"

"No, our customers are usually very nice. We know most of them."

"But occasionally you have customers come in that you've never seen before, don't you?" asked Jacobsson.

"Well, yes, of course. We get walk-ins, too. Every Saturday."

"Do you remember any of the customers from last Saturday?"

"No, I had the day off."

"Who was working that day?"

"Frida and the woman who owns the salon, Britt. There are only two of us on Saturdays."

"How long are you open?"

"Until three o'clock. On Saturdays, that is. Otherwise we close at six. And we're not open on Sundays."

"I want you to be very candid with me. Do you know whether Frida was having an affair on the side? Was she going out with anyone?"

"No, she wasn't. She would have told me if she was. I don't think she would ever go that far."

"How was Frida at work?"

"She was a really good hairdresser, and the customers liked her a lot. She had a very winning way about her. She was cheerful and sociable."

"Do you think any of the customers might have felt she was encouraging them?"

"I don't know. Of course she talked and laughed a lot. I guess that could be misinterpreted."

"Could you describe the evening at the Monk's Cellar?"

"We had dinner in the restaurant. Then we went into the vinyl bar. It was full of people, and we were having a great time. Frida met a man, and she sat and talked to him for a really long time."

"Did he introduce himself to the rest of you?"

"No, they were sitting at the bar the whole time."

"What did he look like?"

"Ash-blond hair. Tall. He looked quite fit. A slight stubble. Very dark eyes, I think."

"What was he wearing?"

"He had on a polo shirt and jeans. Really nice-looking clothes."

"How long did they talk to each other?"

"For about an hour. Then Frida came back to the table and said that he had to leave."

"Did she tell you anything about him?"

"He was from Stockholm. He and his father were going to buy a restaurant in Visby. Apparently they owned several cafés in Stockholm."

"Did she say what his name was?"

"Yes, his name was Henrik."

"No last name?"

"No."

"Where was he staying here on Gotland?"

"I don't know."

"How long was he going to stay?"

"I don't know that, either."

"Did he seem to know anyone at the Monk?"

"I don't think so. I didn't see him talking to anyone besides Frida."

"You didn't recognize him?"

"No."

"What else did Frida say about him?"

"She thought he was sweet. He asked for her phone number, but she didn't give it to him."

"When did he leave the Monk?"

"He left right after she came back to our table. We probably stayed another half hour after that. Until they closed."

"Did you notice when he left?"

"No, Frida said that he had to go."

"How was Frida when you said good-bye to her?"

"The same as always. We said good-bye, and she headed off toward home on her bicycle."

"Was she drunk?"

"Not especially. We were all a little tipsy."

Jacobsson chose to change tracks. "How did Frida get along with her husband?"

"Great, I think. At least I never heard about any big problems. No relationship is perfect, you know. The children kept them really busy, of course."

"Just one more question. Do you have any idea who might have wished to hurt her?"

"No. I don't have a clue."

MONDAY, JUNE 18

The second homicide was a juicy story for the tabloids. The fact that the panties of both victims had been stuffed in their mouths made the crimes even more sensational, of course. After the Sunday evening news had reported on the new information, all the other media picked up the story. Naturally, speculations about a serial killer were rampant. They were splashed in big headlines across the front pages of the newspapers on Monday morning. Frida Lindh's face was all over the tabloids, which screamed:

SERIAL KILLER RAVAGING GOTLAND.
KILLER LOOSE IN VACATION PARADISE.
MURDER IN SUMMER HAVEN.

On the TV news programs, the murders were the top story. The decision to publish the information about the panties had been made after a discussion among the news managers at TV headquarters. Everyone had agreed that publicizing that particular detail was the right thing to do. If they weighed the unpleasantness for the families against the public interest, the scales tipped in favor of the people's right to know. The early morning talk shows featured discussions with criminologists, psychologists, and representatives from various women's groups.

The radio fanned the flames by repeating the details in one news program after another.

On Gotland the murders were the topic of conversation on everyone's lips. People were talking about them at work, on the buses, and in the shops, cafés, and restaurants. Fear of the murderer began creeping along the walls of the buildings. There had been plenty of time for a lot of people to get to know Frida Lindh. Such a nice, cheerful woman. The mother of three. Who could have done that to her? Murder was not very common on Gotland, and a serial killer was something you only read about.

Johan and Emma chose an Italian restaurant that was a little out of the way, down one of the lanes radiating out from Stora Torget, the main square.

Since the tourist season hadn't really started yet, the place was still half empty. They sat down at a table in the very back of the restaurant. Emma felt guilty, even though nothing had happened between them. She hadn't told Olle she was having lunch with Johan. She had lied and said she was going to meet a girlfriend. The lie made her conscious of her guilt. She had always been honest with Olle.

Shortly before they were supposed to meet, Emma had almost called Johan to cancel, but even though she knew she was headed into deep water, she couldn't make herself do it. Her interest in Johan took the upper hand.

As she let him pull out a chair for her, she could feel that she was already lost.

They each ordered a different type of pasta. The waiter brought their drinks. White wine and water for both of them.

I need a glass of wine, Emma thought nervously. She lit a cigarette and looked at him across the table.

"I'm glad to see you again," he said.

"Are you?" She couldn't help smiling.

He smiled back. His dimples deepened. Annoyingly charming. Johan's brown eyes were fixed on her. She made an effort not to hold his gaze too long.

"Let's not talk about the murders. At least for the moment," he pleaded. "I want to know more about you."

"Okay."

They talked about themselves. Johan wanted to know everything, both about her and her children. *He seems genuinely interested,* she thought.

Emma asked him about his job. Why had he become a journalist?

"When I was in high school, I was angry about everything in general," he said. "Especially all the social injustices. I had seen them first-hand, even in the suburb where I grew up. The railroad tracks cut right through the community and divided it in two. On one side was the nice residential area for people who had money. On the other side there were nothing but big apartment buildings, tenements covered with graffiti and the basement windows smashed in. That's where most of the drug addicts lived, along with people who were unemployed. Two different worlds. It was really quite disgusting. At the middle-school level, kids from the whole suburb went to the same school, and that was a wake-up call for me."

"In what way?" asked Emma.

"I ended up having friends who lived in those big apartment buildings. I realized that not everyone has the same opportunities. Some of us started a school newspaper, and we wrote articles about the injustices. That was how it all started, with passion and idealism. And here I am now, just a simple crime reporter."

He laughed and shook his head. "When I started at journalism school, I wanted to be a newspaper reporter, like most people, I assume, but I wound up getting an internship in television, and that's where I stayed. And what about you? How did you end up being a teacher?"

"Unfortunately, I didn't have the same passionate involvement that you did. It's the classic story. Both of my parents were teachers. Probably a lot of it had to do with wanting to please them. I've always liked school. And I'm also very fond of children," she said as the thought of her own children flitted past like a guilty reminder that she shouldn't really be sitting here at all.

Johan noticed the shadow that passed over her face. Quickly he changed the subject.

"What do you think about this new murder?"

"It's totally crazy. How could that happen here? On little Gotland? I don't understand it at all. First Helena and now this."

"Did you know Frida Lindh?"

"No. She only lived here a year, right? Although I think there's something familiar about her face."

"She worked at a beauty salon in Östercentrum. Maybe you saw her there."

"Oh, you're right. I took my kids there a couple of times to get their hair cut."

"Do you think Helena might have known her?"

"No idea. I wonder whether it's just a coincidence that the two of them were murdered, or whether there's some sort of connection. I've been thinking about Helena nonstop, turning everything over in my mind. I've tried to figure out what could be behind such a crime, and who could have done it. I went to Stockholm for her funeral, and I met a lot of people there who knew Helena. Her parents, her siblings, her friends. Per's parents were at the funeral, too, of course. No one believed for a minute that he was the killer. Since then all of us who were at the party on that evening at Per and Helena's house have gotten together. We can't think of anything. I wonder if she had met some new man that none of us knew about, someone she started a relationship with and who turned out to be crazy."

She poked her fork at the remnants of the food on her plate.

"Maybe she was trying to break off the relationship because she realized that she loved Per, and then the other man got horribly jealous."

"Maybe," said Johan. "Sure, it's a possibility. Do you know whether she was ever unfaithful to Per?"

"Yes, that actually did happen. At least once, several years ago. She met someone at a party, and they ended up in bed together. They had an affair that lasted several weeks. She was having her doubts at the time about Per. Didn't really know what her own feelings were anymore. She thought things had gotten to be so routine between them. Helena was completely obsessed with that other guy. She talked about nothing else and said that he was like a drug that calmed her down. She even left work a few times to meet him. That wasn't like her."

"What was his name?"

"I don't know. She wouldn't tell me. I thought she was being ridiculous. She refused to say anything about who he was or what he did or where he lived."

"Why is that?"

"No clue. Of course I tried to squeeze the information out of her, but she was really impossible. 'You'll find out soon enough,' she told me."

"So what happened?"

"One day she told me that it was over. I don't know what happened or why. She just said it was over and that she had decided to stay with Per."

"When was that?"

"Hm . . . a few years back. It must have been three or four years ago, I guess."

"Didn't she ever talk about him after that?"

"No. Time passed and I forgot all about it. Until now."

"That's something that should be checked out," said Johan. "Somebody else must know about it. Did you discuss it with any of her friends over in Stockholm when you were there?"

"No, I didn't. It didn't occur to me."

She glanced at her watch. Two thirty. An hour and a half until she had to pick up the kids. She could feel the effect of the wine, but she took another sip and met his gaze.

"I need to keep an eye on the time because I have to catch a bus so I won't be late at the daycare center."

"I can drive you there. I've only had one glass of wine. It'll be okay."

They drove through the town in silence. Emma leaned back and closed her eyes, feeling more at ease than she had in a very long time.

She opened her eyes and let her eyes rest on him.

Good Lord, she thought, *am I falling in love? This is idiotic.* At the same time, she couldn't help enjoying the moment. She felt relaxed in his company, happier and more talkative than she'd been in a long time. She looked at his hands on the steering wheel. Very tan and manly. Short, clean fingernails.

He turned his head to look at her. "What are you thinking about?"

She blushed. "Nothing." She felt a smile tugging at her lips.

Without warning, he turned off the main road to Roma onto a gravel road, stopping at the edge of the woods. She was neither surprised nor frightened, merely felt a fluttering in her stomach.

He didn't say a word, just leaned over and kissed her. She kissed him back. He was startled by her intensity. He touched her hair, her arms, her thighs. Emma felt desire seize hold of her. *Just a few more minutes,* she thought as her tongue began playing a tender wrestling match with his. *Just a little while longer.* Until his hand crept under her shirt and she pushed him away.

"We have to stop. We can't do this right now."

"Just a little more," he begged.

But Emma was firm. Reason began trickling back into her brain.

The rest of the drive to Roma took place in silence.

When they reached the school, he turned to her. "When can I see you again?"

"I can't tell you that right now. The kids are waiting. I have to think about it. I'll call you."

A sense of relief swept over her when she saw Sara waving from the playground.

On his way to school, the pain in his stomach grew stronger. With each step he took, it got worse. When he turned onto Brömsebrogatan and saw the redbrick façade of Norrbacka School, he felt the usual pressure in his chest that made it even harder to breathe. He tried to push the feeling aside. Right now he had to be his normal self. Appear unaffected. There came Jonas and Pelle. Chattering and kicking pebbles back and forth, shoving and teasing each other. Completely natural and confident. Just a few months ago he was one of them, but now everything had changed. They reached the playground at the same time. He stretched and then spat into the road. Glanced furtively at his classmates. The boys ignored him. He could feel his face turning red and looked down at the ground as he quickly crossed the playground. The feeling of desperation grew in his stomach. How could everything have changed in such a short time? School was now nothing more than a big, black object of hatred. Total darkness. Would it ever pass?

How he wished he could turn back the clock! To the way things were last fall. Back then he went to school and played with his friends as if it were the most natural thing in the world. They played soccer and hockey during recess. Back then school was the most fun part of his life. That's where he always longed to be whenever he was home. In school everything was normal. Everyone around him was happy and nice. It wasn't like at home, where he couldn't understand all the weird moods and he didn't know how he was supposed to react to them. At home he was often walking on eggshells, trying to please his mother. Not make any trouble. He had gotten used to the fact that his parents hardly ever talked to each other anymore, and to the odd atmosphere at the dinner table. The main thing was to get away as quickly as possible without annoying anyone. In the past it had never felt so dangerous at home. Back then he had friends to visit. Kids he could go out and play with. But not anymore. That's why the unpleasant atmosphere at home was making him feel so much worse. He had nowhere to go. Instead, he would escape to his room. Into himself. He read books. Worked on complex and difficult puzzles that took a long time to solve. Did his homework with great care. Lay in bed and stared at the ceiling. Mostly he felt lonely and worthless. No one wanted to be around him anymore. No one asked about him. He wasn't wanted, either at home or at school. His sister had her own friends and spent most of her free time at the stables. Who wanted to be with him?

By now he had reached the classroom door. He hung his jacket and book bag on a hook.

When the bell rang for first period, he felt relieved. Even though he knew the feeling was only temporary.

Karin Jacobsson could hear a commercial for Radio Mix Megapol playing in the background as she stepped inside the beauty salon. The only customer was a middle-aged woman who was having her curls wrapped in foil papers.

In a basket on the floor in one corner lay a shaggy little dog who wagged his tail when he caught sight of Jacobsson.

The hairdresser was wearing a blouse and skirt made of natural-colored linen and red shoes. Her legs were slender and tan. She turned toward the door when Jacobsson came in. "Hi," she said with an inquisitive look at Jacobsson.

Karin introduced herself.

"I'm just about finished here," said the hairdresser in a friendly voice. "Why don't you have a seat." She nodded toward a brown sofa.

Jacobsson sat down and leafed through a glossy magazine filled with different types of hairstyles.

It was not a large room. Three black leather chairs for the salon customers stood lined up along the opposite wall. The woman in the only occupied chair kept casting curious glances at Jacobsson. The walls were painted a light color but were bare. Very little had been spent on the decor. Mirrors and a clock on one wall, but otherwise nothing. It was more like a typical barbershop for men, spartan and slightly old-fashioned. After a few minutes the hairdresser was through wrapping up the woman's hair. She placed a dryer over the customer's head, supplied her with some coffee and several magazines, and then motioned Jacobsson to follow her behind a curtain.

"How can I help you?" she asked after they were seated at a little coffee table.

"I'd like you to tell me about Frida Lindh."

"All right, but what can I say? She worked here for six months. I took a risk by hiring her. She was from Stockholm, and I didn't really know much about her. The only experience she had was a part-time job for a couple of years at a salon in Stockholm, but that was a long time ago, so I had my doubts. She turned out to be a big hit, at least financially. She was talented, she worked fast, and she was cheerful and nice to the customers. They really liked her. She rented a chair here, and after only a few weeks she was totally booked up. She also brought in new customers that the rest of us took care of if she didn't have time."

"What did you think of her yourself?"

"To be honest, I didn't particularly like her. Simply because she was a little too flirty with the male customers. And it was mostly men who made appointments with her."

"Why did you react so strongly?"

"Well, of course I think that anyone who works here should have good relations with the customers, but Frida didn't know where to draw the line. She would giggle and chatter loudly about all sorts of things with her customers, and I often thought she got too personal with them. In this place it's impossible not to hear what everyone else is saying, and sometimes it could be rather embarrassing. She quite simply went too far."

"In what way?"

"For instance, sometimes she and the customer would tell jokes with all sorts of sexual innuendoes. I don't think that's proper. Visby is a small town, and lots of people here know each other well."

"Did you ever speak to her about this?"

"Actually I did, just a week or so ago. Frida and a male customer were joking around, and she started laughing so hard that she couldn't even cut his hair. It was a Saturday, and we had so many walk-ins that people were lined up waiting, but she acted as if she didn't even see them. The customer got so lively and carried away by her giggling that he just kept going on and on. It took her over an hour to finish a typical man's haircut. That's when I had a talk with her."

"How did Frida react?"

"She apologized and promised me it would never happen again. And I believed her."

"When did this happen? You said it was a week ago?"

"Yes, it must have been last Saturday."

"Did you know the customer from before?"

"No, he was new. I'd never seen him before."

"Can you describe him?"

"I guess he was a little older than she was. Tall and good-looking. That was probably why she started acting that way."

"Do you think he was from Gotland?"

"No, he didn't speak with a Gotland accent. I noticed that because they were carrying on and making so much noise. He sounded like a Stockholmer."

"Did they seem to know each other?"

"I don't think so."

"Do you happen to remember what he was wearing?"

"No, actually I don't. He was probably very neatly dressed. I would have noticed if there was anything special about his clothes."

"And with your walk-in customers you don't write down their names?"

"No, not the walk-ins. We don't do that."

"Have you seen that customer since then?"

"No."

"Did you notice anything else here in the salon? Anyone who showed a particular interest in Frida?"

"No. Of course she was very popular, but I didn't notice anything special. But I can ask Malin. She works here, too."

"We've already talked to her. Are there any other employees?"

"No, just the three of us. Well, two now."

At that moment a buzzer went off in the salon. It was the timer on the hair dryer.

The hairdresser stood up. "You'll have to excuse me, but I have to go back to work. Is there anything else?"

"No," said Jacobsson. "If you happen to think of anything, don't hesitate to call. Here's my card."

"Is there any reason why Malin and I should be afraid? Do you think one of our customers might be the murderer?"

"Right now it doesn't look as if there's anything to indicate that. Although it wouldn't hurt to be extra alert about anyone you happen to see in the area. If you see or hear anything suspicious, give us a call."

Knutas sat in his office, filling his pipe. Once again he went over in his mind what he knew about the two homicides. There were two things in particular that were puzzling him: the murder weapons and the panties.

Helena Hillerström was killed with the family axe. The perpetrator had stolen it from the shed, just as Bergdal had said. How did that happen? How close had he been to Helena? He must have been spying on her for a while. Provided it wasn't someone she knew, of course— one of the guests at the party, for example.

Frida Lindh was killed with a knife. Why did the perpetrator use two different types of weapon? Maybe he didn't want to walk around town carrying an axe. A knife was much easier to conceal. It could be as simple as that. Presumably he had waited for her near the cemetery. That meant that he knew where she lived. Was it someone she knew? The mysterious man at the bar in the Monk's Cellar had not yet turned up.

The bartender remembered him quite well but couldn't recall having seen him before—or since that night, either. The interviews with the other employees who were working that Friday night at the restaurant had produced no results. If the murderer had been spying on her for a while and then decided to kill her, why did he choose that moment to act? He was taking a big risk by killing her in the middle of town, where he might easily be seen. There was also a big risk that the body would be quickly discovered.

Then there was the part about the panties. Knutas had reviewed similar incidents elsewhere in Sweden and even abroad. In every case in which the perpetrator had done something similar, he had also raped the victim or subjected her to some other kind of sexual assault. Whether Frida Lindh had been raped or not was something he wouldn't know until the preliminary autopsy report was ready, but there was nothing to indicate that she was.

A group of experts from the National Criminal Police was working to find information about previous assailants with similar MOs. His own core team of Wittberg, Norrby, Jacobsson, and Sohlman was fully occupied with conducting interviews and compiling reports on the interviews they had already completed. The forensic medicine department in Solna would issue a preliminary statement about Frida Lindh, and they were still waiting for the response from SCL. Everything had been set in motion. Yet he was filled with impatience. No matter how he twisted and turned everything, he kept coming to the same conclusion. All indications were strong that the victims had known the perpetrator. That was also most often the case in homicides.

Frida Lindh had a very small circle of acquaintances on Gotland. Of course lots of people knew her, but her actual circle of friends was not large. It wasn't at all unlikely that she had met her killer at the beauty salon.

As for Helena Hillerström, she didn't have many friends on Gotland, either. Apart from her relatives, the people she knew were mostly confined to those who had been at the party. Once again it was the face of Kristian Nordström that appeared in his mind. Nordström had been interviewed once, but Knutas wanted to talk to him again. He decided to go out and pay him a visit. Unannounced.

It was four o'clock in the afternoon. Real summer heat had finally arrived, and with a vengeance. It was eighty-two degrees without a breath of wind. His Mercedes was in its usual spot outside police headquarters, and Knutas saw to his great regret that at the moment it was parked in direct sunlight. When he opened the car door, it felt like stepping into a sauna. He tossed his jacket onto the backseat and practically burned himself when he got into the driver's seat. The car had no air-conditioning. He rolled down the window, which helped a lot, but his jeans were sticking to his legs. *I should have worn shorts,* he thought. The heat made him irritable, and he was having a hard time concentrating. He pulled out onto Norra Hansegatan, and several minutes later he had left the town behind. He was headed north on the road to Brissund, six miles outside of Visby.

When he reached Kristian Nordström's address, he was struck by the spectacular view. The modern wooden house stood in lonely majesty on a high cliff facing the sea and Brissund's old fishing village. The house was built in a semicircle that followed the curve of the hill, as if the structure were climbing up the slope. Enormous glass windows covered every wall, and a truly huge wooden deck faced the water. Parked outside was a newer-model car, a dark green Jeep Cherokee.

Knutas was sweating. He got out of the car, pulled out his pipe, and stuck it between his teeth without lighting it. He walked over to the front door, which was painted blue. *Just like in Greece,* thought Knutas, and rang the bell. It had been a long time since he had traveled abroad. He could hear the doorbell ringing inside the house. He waited. Nothing happened. He rang the bell again. Waited. Sucked on the stem of his pipe.

He decided to take a little stroll around the house. The sea was calm. The sun was blazing. He heard a buzzing in the air. He peered up at the sun, shading his eyes with one hand. Thousands of tiny black dots formed a giant swarm and were raining down from the sky. It was rather disgusting. He looked down at the ground and realized they were lady-bugs. The lawn in front of the house was glittering with the tiny red bugs with their black-spotted shells. A ladybug sat on every single blade of grass. How strange. He looked up at the sun again. They looked like snowflakes drifting down in winter. That's what they were: ladybug snowflakes.

He stepped up onto the wooden deck in back. The house seemed empty and deserted. He peered into one of the windows that reached all the way to the ground.

"Can I help you with something?"

Knutas almost dropped his pipe on the newly varnished planks of the deck. Kristian Nordström had popped into view from around the corner.

"Hello," said Knutas, reaching out to shake hands. "I wanted to have a little talk with you."

"Certainly. Shall we go inside?"

Knutas followed the tall man into the house. It felt cool in the hall-way.

"Would you like something to drink?" asked Nordström.

"A glass of water would be great. It's damn hot outside."

"For my part, I think I need something stronger."

Kristian Nordström poured himself a Carlsberg Elephant beer and handed the inspector a big glass of ice water. They sat down on leather armchairs that stood near one of the panoramic windows. Knutas took out his worn old notebook and a pen.

"I know you've told us all this before, but how well did you know Helena Hillerström?"

"Quite well. We've known each other since we were teenagers. I've always liked Helena."

"How much time did you spend together?"

"In high school we were part of a group that did everything together, both at school and in our free time. Several of the people who were at the party over Whitsun were part of that group. We did our homework together, went to the movies, and hung out together after school and on Saturday and Sunday nights. I'd say we spent a lot of time together during those years."

"Was there ever anything else between you and Helena, other than friendship?"

His reply came quickly. Maybe a little too quickly, thought Knutas.

"No. As I already told you, I thought she was pretty, but nothing ever happened between us. Whenever I was single, she was seeing someone else, and vice versa. We were never single at the same time."

"What were your feelings for her?"

Kristian looked him straight in the eye when he answered. A certain irritation was evident in his voice. "I've already told you. I thought she was great. An attractive girl. But she didn't mean anything special to me."

Knutas decided to change tactics. "What do you know about her previous boyfriends?"

"Oh, not much, really. She had a lot of them over the years. She was almost always with someone. Usually not for more than two or three months at a time. They were guys from school, or sometimes she'd meet them somewhere else. Guys from the mainland who came over here for the summer. She'd have an affair with one of them for a few weeks, until it was time for the next guy. She was usually the one to end it. I think she probably managed to break a lot of hearts."

Knutas sensed a hint of bitterness in his voice.

"Then there was that teacher she used to meet with in secret."

Knutas frowned. "Who was that?"

"The PE teacher at school. What was his name? . . . Hagman. Göran? No, Jan. Jan Hagman. He was married, so there was a lot of talk about them."

"When did this happen?"

Kristian seemed to give it some thought. "It must have been in our second year in high school, because the first year we had a different teacher, who retired after that. Helena and I were in the same class in high school, too, specializing in the social sciences."

"How long did their relationship last?"

"I don't really know, but I think that it went on for quite a long time. For more than six months, at least. I think it started before Christmas, because Helena told Emma that she was going to see him during Christmas vacation. Emma told me about it when she got a little drunk at a party. I don't think she was supposed to say anything. On the other hand, she was probably worried about Helena. They were best friends, you know. He was married, with kids, and he was much older. I remember that they were together on a school trip that we took to Stockholm before summer vacation started. Hagman was one of the teachers who went along with us. Someone noticed when Helena slipped into his room at night, and the news spread to the other teachers. When we got back from the trip, a lot of rumors started circulating about them. Then it was summer, and everyone went away on vacation. After that, I at least heard no more about it. When fall came, he was no longer teaching at our school."

"Did you ever talk to Helena about her relationship with this teacher?"

"No, actually I didn't. All of us could see that she took it really hard. I remember that she wasn't around all summer. When we went back to school after vacation, she looked like she'd lost at least twenty pounds.

She was pale and wan, while everyone else looked healthy and tan. I'm sure everybody remembers that, because it was so unlike her."

"Why didn't you mention any of this before?"

"I don't know. I didn't think about it. It happened so long ago. More than fifteen years ago."

"Do you have any idea who might have killed her? Has anything else occurred to you since we last talked?"

"No," replied Kristian. "I have no idea at all."

Kristian Nordström walked with Knutas to the door. The heat washed over them as they came out of the cool house onto the stairs. Outside, all of nature was clad in the tender green of early summer.

As Knutas drove back to Visby in the afternoon light, thoughts kept swirling through his mind. What did the story about the teacher mean? Why hadn't anyone mentioned it before, not even her best friend Emma?

It had happened a long time ago. And yet . . .

After reaching police headquarters, Knutas noticed how hungry he was. Going home for dinner was out of the question. After obtaining this new information, he wanted to call a meeting at once. He punched in his home phone number to say he would be late.

His long-suffering wife received the news calmly. Years ago, she had quite simply given up counting on him for dinner during the week. *Maybe that's why our marriage works so well,* Knutas managed to think as he took the stairs up to the criminal investigations department. The fact that they each had their own role in life, without expecting to share every single second, definitely made their life together much easier.

The detectives who were present in the building called up their usual pizzeria to put in a collective order. Between bites Knutas reported on his meeting with Kristian Nordström and told the others what he had said about Helena Hillerström's love affair with the PE teacher, Jan Hagman.

"Did you say his name was Hagman?" exclaimed Karin Jacobsson. "I talked to him not long ago. We went out to his house in Grötlingbo." She turned to Thomas Wittberg. "Don't you remember? His wife had committed suicide."

"Oh, that's right. It was only a few months ago. She hanged herself. He was rather strange, that guy. Introverted and hard to make contact with. Do you remember, we thought it was odd the way he didn't seem the least bit upset or even surprised that his wife had taken her own life?" said Wittberg.

"We did an investigation, of course," said Jacobsson. "But everything pointed to suicide, and when the autopsy report came back, we were convinced that's what happened. She had hanged herself in a barn they had on their property."

"We need to check up on him," said Knutas.

"But why should Hagman have anything to do with these murders?" asked Wittberg. "It was twenty years ago that they were together. I don't see why we should spend any time on such an old story. An affair with a high school teacher? She was thirty-five years old when she was killed, for God's sake."

"I agree that it seems like a long shot," said Norrby.

"That may be, but I still think it would be worthwhile to talk to Hagman," said Knutas. "What do you think, Karin?"

"Yes, of course. We don't have anything else concrete to go on. Although it's strange that none of the people we interviewed ever said anything about this PE teacher. And why would Kristian Nordström decide to mention it now?"

"He told me that it just didn't occur to him," said Knutas. "That it happened so long ago. And no one else said anything about it, either." He pushed aside his pizza box.

"If we turn our focus back to the present, is there anything new to report about the victims?" asked Jacobsson.

"Well, yes, the group that's mapping out their lives is hard at work. Kihlgård from the National Criminal Police is on his way over here.

He was asleep when I phoned," said Knutas. "Taking an after-dinner nap, as he called it."

Norrby rolled his eyes. "Yeah, thanks a lot. I'm glad some people have time to rest."

The murmuring that spread through the room was cut off by the door opening.

Kihlgård's big, wide body filled the whole doorway. "Hey, sorry I'm late." He greedily eyed the pizza boxes. "Anything left for me?"

"Here, take mine. I can't eat the whole thing." Jacobsson slid her pizza box over toward him.

"Thanks," Kihlgård growled as he rolled up the rest of the pizza and bit into it. "This is good," he managed to say between bites. The others had stopped talking and were watching him with fascination. For a moment they even forgot why they were there.

"Didn't you already eat?" asked Knutas.

"Sure, but it's always good to have a little pizza." Kihlgård chuckled before taking another bite. "So where were you? Tell me about this teacher story."

Knutas reported one more time on his conversation with Kristian Nordström.

"Hm. I see. We're in the process of mapping out the lives of the two women, and so far we haven't heard anything about this," said Kihlgård. "It's true that she had a lot of relationships, but not with any teachers, as far as I know. But this was supposedly much earlier, in high school, right?"

"Yes. Apparently they started a love affair sometime during the fall semester when Helena was in her second year. According to Nordström, they made plans to meet during Christmas vacation. Then the relationship must have continued through the whole spring, because it ended sometime during the summer. The teacher, Jan Hagman, was married and had children and evidently decided to stay with his wife. When the fall came, he started teaching at a different school."

"Do we know whether he still lives on the island? The teacher, that is?" said Kihlgård, using his radar eyes to search the collection of pizza boxes on the table. There might be a piece of crust left.

"Yes, he lives in the southern part of Gotland. Jacobsson and Wittberg were out there a few months ago. His wife committed suicide."

"Is that right?" Kihlgård raised his eyebrows. "So the guy's a widower. How old is he?"

"Hagman was supposedly in his forties when they were together, which means that he was more than twice Helena's age. Today he should be around sixty."

The evening sun flooded in over the kitchen benches, lighting up the children's hair in its glow. Emma leaned down over Filip and drew in his scent with a feeling of pleasure. His soft blond hair tickled her nose.

"Mmmm, you smell good. Mamma's little sweetie," she said tenderly, and then moved over to her daughter. Sara's hair was thicker and darker, like her own. She took in another deep breath. The same tickling in her nose.

"Mmmm," she said again. "You smell so wonderful, sweetheart." She stroked her daughter's head. "You're both my little darlings. That's what you are."

Emma sat down next to them at the counter in the middle of the big open kitchen. It was the room she liked best in their house. She and Olle had built the kitchen themselves. Part of it, where they were now sitting, was the work area, with clinker bricks on the floor, beautiful tiles above the sink, and a big island with a free-hanging vent over the stove. She loved to stand there and cook. At the same time, she could savor the view through the windows facing the garden. There was even room for four place settings, perfect for a quick breakfast or a drink before dinner with good friends. A couple of steps led down to the dining area with the oiled pine floor, the sturdy beams in the ceiling, and the big rustic table. The windows that opened onto all sides meant that her kitchen plants flourished there, just as she did.

The children were perched on tall bar stools, drinking chocolate milk and eating warm cinnamon rolls. It was their treat after the sting of shampoo in their eyes and water that was alternately too cold or too hot as their mother sprayed it over them in the shower they had just taken.

Emma watched them as they ate. Sara, seven years old and just finished with first grade. Cheerful, popular, a good student, with dark eyes and rosy cheeks. *Things have been going well so far,* she thought gratefully. Her gaze shifted to Filip, who was six. Blond, with a fair complexion, blue eyes, and dimples in his cheeks, good-natured but rowdy. Only a little more than a year between them. She was happy about that now.

It was rough in the beginning, though, with a child on each arm. Sara hadn't even learned to walk yet when Filip was born, and Emma wasn't finished with her degree. She had kept on plugging away during her last year at the teachers' college, with one baby at her breast and another in her belly. Now she couldn't understand how she did it, but it had all worked out—with a lot of help from Olle, of course. At the time he was also in his last year, working on a degree in economics, so they had taken turns tending to the babies and studying. It had been a struggle, what with the kids, little money, and difficult studies. Back then they were living in a sublet apartment in Stockholm. She smiled when she thought about how she had lugged around a double baby buggy, bought bruised tomatoes cheap at the Rimi supermarket, and how they had used cloth diapers with plastic ties. It was a matter of saving money as well as doing their part for the environment. In the evenings Olle would sit and fold diapers while he watched the news on TV and she nursed the baby. What a struggle it had been. Yet at the same time, their love had blossomed, and they had shared everything with each other.

Back then she thought they would stay together forever. Now she was no longer so sure.

Sara gave a big yawn. It was eight o'clock. Time for bed. After the kids brushed their teeth, Emma read them a short story and kissed them good night. Then she sat down on one of the sofas in the living room. She didn't bother to turn on the TV, just looked out the window. The sun was still high in the sky. *Strange how a person's perspective changes with the light,* she thought. Right now, with the garden bathed in light, it seemed absurd to put the children to bed. In December it would seem like bedtime at four in the afternoon.

She poured herself a cup of coffee and curled up in a corner of the sofa. Then her thoughts wandered back in time.

Of course things were good between her and Olle for a long time. When the kids were little, she had scrupulously made sure that they had their cozy dinners on Friday night, in spite of the children crying and the necessity of changing diapers. Many a night they had sat at the table with the candles lit while one of them rocked the children to sleep and the other ate before the food got cold. But sometimes things worked out well, and those moments were precious, she thought.

They hadn't neglected each other just because they had children. That was a mistake that plenty of couples in their circle of friends had made, and it often resulted in divorce. But Emma and Olle kept on having fun together, laughing and joking, at least for the first few years. Back then Olle would often buy her flowers and tell her how beautiful she was. She had never felt so fulfilled with anyone else.

Even after she put on almost sixty-five pounds when she was pregnant with their first child, he had looked at her naked body with admiration and said, "Sweetheart, you're so sexy."

She had believed him. When they strolled through town she had felt so pretty, at least until she caught sight of her own image in a shop window and realized that she was three times bigger than her husband.

They had carefully guarded their love, and she had been in love with him for a long time.

During the past two years, something had happened. She couldn't really pinpoint when the change occurred; she just knew that it had.

It started with their sex life. She thought it seemed more and more dreary and increasingly predictable. Olle did what he could, but she had trouble feeling any real desire. Of course they still made love with each other, although less and less frequently. Most often she was only interested in putting on a soft nightgown and reading a good book until her eyes fell shut. Deep inside, a feeling of discontent began gnawing at her. Would they ever get back to the sex life they had shared before? She had her doubts.

Other things had changed, too. Nowadays Olle had a tendency to work like a dog during the week, and that seemed to be enough for him. He apparently had no need to think up fun things to do with her anymore. If they happened to go out to eat or to a movie, she was the one who had to make the arrangements. Olle was happy to stay at home. The bouquets of tulips and the personal compliments were getting to be few and far between. That was a big difference compared to the first years, and it became even greater with time.

She looked out the window again. Olle was at a conference on the mainland. He'd be gone for three days. He had called twice today, sounding worried. He wanted to know how she was doing. Of course she appreciated his concern, but at the moment she just wanted to be left in peace.

Her thoughts shifted to Johan. She couldn't see him again. It was impossible. Things had already gone too far. But she was astonished by how he made her feel. She had forgotten what that was like. She had such a wild desire for him. In some strange way it had felt so right. As if she were entitled to feel that way and her whole body were meant to burn like that. Johan made her feel alive, like a whole person.

The realization was painful.

TUESDAY, JUNE 19

Knutas quickly greeted his colleagues as he entered the conference room, arriving out of breath and fifteen minutes later than all the others. He had overslept this morning. Kihlgård had called to wake him.

He sank onto a chair and almost tipped over the coffee cup that stood in front of him on the table. "So what have you found out about Hagman?"

Kihlgård was sitting at one end of the table with a cup of coffee and a huge open-face cheese sandwich on top of a plate that was much too small for it. Knutas stared at the sandwich in disbelief, thinking that he must have sliced the loaf of bread lengthwise.

"Well, we've found out a few things, all right," said Kihlgård after taking a big bite followed by a gulp of coffee, making a loud slurping noise. "He worked at a high school called the Säve School up to and including the spring semester of 1983. Then he left voluntarily, according to the principal, who is actually the same one they had back then. That was a lucky break for us," Kihlgård said with satisfaction, and then took another bite of his sandwich.

The others in the room waited impatiently for him to finish chewing and swallow.

"The fact that he was having an affair with a student quickly spread, and it became an enormously difficult situation for Hagman. People started to talk, of course. As mentioned, he was married and had two kids. He took a job at a different school and moved his whole family to Grötlingbo. That's in southern Gotland," Kihlgård explained, as if he had forgotten that everyone in the group except himself was a Gotland native.

He glanced at his notes. "The school where he taught there is called

Öja School. It's near Burgsvik. Hagman worked there until he took early retirement two years ago."

"Does Hagman have a police record?" asked Knutas.

"No, not even a speeding ticket," replied Kihlgård. "But it's true that he did have a love affair with Helena Hillerström. The principal confirmed it. All the teachers knew about it. Hagman resigned before the school had a chance to take any action against him."

Kihlgård leaned back, holding his sandwich in his hand and looking around expectantly.

"Let's go out and have a talk with him right now," said Knutas. "I'd like you to come with me, Karin, all right?"

"Sure."

"Would you mind if I came, too?" asked Kihlgård.

"No, not at all," said Knutas, surprised. "You're welcome to come along."

Johan and Peter had finished editing a rather lengthy report about the mood on the island after the latest murder. They had conducted several good interviews: a nervous mother, a restaurant owner who had already noticed a drop in business, and several young girls who were afraid to go out at night. Even so, their editor wasn't happy. That Max Grenfors. Never completely satisfied if a story didn't take the exact form that he himself would have given it. *What a son of a bitch,* thought Johan. At least he had agreed to let them stay a few more days, even though nothing new had happened. There were still plenty of things to get done. Johan had scheduled another interview for tomorrow with Detective Superintendent Anders Knutas to find out the latest developments in the investigation.

The fact that Johan could stay on the island meant that he would have more opportunities to see Emma. If she wanted to see him, that was. He was afraid that he had scared her off by moving too fast. At the same time, a feeling of guilt was gnawing at him. She was married, after all. In spite of that, he thought about her practically all the time, saying her name out loud. Emma. Emma Winarve. It felt so right on his lips. He had to see her again. At least one more time.

He decided to take a chance. Maybe she was home and her husband wasn't. She picked up after only one ring, sounding out of breath.

"Hi, it's me. Johan."

A brief pause.

"Hi."

"Are you alone?"

"No, the children are here. And my mother-in-law."

Shit.

"Could we meet?"

"I don't know. When?"

"Right now."

She laughed. "You're crazy."

"Can your mother-in-law hear what we're saying?"

"No, they're outside."

"I have to see you. Do you want to see me?"

"I want to, but I can't. This is insane."

"Who cares if it's insane. It's fate."

"How do you know I feel the same way?"

"I don't. But I'm hoping you do."

"Oh God, I really don't know."

"Please. Can you get away?"

"Wait a second."

He heard her put down the phone and walk away. It took about a minute. Maybe two. He held his breath. Then she was back and picked up the phone.

"Okay, I can do it."

"Shall I pick you up?"

"No, no. I'll drive into town. Where should we meet?"

"I'll meet you at the parking lot by Stora Torget. In an hour?"

"Okay."

I don't know what I'm doing, thought Emma when she hung up the phone. *I'm totally out of my mind.* At the moment, though, she didn't care. It had all worked out much too easily. She told her mother-in-law that one of her women friends was depressed and couldn't stop crying and that she had to go see her right away. "That's all right," her mother-in-law had assured her. She would take care of the children and make them pancakes for dinner. How awful, that poor woman. Of course Emma had to go. Her mother-in-law offered to stay all evening and even overnight if necessary. Olle wouldn't be home until the next day.

Emma rushed off to take a shower. They had been out in the sun all day, so she was hot and sweaty, she explained, at the same time that warning lights were going off in the back of her mind. She washed her hair, rubbed scented lotion into her skin, and applied a few drops of perfume as she felt her heart pounding with excited anticipation. Swiftly she put on her best bra and a blouse and skirt. She kissed the children and said good-bye. She drew in a deep breath and promised to call later. By the time she sank into the driver's seat she was starting to sweat again.

As she drove out onto the road to Visby, she turned up the car stereo as loud as it would go and rolled down the window. She let the warm air of early summer sweep into the car and blow her feelings of guilt right out the window.

When she turned the car into the empty parking lot, she caught sight of him outside the state liquor store. He was dressed in jeans and a black T-shirt. His hair was disheveled.

What happened next seemed so natural. They didn't need to say a thing. They simply walked side by side along the street, and their steps took them automatically toward the hotel where Johan was staying, as if it were the most natural thing in the world. Through the lobby, up the stairs, over to the door, and then they were inside. Alone for the first time in a private space. They still didn't say a word. He took her in his arms the minute he closed the door. She noticed that he locked it.

Knutas drove fast along the road to Sudret. Karin Jacobsson and Martin Kihlgård were sitting in the back seat. They had decided to take county highway 142, which cut straight across the center of the island past Träkumla, Vall, and Hejde, then across the Lojsta heath, where the Gotland ponies live almost wild out on the moors. Jacobsson, who had worked as a guide in her younger days, told Kihlgård about the ponies, or the "forest rams," as they were also called.

"Did you see the sign that said 'Pony Park'? If you keep going in that direction for a few miles, you come to the part of Lojsta reserved for the ponies. They roam around out there in herds all year round and in all kinds of weather. There are about fifty mares and one stallion. The stallion stays for between one and three years, depending on how many mares he manages to impregnate. There are usually about thirty foals each year."

"How do they get any food?" asked Kihlgård, with his eyes fixed on the corner of a candy bag containing gummy cars. He was trying to open it. Finally he gave up and tore off the corner with his teeth.

"Hay is brought in during the winter, but otherwise they eat grass and whatever the forest has to offer. They're brought in to the vet a couple of times a year, to take care of their hooves, and the whole herd is rounded up each year for the pony competition in July."

"What's the point of having ponies if they just roam around outdoors all the time?"

"It's to preserve the breed. The Gotland pony is Sweden's only remaining domestic pony. Their lineage can be traced all the way back to the Stone Age. In the early twentieth century they were on the verge of extinction. That's when people began raising them again, and now their numbers have swelled. Today there are a couple of thousand ponies on Gotland and at least five thousand in the rest of Sweden. They're very popular as saddle horses, because they're so small, only about four feet high at the shoulder—perfect for children, especially because of their temperament. They're gentle horses, good workers with lots of stamina. They're also great for harness racing. My brother has horses here. I usually go with him when it's time for the competition. We meet early in the morning, a group of about thirty, and we help to round up the ponies. It's a marvelous experience," said Jacobsson, with a look of nostalgia in her eyes.

They continued chatting as they drove. Kihlgård offered to share his gummy cars, although most of them ended up in his own mouth. Jacobsson appreciated Kihlgård's expertise as well as his good humor. She was also fascinated by his eating habits, which were quite interesting, to say the least. He seemed to be eating all the time, no matter what the hour. He usually had something in his mouth, and if he didn't, he was either on his way to or from a meal. In spite of this, he wasn't overweight. Maybe just a little stocky.

Knutas really had nothing against Kihlgård, but the man was starting to irritate him. He was so outgoing and congenial that he had quickly become very popular among the employees at police headquarters. That was fine, of course, but he did take a lot of liberties. Kihlgård had an opinion about everything, and he kept trying to meddle in the way Knutas was managing the investigation. Knutas had noticed how his colleague kept trying to insert little criticisms and slip in his own views. Even though he would refuse to acknowledge it, Kihlgård displayed something of a big-brother attitude. The police in Stockholm probably thought at heart that it was a step down to be an officer on Gotland. Did anything ever happen over there? It was true that most of the crimes on the island consisted of break-ins and drunken brawls that couldn't compare with all the aggravated and complicated crimes that were committed in Stockholm. Anyone who worked in the National Criminal Police was, of course, a better and more skilled officer. There was a certain conceitedness about Kihlgård that shone through, in spite of the fact that he was supposedly such buddies with everyone. Under normal circumstances, Knutas didn't think of himself as high-powered, but now he was starting to sense a battle for territory, and he wasn't happy about it. He had decided to rise above it all and take a positive attitude toward his older colleague, though that wasn't always easy. Especially since the guy was so stubborn about chomping on something at all times. And why did he get into the backseat with Karin? He was such a big man that he should be sitting up front. The two of them seemed to be having a great time back there. What were they whispering about? Knutas felt his irritation growing. His thoughts were interrupted when Kihlgård stuck out the candy bag with three pitiful gummy cars left in the bottom.

"Would you like one?"

The road wound its way through the interior of the island. Farm houses whizzed past, along with pastures filled with white cows and black sheep. In a farmyard three men were running around chasing a huge pig that had apparently gotten out. They drove through Hemse, then Alva, and finally Grötlingbo in the center of Sundret before they took the road heading for the sea and Grötlingbo Point.

They discussed what approach to take when they arrived.

What did they know about Jan Hagman? Very little, actually. He had taken early retirement, and he was a widower as of a few months ago. He had two grown children. And he was interested in young girls, or at least he had been.

"Did he have anything going on with other students?" asked Jacobsson.

"Not that we know of, but of course he might have," said Kihlgård.

Four big wind power stations dominated the bare landscape at Grötlingbo Point. Low stone fences lined the road that led straight out to the sea. The special type of Gotland sheep that stayed out in the pastures all year round, with their thick coats and curving horns, were grazing among the scruffy juniper bushes, the windblown dwarf pines, and the huge boulders that were scattered about. Hagman's farm was almost at the very end of the point, with a view across Gansviken. It was easy to find among the few houses that stood out there. Since Jacobsson had been there before, she gave directions.

They arrived unannounced.

The name HAGMAN was on the homemade mailbox. They parked in the yard and got out. The farm consisted of a run-down, white-painted wooden house with gray trim and corner posts. It had undoubtedly been a fine house at one time, but now the paint was peeling.

A short distance away stood a large barn that looked as if it might collapse at any minute. *So that's where his wife hanged herself,* thought Knutas.

As they approached the house, he glimpsed a movement behind the curtains in one of the second-floor windows. They climbed the steps to the partially rotting porch and knocked. There was no doorbell. Three times they had to knock before the door opened.

A man who was much too young to be Jan Hagman stood in the doorway. He gave them an inquiring look. "Yes?"

Knutas introduced himself. "We're looking for Jan Hagman," he said.

The man's friendly expression gave way to alarm. "What's wrong?"

"It's nothing serious," Knutas said in a soothing tone. "We just want to ask him a few questions."

"Does it have to with Mamma? I'm Jens Hagman. Jan's son."

"No. This is about something else entirely," Knutas assured him.

"I see. Well, Jan is out chopping wood. Wait a second." He turned around and pulled out a pair of wooden clogs that he slipped on his feet. "Come with me. He's out back."

As they rounded the side of the house, they could hear the rhythmic blows of an axe. The man they were looking for stood bending over a chopping block, seeming to be intently focused. He raised the axe and brought it down. The blade sliced through the wood, which split in half and fell to the ground. The man's thick hair fell over his face as he worked. He was wearing shorts and a cotton shirt. His legs were hairy and already very tan. The muscles in his arms bulged when he brought the blade down. Big patches of sweat spread across his shirt.

"Jan! The police are here. They want to talk to you," yelled the son.

Knutas frowned, thinking that it was strange for the son to persist in calling his father Jan.

Jan Hagman lowered the axe, then set it aside. "What do you want? The police have already been here once before," he said, sounding surly.

"This isn't about your wife's death. It's about something else," said the superintendent. "Could we go inside and sit down?"

The tall man gave them a guarded look without saying a word.

"Let's do that," said the son. "I can make some coffee."

They went inside the house. Knutas and Jacobsson sat down on the sofa while Kihlgård sank into an armchair.

They sat in silence, looking around. It was a gloomy room in a gloomy house. A dark brown wall-to-wall carpet lay on the floor. The walls were covered with dark green wallpaper. Paintings clustered thickly on three of them, mostly scenes of animals in a winter landscape: deer in the snow, ptarmigans in the snow, elk and hares in the snow. None of the officers was any sort of art connoisseur, but they could all see that these paintings were hardly of the same caliber as a work by Bruno Liljefors, for example. The fourth wall was devoted to guns of various types. To Karin Jacobsson's horror, she noticed a stuffed green parakeet sitting on a perch on top of what looked like a handmade lace doily on the side table.

The house had a silent, oppressive atmosphere, as if the walls were sighing. Heavy curtains with intricate tie-backs blocked most of the light from the windows. The furniture was dark and ungainly and had seen better days.

Just as Knutas was wondering how he was going to get himself out of the sagging old sofa without asking for a hand up, Jan Hagman appeared in the room. He had changed into a clean shirt but had the same surly expression on his face. He sat down in an armchair next to one of the windows.

Knutas cleared his throat. "We're not here with regard to the tragic death of your wife. Ahem . . . And of course we're sorry for your loss," said Knutas, coughing again.

Now Hagman was giving him a hostile stare.

"This has to do with a different matter," the superintendent went on. "I assume that you've heard about the two women who were murdered here on Gotland. The police are working their way back in time, to investigate the backgrounds of the women. It has come to light that you had a relationship with one of them, Helena Hillerström, in the early eighties when you were working at Säve School. Is that true?"

The oppressive atmosphere in the room became even more intense. Hagman's expression didn't change.

A long silence followed. Kihlgård was sweating and fidgeting, making his chair creak. Knutas waited, keeping his eyes steadily fixed on Hagman's face.

Jacobsson was longing for a glass of water. When the son came into the room carrying a coffee tray, it felt as if someone had opened a window.

"I thought you might want some coffee," he said stiffly, and he set down on the table his tray with the cups and a plate of store-bought jam cookies.

"Thank you," murmured the three officers in unison, and the tense mood was pushed aside for a moment by the clattering of china as the coffee was served.

"You need to leave us alone now," said the father harshly. "And close the door after you."

"All right," said his son, and left the room.

"So, what about this whole episode with Helena Hillerström?" asked Knutas again after the door closed.

"It's true. We had a relationship."

"How did it start?"

"She was one of my students, and we got on well during class. She was so cheerful and . . ."

"And?"

"Well, she made it more fun to teach."

"How did the relationship start?"

"It happened at a school dance in the fall. Helena was in her second year. This was in 1982."

"What were you doing there?"

"I was one of the teachers who was there as a chaperone."

"What happened between you and Helena?"

"That night when we were cleaning up after the dance was over, she stayed behind to help. She loved to talk, you know . . ." Hagman's voice faded out, and his expression softened.

"What happened?"

"She needed a ride home after the party, and we lived in the same part of town, so I offered to drive her home. After that I don't really know how it happened. She kissed me. She was young and attractive, and I'm just a man, after all."

"And after that?"

"We started meeting in secret. I was married, you know, and had children."

"How often did you meet?"

"Quite often."

"How often?"

"Well, it was probably two or three times a week."

"What about your wife? Did she notice anything?"

"No. We usually met in the daytime, in the afternoon. And my children were big enough to look after themselves."

"How was your marriage?"

"Not good. It was completely dead. That's why I didn't feel guilty. Not because of my wife, at any rate," said Hagman.

"What was Helena like as a person?" asked Kihlgård.

"She was . . . I don't know what I should say." He hesitated. "She was wonderful. She made me feel alive again."

"How long did the relationship last?"

"It ended at the beginning of summer vacation."

Hagman looked down at his hands. Karin Jacobsson had noticed that he kept twiddling his thumbs, almost nonstop. She remembered that he had done the same thing the last time she was here, after his wife's death. *Imagine that there are people who still do that,* she thought.

"Late in the spring, in May, I think, the class went on a trip to Stockholm. Several other teachers went along."

"What happened?"

"After dinner one evening, Helena and I weren't very careful. She went back to my room with me. Apparently someone saw us and reported it to one of the other teachers. The teacher told me what she had heard. There was nothing I could do but confess. She said it wouldn't go any farther if I promised never to see Helena again. So I promised."

"Then what happened?"

"We got back from the trip, and I broke up with Helena. But she didn't understand. It wasn't long before we started seeing each other again. I couldn't help myself. Late one night one of my colleagues came upon us in the locker room. That was the week after summer vacation had started for all the students. We teachers had to work one more week."

"How did the school administration react?"

"The principal didn't make a big ruckus about it. He arranged for me to take a job at a different school. There was a lot of talk, and they really let me have it. In most people's eyes I was a real loser. My wife found out, of course. I wanted a divorce, but she refused. We decided to move away. My new job was in Öja, so we bought this farm. It was a good place, quite close, and we could escape from all the gossip. I couldn't keep on seeing Helena. When her parents found out about it, they went crazy. They wrote me a letter threatening to kill me if I ever came near their daughter again."

"How did Helena react?"

Hagman sat in silence for a long time. He frantically twiddled his thumbs. At last the silence became very uncomfortable, and Knutas was just about to ask the question again when the answer came.

"I never heard from her again. She was so young. I suppose she just went on with her life."

"Didn't you try to contact her?"

Hagman raised his head and looked Knutas straight in the eyes when he replied. "No. Never."

"When was the last time you saw her?"

"It was that night. In the locker room."

"And you chose not to leave your wife?"

"That's right. She wanted to forget all about it and move on. I don't know why. She never loved me. She didn't love the children, either," said Hagman, glancing toward the closed door, as if he wanted to be sure that his son couldn't hear.

"Did your children ever find out what had happened?"

"No, they didn't notice a thing. Jens wasn't even living at home. He had moved in with my sister and brother-in-law in Stockholm right after middle school. He wanted to go to high school over there. Since then, he has always lived in Stockholm. He just comes here to visit.

My daughter, Elin, lives in Halmstad. She met her boyfriend after high school and then moved there."

Again there was silence. Knutas noticed a ladybug crawling up one of the table legs. *They're everywhere,* he thought.

Kihlgård broke the silence. "Have you had any relationships with students other than Helena?" he ventured.

The change was immediate. Hagman's knuckles turned white as he gripped the arms of his chair. He gave Kihlgård a furious glare. "What the hell do you think you're saying?" He spat out the words as if they were missiles.

Kihlgård glowered back at him. "I want to know if there were any other students you slept with."

"No. There weren't. All I wanted was Helena." Hagman took in a deep breath through his nose.

"Are you sure about that? If you had a relationship with any other student, it's bound to come out eventually. Things would go a lot faster if you admit it to me right here and now."

"Didn't you hear what I said? There was only Helena. And there has never been anyone since then, either. That's enough now. I have nothing more to say."

Hagman's face had turned pale under his tan. He got up from his chair.

Knutas realized that they might as well leave. The man was so upset that they weren't going to get anything more out of him anyway. Not this time.

The school bell rang just as he was about to start on the next math problem. He had been concentrating so hard on the problems in his book that he forgot all about the time. Math was the only subject that could swallow him up completely—and change the world for a moment so that he forgot both time and space. It made him feel almost happy.

His classmates all around him were standing up. Chairs scraped, books were gathered up, desk lids were slamming shut. Everyone started talking at once. He caught a few scattered remarks.

How could the same bell signal heaven one time and hell the next? There were times when he loved it. The bell could signify liberation, a warm embrace that rescued him in his hour of need and helped him to escape to his temporary refuge in the classroom. Other times he hated it more than anything else in the world. He would feel nervous and scared. He would start to shake and sweat. It filled him with a fear of what was to come.

Right now his thoughts were flitting around in his head like caged birds as he slowly gathered up his books. He looked down at the desk lid.

How would things go this time at recess? Would he be able to escape? Should he stay back as long as possible? Then maybe they would get tired of waiting for him. Or should he race off as fast as he could and try to dash out so that he could reach his hiding place?

Uncertainty gnawed at him as he mechanically gathered up his books. When he reached the classroom door, the pain in his stomach started up in earnest. It was practically suffocating him. He went out the door with a feeling of doom inside his body.

The hallway was filled with children. Rows of hooks and bags and boots and jackets and hats and backpacks and dark blue and red gym bags. Everything that represented the school, everything he hated. He had to pee. He'd better run to the bathroom.

First he had to find his gym bag. His eyes studied the shiny clothes hooks. His was in the long row on the red tile wall. None of the hated demons seemed to be around.

When he reached his bag, he grabbed it from the hook, spun on his heel, and dashed into the bathroom, which turned out to be empty. He sighed with relief when he was inside. He would sit here on the toilet until the bell rang again and recess was over. Of course, that would mean that he would arrive several minutes late for gym class. The teacher, Mr. Sturesson, would yell at him, but it was worth it.

WEDNESDAY, JUNE 20

Johan lay in bed in his hotel room, staring up at the ceiling. He had just had a long talk with his mother. The conversation had largely consisted of her crying and saying how hard everything was, while he did his best to comfort her. In addition to the grief and emptiness after his father's death, his mother had begun to notice other consequences of a purely practical nature. If a fuse blew or the drain was stopped up, she was at a loss to know what to do. Her finances were getting worse, and she couldn't even afford the things to which she had become accustomed; she had to budget carefully to make everything work out. The consoling visits all her relatives and friends had made in the first weeks after her husband's death had become less frequent over time and then virtually stopped altogether. Friends who still had a spouse didn't invite her over as often as they had in the past. Actually, almost never. Johan felt sorry for her but didn't know how he could fix her life. It was frustrating. He just wanted her to be happy.

He still hadn't had time to deal with his own grief over his father's death. In the period right afterwards he was fully occupied with all the practical details. The funeral, the probate, and all the documents that had to be completed. His mother had been apathetic, and since he was the eldest in the family, his siblings had turned to him for solace, each in their own way. He had been kept busy taking care of everyone else, and then things had gotten hectic at work, and he hadn't taken the time that he probably should have to deal with his own grief.

He had truly loved his father. They could talk about anything. He needed him now, when he was feeling so confused, to talk about Emma. Self-reproach was wearing him down. Who was he, after all? Was he such a loser that he couldn't find anyone who was free? Available? What right did he have to come barging into Emma's life? He had no right. There was a man who lived with Emma, who shared her daily life, a man about his own age who took good care of his family. What had he done except seduce that man's wife and the mother of his children? He might even have mortally wounded him, or at least caused serious injuries, bound to leave permanent scars.

He got up and lit a cigarette as he paced back and forth in the room. What if Emma was actually happy with her family? What if she and her husband were just going through a down period? That wouldn't be surprising after everything that had happened.

He opened the minibar and took out a beer. His thoughts kept on churning, inexorably.

What if she really wasn't happy in her marriage? What if she was going around in a marriage that was dead? Stone cold dead. What if she had never been happy with her husband? Maybe the children were suffering because their parents were always fighting. Sullen faces and difficult moods. Angry voices. Arguments about petty things. A tense atmosphere at the dinner table. What did he know about how things were between them? Emma hadn't said a word. Good Lord, they didn't really even know each other. They had only met a few times. Why was she filling his thoughts so much? He was scaring himself.

A sense of disquiet was twisting and turning inside of him. He needed air. He pulled on his running shoes and went out.

On the street, people in their summer clothes were strolling around and eating ice cream as if they didn't have a care in the world. He walked down toward the harbor, past the boats. There were more and more of them every day. He sat down on the edge of the dock and looked out across the sea, which was glittering in the sun. He drew the fresh air deep into his lungs. How good it made him feel, being close to the sea.

What real meaning did his own life have? He worked hard, but his days were pretty much all the same. He turned in one news story after another. A new drug story here, a new murder there, robberies and assault and battery. Year in and year out. He lived in his little apartment, hung out with his friends, partied on the weekends.

For the first time he had met a woman who had truly shaken him up. Got under his skin. Made him stop and think. The seagulls were screeching as a ferry arrived from the mainland. More vacation-happy people on their way to wonderful Gotland. Why didn't he just move over here? He could get a job at one of the newspapers, *Gotlands Alle-handa* or *Gotlands Tidningar.* He had always wanted to write but never got the chance. Over here he could report on other things, get close to the people.

Just think of all the things Gotlanders didn't have to put up with that Stockholmers had to live with every day. The traffic, the lines, the stress, the subways. Everything had to move fast, really fast. Even last time, when he got back home after his first trip to the island, he had clearly noticed the difference. The very instant he stepped off the ferry in Nynäshamn, he started walking faster. He felt annoyed in the shops if things took too long. Stress went hand in hand with living in a big city. People didn't look at each other in the same way as on Gotland. Here they had time for small talk and eye contact. Life was slower and gentler. More pensive. Besides, he had always liked Gotland, with its marvelous nature and the sea that was close by no matter where you were. And Emma was here. He could move here for her sake. Would she want that? He didn't know. He would have to wait and see. The important thing was for them to see each other more.

THURSDAY, JUNE 21

The whirring of the potter's wheel was the only sound to be heard. Gunilla Olsson was straddling the simple wooden chair, hard at work, with one foot on the pedal that controlled the speed of the wheel. High speed at first as she started on a new lump of clay, then slower.

The evening sun shone through the windows that ran along one whole wall. It was the day before Midsummer Eve and the lightest day of the year. Outside, the geese still hadn't figured out that it was time to go to sleep. They were waddling around, eating the grass and cackling in chorus.

She plopped another lump of Gotland clay onto the wheel, wet her hands by dunking them in the bucket next to her, and let her fingers rest lightly but firmly on the clay as the wheel spun round and round.

The studio was filled with shelves holding ceramic objects: pots, pitchers, plates, bowls, and vases. The wooden walls were spattered with traces of dried clay. A mirror hung on one wall. It was dusty and spotted, offering almost no reflection at all.

Gunilla began humming a song as she sat there. She straightened her back a bit and tossed her braids over her shoulder. She would make two more pots. Then that should be enough.

The commission that she was trying to finish had taken weeks of intensive labor. It would bring in a nice sum of money that should last her through most of the winter. She had decided to grant herself a few days off during the Midsummer holiday. She was going to enjoy the time in peace and quiet with Cecilia, one of her artist colleagues who also lived alone. They had known each other only a few months. They met at an art exhibit in Ljugarn over Easter and quickly became good friends. Now they were going to spend Midsummer Eve at Cecilia's cabin in Katthammarsvik.

It had been years since Gunilla had celebrated a Swedish Midsummer. This past winter she had returned to Sweden and settled in När after a decade abroad. When she was in art school she had met Bernhard, a wild, freethinking art student from Holland. She quit her studies and followed him to the Hawaiian island of Maui to start a new life in sunshine and freedom. There they had lived in a commune and worked on their art. Life was perfect. Then she got pregnant, and everything changed. Bernhard left her for an eighteen-year-old French girl who thought of him as a god.

Gunilla had come back home to have an abortion. She was depressed and had no friends, so she put all her energy into her work. Things had gone well. She had had several exhibits and sold a lot of pieces, and now things were rolling. Lately she had also acquired several new friends. Cecilia was one of them.

She was aroused from her reverie when the trumpeting of the geese got louder outside. Now she could hear them shrieking indignantly. *Shit,* she thought, not wanting to interrupt her work just as she was shaping the upper part of the pot. What was wrong with them?

She stood up halfway and peered out the window. The geese were crowding together out in the yard. Her gaze swept from one side of the yard to the other. She couldn't see anything out of the ordinary. She sat back down, resolving to finish the last two pots. She might be a dreamer, but she had always been very disciplined.

The geese were quiet now, and once again the rhythmic whirring of the wheel was the only sound.

She had her eyes fixed on the lump of clay in the middle of the wheel. The shape of the pot was almost done.

Suddenly she froze. Something was moving outside the window. Or someone. Like a shadow slipping past. Or was she imagining things? She wasn't sure. She stopped working and listened, waiting without knowing for what.

Slowly she turned around on her chair. Her eyes surveyed the room. She looked toward the entrance. The door to the yard was slightly ajar.

She saw a goose strut past. That made her feel calmer. Maybe it was just a goose.

She stepped on the pedal again, and the wheel began turning.

The floor creaked. Now she knew that someone was there. Her eyes caught sight of the mirror on the wall. Was that where she had seen something? Again she stopped her work and listened closely. All her senses were on alert. She eased her foot off the pedal. Automatically she wiped her hands on her apron. Another creak. Someone was in the room but wasn't saying anything. The room was breathing danger. The thought of the two murdered women darted like a swallow through her mind. She sat totally still. Didn't dare move.

Then she saw a figure in the spotted mirror on the wall.

She felt enormous relief. Her lungs released the air that they had been holding inside. She took a big breath.

"Oh, it's only you," she said with a laugh. "You really scared me."

She smiled and turned around.

"You know, I heard a noise, and it made me think instantly about that lunatic who's been killing women."

That's as far as she got before the axe struck her in the forehead and she fell over backward. As she fell, her arm pulled down the newly shaped pot that was warm from her hands.

FRIDAY, JUNE 22

When Gunilla didn't answer the phone on Thursday evening or on the morning of Midsummer Eve, Cecilia started to worry. It was true that Gunilla sometimes seemed unusually naive and up in the clouds, but before, on those occasions when they had agreed to meet, she had always been punctual. Gunilla was also a morning person, and she had said that she would be leaving by eight. She had joked about waking Cecilia up with breakfast in bed, but Cecilia had just finished eating her Midsummer breakfast.

Why doesn't she phone? she thought. Gunilla had said she would give her a call last night. Maybe she had been working and then it got to be too late. Cecilia knew how that could happen. She was an artist herself.

Cecilia was already at the cabin in Katthammarsvik. She had arrived the night before, loaded down with food and wine. They were going to have herring and new potatoes for lunch and later grilled salmon burgers for supper. No dance floor, no party, and above all no other people. Just the two of them. They would drink wine and discuss art, life, and love. In that order.

She had made a little Midsummer pole that they could decorate with flowers and birch leaves. They would sit outside and eat, enjoying the peace and quiet. The weatherman on the radio had promised high pressure all weekend.

Where on earth was Gunilla? It was past eleven, and Cecilia had called several times. She had tried her house, her studio, and her cell phone.

Why wasn't she answering? Maybe she had fallen ill suddenly, or even injured herself. Anything could have happened. Cecilia grappled with these thoughts in her mind as she worked on the preparations for Midsummer. When the clock struck twelve, she decided to go over to Gunilla's house, fifteen miles away.

Cecilia got into her car with a growing sense of trepidation.

When she turned into the yard, all the geese were running back and forth, cackling hysterically. The door to the ceramics workshop was slightly ajar. She pushed it open and went in.

The first thing she saw was the blood. On the floor, on the walls, on the potter's wheel. Gunilla lay on her back in the middle of the workshop, stretched out on the floor with her arms above her head. Cecilia's scream caught in her throat.

Knutas's eyes were filled with tenderness as he looked at his wife. He stroked her sunburned, freckled cheek. She had more freckles than anyone else he had ever known, and he loved every single dot on her. The sun was warming the ground, so the children could run around barefoot. The long table was set with the blue-flowered Rörstrand dishes, the napkins had been festively stuck in the glasses, and the silverware shone. Ceramic pitchers were filled with summer wildflowers: daisies, cranesbills, almond blossoms, and fiery red poppies. The herring was arranged on a platter: herring in mustard sauce and in aquavit, pickled herring, and his own homemade herring in sherry, which burned sweetly on the tongue. The new potatoes that had just been set on the table were steaming in their deep bowls, white and tender, with green sprigs of dill that brought out the sweet taste of summer.

The bread basket was filled with crisp bread, rye crackers, and his mother's famous unleavened flat bread that could entice people to come to Gotland just for the sake of buying some of it. It was sold only at his parents' farm in Kappelshamn.

He looked out at the yard, where the guests were decorating the Midsummer pole. It rose up, tall and stately, in the middle of the lawn. The children were eagerly helping.

His sister and brother had come with their families. Both his parents and parents-in-law were there, along with some neighbors and good friends. It was a tradition for him and his wife to give a Midsummer party at their summer house.

Something was tickling his hand. A ladybug was crawling up toward his wrist. He brushed it off. This Midsummer celebration was a badly needed break from the murder investigations, especially since he didn't feel that they were making any progress. It was frustrating not to be getting anywhere while at the same time the perpetrator might be planning his next murder. *We need to go farther back in time,* thought Knutas.

He had discussed this with Kihlgård. His colleague clearly had his own theory: He seemed convinced that the perpetrator was someone the women had met quite recently, yet he hadn't succeeded in producing any concrete proof. On the other hand, the good inspector from the National Criminal Police didn't hesitate to comment on the work of the Visby police. Kihlgård had an opinion on everything, from petty little routines to their interrogation methods and the way they conducted their investigative work. He had even complained that the coffee from the headquarters vending machines was too weak. Ridiculous, all of it. Right now the important thing was to focus on the hunt for the killer.

Not today, though. He needed this break, a few hours of congenial socializing with family and friends. He was even planning to get loaded. The homicide investigation could wait until tomorrow. Then he would urge the team to search further back in the past of the victims.

A sense of unease came over him, but it vanished when his wife brought out the frosty bottles of ice-cold aquavit and set them on the table. He felt a rumbling in his stomach. He sliced off a piece of ripe Västerbotten cheese and quickly stuffed it into his mouth before ringing the old cowbell they always used to announce that it was time to eat.

"Come and get it, everybody," he shouted.

After the guests had helped themselves from the platters, they all raised their glasses of aquavit, and Knutas welcomed everyone by making a toast to summer.

Just as he put the glass to his lips, the cell phone in the inside pocket of his jacket started ringing. Reluctantly he lowered his arm. *Who the hell would be calling me now, in the middle of the Midsummer holiday?* he thought angrily. It could only be someone from work.

His summer house was way up in Lickershamn, in the northwestern part of Gotland. The murdered Gunilla Olsson's house was in När, in the southeast. It would take Knutas an hour and a half to drive there.

It was just after one in the afternoon, and it was the warmest Midsummer in many years. The thermometer said that it was eighty-four degrees. Along the way he picked up Karin Jacobsson and Martin Kihlgård in Tingstäde, where Karin's parents lived. She had invited Kihlgård to their Midsummer celebration.

The other group members from the NCP had gone home to Stockholm for the holiday. Kihlgård had stubbornly insisted on staying on the island. After all, something might happen.

"This is exactly what we needed," he said in the car as the summer landscape, covered with flowers, rushed past the windows. "Something new had to happen before we could make any progress. We were at a complete standstill."

Kihlgård had consumed both herring and aquavit, and alcohol fumes enveloped him as he talked. Knutas's face turned white as chalk. He pulled over to some trash cans standing along the road and came to an abrupt stop. He jumped out of the car, tore open the back door where Kihlgård was sitting, and hauled him out.

"How can you sit there and say that? Are you out of your mind?" he yelled.

Kihlgård was so flabbergasted that he didn't know how to react. Then he got defensive.

"What the hell are you doing? I'm right, you know. Something had to happen, for God's sake, because we weren't getting anywhere."

"What the fuck do you mean?" bellowed Knutas in reply. "How the hell can you stand there and say that it's a good thing a young woman was killed by some deranged lunatic? Are you off your rocker, too?"

Jacobsson, who was still sitting in the car, now got out to intervene. She grabbed hold of Knutas, who had a firm grip on Kihlgård's shirt collar. Two buttons had flown off somewhere.

"Are you both crazy?" she shouted. "How can you act like this? Don't you see that people are watching?"

Both men backed off and turned their glaring eyes toward the road. On the other side was a farm, and a group of people, all dressed up with flower wreaths on their heads, were staring at the police car and the angry men.

"Oh, shit," said Knutas, and pulled himself together.

Kihlgård straightened his clothes, gave the audience a little bow, and climbed back into the car.

They continued on in silence. Knutas was furious, but he decided it would be best to leave this discussion until a later time. They were all undoubtedly feeling the frustration of failing to capture the killer.

Jacobsson was now sitting in the front passenger seat. She didn't say a word. Knutas could tell that she was mad.

To avoid listening to Kihlgård's muttering, Knutas turned on the radio. Then he rolled down the window. Another murder. This was terrible. One more woman. Axe wounds and panties in her mouth. When would it all end? They had gotten nowhere. On that point he had to agree with Kihlgård. He began mentally preparing himself for the sight that would soon greet him. He glanced to his right. At Karin. She was sitting there in silence, looking straight ahead.

"What are you thinking about?" he asked.

"We have to catch this guy. Now," she said resolutely. "This is going to scare people to death."

The police had already cordoned off the area when they arrived at the farm. Sohlman and his colleagues were busy securing evidence.

They parked the car in the gravel-covered yard and then hurried up the steep stone steps. When they entered the studio, all three of them instinctively recoiled. Blood was splattered on the walls, the floor, and the shelves. The sweet, nauseating smell of the corpse made them hold their hands up to their mouths. Jacobsson turned around and threw up on the steps.

"Goddamn it all," Kihlgård managed to say. "This is the worst I've ever seen."

The woman's naked body lay on the floor, bathed in blood. The deep wounds on her throat, abdomen, and thighs gaped wide open in the sunlight. With a great effort, Knutas forced himself to walk over to the body. It was true: In her mouth was stuffed a pair of white cotton panties. Jacobsson appeared in the doorway again, leaning on the doorframe. The police officers surveyed the scene, feeling powerless.

There was only one entrance, and that was through the doorway they had just entered. On the floor lay a shattered mirror. The pieces glittered in the sunshine. A short distance away was a lump of clay.

"She must have been sitting here working," said Knutas. "Do you see that lump of clay over there?"

"Yes," replied Jacobsson, and then turned to Sohlman, who was squatting down next to the body. "How long do you think she's been dead?"

"The body's completely rigid. Taking into consideration the rigor mortis, I'd guess she's been dead at least twelve hours, but not much longer than that. The body is still warm."

"Who called it in?"

"A friend of hers. Cecilia Ångström. She's in the house."

"I'm going over there," said Knutas.

From the outside, Gunilla Olsson's house looked too big to be the home of just one person. It was a two-story limestone building that appeared to be very old.

Knutas went in the front door, trying to shake off the image of the act of violence he had just been forced to see.

At the kitchen table sat a young woman with her head bowed. Her long dark hair hid her face. She was wearing a light-colored summer dress with spaghetti straps. A female uniformed police officer was sitting next to her, holding her hand. Knutas greeted them. He knew the officer slightly. The young woman was about twenty-five, Knutas guessed. She looked at him with a blank expression. Her face was streaked with tears.

Knutas introduced himself and sat down across from her. "Can you tell me what happened?"

"Well, Gunilla was supposed to come over to my house today. We were planning to celebrate Midsummer together, at my cabin in Katthammarsvik. She was supposed to arrive right after breakfast. When I didn't hear from her and she still hadn't shown up by noon, I started getting worried. She didn't answer any of the numbers that I called. That's when I decided to come over here."

"When did you get here?"

"It must have been close to one."

"What happened?"

"The door to the studio was open, so I went in. I found her there. She was lying on the floor. There was blood everywhere."

"What did you do?"

"I went out and got in my car and locked the doors. Then I called the police. I was scared and wanted to leave, but they told me to stay here. The police arrived in about half an hour."

"Did you see anyone?"

"No."

"Did you notice anything strange?"

"No."

"How well did you know Gunilla?"

"Quite well. We've been friends for a couple of months."

"And you were going to celebrate Midsummer together, just the two of you?"

"Gunilla was in the middle of working on a big commission. She'd been working really hard for the past few weeks and just wanted some peace and quiet. I felt the same way. That's why we decided to spend Midsummer together."

"When did you last talk to her?"

"The day before yesterday. She was supposed to call me last night, but she never did."

"Do you know whether she had planned to do anything special yesterday? Or whether she was going to meet anyone?"

"No. She was going to work all day and in the evening, too."

"Do you know where her family lives? Her parents? Her siblings?"

"Her parents are dead. She has a brother, but I don't know where he lives. Not on Gotland, at any rate."

"Did she have a boyfriend?"

"No, not as far as I know. She hadn't been back home very long. She lived abroad for a long time. She came back to Sweden in January, I think."

"I see." Knutas patted Cecilia Ångström's arm and asked his colleague to drive her to the hospital. "We'll talk some more later," he said to Cecilia. "I'll be in touch."

He left the kitchen and walked through the rest of the house. His courage sank as he looked out a window. Not a neighbor for as far as the eye could see. The living room was big and bright. Colorful paintings hung on the walls, works by artists he didn't know. He went upstairs and into the bedroom, where there was a big, inviting bed. Next door was a guest room that seemed unused, then a study, a big bathroom, and a sitting room.

He didn't discover anything unusual, at least not at first glance. No damage or vandalism, from what he could see. Sohlman would go over the house later, so he didn't want to touch anything.

The downstairs was equally bright and airy. Next to the kitchen was a big dining room with a fireplace. There was also another bedroom and one more room, filled with books and a big armchair for reading. *She certainly had a lot of room to herself,* he thought.

He was interrupted by Karin Jacobsson, who appeared in the doorway.

"Come here, Anders," she called out to him breathlessly. "We've found something."

No more than five minutes left in the school day. After school he usually went straight home. Hurry up. Hurry up. The key on a string around his neck. Since the only chance he had of escaping his tormentors was to get such a big head start that they couldn't catch him, he would always start preparing several minutes before the last class was over. Cautiously he began gathering up his things. Quietly he closed his book. Then he put his pencil in the little slot in his pencil case and the eraser in its slot. The whole time he kept his eyes fixed on the teacher, who mustn't notice anything. Slowly he closed the zipper on his pencil case. He thought it scraped as loudly as thunder through the classroom, but again the teacher didn't notice a thing. It was normally dead quiet in the room because the teacher was strict and wouldn't stand for any talking or playing around during class. Now she turned her back. Good. Carefully he opened the desk lid. Just slightly, enough so that he could slide his books inside. Then his pencil case. All right. His heart was thudding, hard and fast. The bell was going to ring soon. If only the teacher wouldn't notice anything before then. Lisa, who sat next to him, saw what he was up to but didn't care. She treated him like all the others did, ignoring him completely. Just like all those other chickens. No one dared make friends with him, out of fear that they, too, would fall victim to the hated demons.

Johan slammed down the phone after talking to his source in Nynäshamn. How did the old guy find out everything so fast? He wondered who it was that was willing to feed him such good information.

He quickly grabbed his notebook, cell phone, and pens and rushed out of the room. Another murder had been committed. Three homicides in less than three weeks. It was frightening and totally improbable. His editors in Stockholm wanted him to go straight down to the farm in När and file a firsthand story from there for both the *Aktuellt* and *Rapport* news programs by phone. It was a matter of finding out as much information as possible before the broadcast. According to his source, it was the same scenario as the two previous cases: a murdered woman in her thirties, hacked to death and with a pair of panties in her mouth.

He called Knutas while he waited for Peter to pick him up at the hotel. The cameraman had been out, giving one of Gotland's many golf courses a try, and Johan had interrupted him in the middle of a game. Knutas didn't answer. Jacobsson didn't, either. So he tried the duty officer, but he referred Johan to the head of the investigation, which meant Knutas. *Shit.* The duty officer would say only that something had happened on a farm in När. He refused to give any further details. The police were on the scene and needed to be able to work undisturbed. Johan impatiently lit a cigarette and cast a glance down the street. What was taking him so long?

A reporter from the central desk would be arriving on the first plane he could get. Over the next few days he would represent Swedish TV's national news while Johan would continue to work for the regional division. The national reporter showed up only when things were hot. Like right now, when the inconceivable had happened: a third murder. Under normal circumstances, Johan would have felt offended that the national news wasn't satisfied with using his reports in their program. Now he was glad. If he had to be working for all the news broadcasts at once, he wouldn't have time to see Emma.

"Hurry up. Come on."

Jacobsson sounded agitated. Knutas followed her out to the yard. In a clump of trees a short distance away, Sohlman and Kihlgård were bending over something. He trotted over to join them.

Sohlman was using tongs to pick up some object from the ground. It was oblong in shape and made of plastic. He turned it this way and that. Sweat was running down his back in the heat.

"What the hell is it?" grunted Kihlgård.

"It's an inhaler for asthmatics."

"Was Gunilla Olsson asthmatic?" asked Knutas.

His colleagues shrugged their shoulders.

Knutas ran back to the house. Cecilia Ångström and the police-woman were just about to leave.

"Do you know whether Gunilla had asthma?" asked Knutas.

"I don't think so," replied Cecilia hesitantly. "No, she didn't," she then said more firmly. "She couldn't have. We were at a party a few weeks ago, visiting some of my friends, and they have both a dog and a cat. Gunilla didn't say anything about it bothering her."

"Do you have asthma?"

"No."

Knutas went back outside to his colleagues, who turned to him with a look of inquiry.

"All right," he said. "It is very possible that we now know something new about our killer. He might have asthma."

Johan didn't know much about När, other than that it was the home district of the Ainbusk Singers. In his attempts to find Gunilla Olsson's farm, he and Peter ended up on the road leading to the windy harbor of Närshamn. The little fishing village reminded them of Norway or Iceland. A wharf jutted out into the sea. On it was a long barracks with fish stalls inside. There were fishing trawlers, stacks of polystyrene fishing crates, and piles of netting. The boats that weren't out at sea rocked on their moorings beside the wharf. In the distance they saw a couple of tourists pedaling their bikes against the wind, heading for the light-house on Närsholmen. The waves broke in a steady rhythm that seemed predetermined.

Johan rolled down the window. The smell of seaweed awakened memories. He felt an urge to walk right out to the end of the wharf and let the wind fill him with energy. Thoughts of Emma floated around him, seizing hold of his heart, his brain, his genitals, and his stomach. Right now, though, a different reality was demanding his attention. Peter turned the car around.

"Goddamn it. We took the wrong road."

After getting lost two more times, they finally reached the farm. As windy as it had been down at the harbor, it was completely still outside the murdered woman's house. The police had cordoned off a large area, and a number of curiosity seekers had interrupted their Midsummer celebrations to gather outside the police tape.

From the village came the faint sounds of accordion music. The Midsummer celebrations were in full swing just a short distance away from the murder scene.

Johan made inquiries and learned that Knutas had left the woman's residence only fifteen minutes earlier. Jacobsson had left, too. They were the only ones he had good contact with among the Visby police.

Johan called Knutas, who confirmed that a thirty-five-year-old woman had been killed at her home. The precise time of the murder was unclear. The police refused to comment on how she had been killed.

Knutas, who knew that the journalists could quickly find out the victim's identity, asked Johan not to include her name or photo in his report. The police had not yet been able to contact her family.

Before it was time for his report, Johan managed to talk to a young guy in the crowd that had gathered outside the police tape.

Yes, it was true that a girl lived here alone. She was in her thirties, the guy told him. She worked with ceramics.

It was a few minutes before six when he called the *Aktuellt* editor in Stockholm. He was linked up to the studio and reported live on what he had learned to the TV audience.

When the phone spot was done, he had to try to find more material for the later broadcasts. A press conference at police headquarters was scheduled for 9:00 P.M.

By then the national reporter should have arrived, and they could work together. That suited him fine.

Peter walked around outside the police tape, shooting footage. The police refused to say anything more. Johan decided instead to talk to the people standing on the narrow dirt road outside the farm. Some had arrived on bicycles, a couple of teenagers came on delivery mopeds, and a few cars had stopped and parked along the road. Most of them turned out to be neighbors who had seen the police cars gathering around the farm.

Johan approached a short, plump, middle-aged woman wearing shorts and a polo shirt. She had a dog with her, and she was standing by herself, slightly apart from the other spectators.

He introduced himself.

"Did you know the woman who lived here?" he asked.

"No," replied the woman. "Not really. I heard that she was murdered. Is that true? Was it the same person who killed those other two women?"

She kept on talking without waiting for an answer.

"This is crazy. It's like in a movie. It can't possibly be true."

"What was her name?"

"Gunilla Olsson."

"Did she have any family?"

"No, she lived here alone. She was a potter. She worked in that studio over there." The woman pointed to a low building with big windows inside the restricted area.

"How old was she?"

"Thirty-four or thirty-five."

"Do you live around here?"

"Yes, farther up the road."

"How well did you know each other?"

"I knew her mother when she was alive. We were in the same sewing circle, but I never had much contact with the daughter. We would say hello to each other whenever we happened to meet, but it didn't seem like she wanted to talk much. She mostly kept to herself. She moved in quite recently. It must be, what, six months ago? She lived abroad for a long time. Far away, in Hawaii. Her parents lived in Ljugarn, so that's where she grew up. They've been dead several years now. They died in a car accident while Gunilla was living so far away. And just imagine, she didn't even come home for their funeral! They lost nearly all contact with each other after she grew up. She didn't even want to have the same last name as they did. As soon as she was old enough, she changed

her name to Olsson, even though her parents' name was Broström. I
know that her mother was very upset about that. She has a brother, too,
but he lives on the mainland. I think his name is still Broström. It's the
daughter that the parents had the most trouble with."

"What sort of trouble?"

"She skipped school a lot and wore strange clothes. And every time
I saw her, she had changed her hair color. Her father was a pastor. I
think it was especially hard for him. She was . . . what should I say?
Rebellious. That was when she was young, of course. Later she moved
to Stockholm and went to art school, and then I know she left to live
abroad."

Johan was astonished by this woman who had turned out to be a
virtual news bureau all on her own. Peter had joined them, and the
camera was rolling as the woman talked.

"In any case, she had a couple of shows this past spring," she went
on. "I think it was all going really well for her. And she did make beautiful things."

The talkative woman patted her dog. He had started to whine with
impatience.

"This whole thing is just so awful. A person hardly even dares go
out anymore. I went to one of her exhibits, and I tried to talk to her
there, but I didn't have much luck. She barely answered me."

"Do you know whether she had any kind of relationship?"

"No. But now that you mention it, I've seen a man that I didn't recognize around here lately. I take a lot of walks with my dogs, and I've
seen him several times."

"Is that right? Where was that?"

"The first time was maybe a few weeks ago. I was walking past one
evening when he came out of her house."

"Did you speak to him?"

"No. I don't think he noticed me."

"Can you describe him?"

"He was tall with very blond hair."

"How old was he?"

"I think he was quite young. Maybe about thirty. I've seen a man here a couple of times since then, and I'm almost positive he was the same one."

"When was that?"

"About a week after I saw that man the first time, I caught sight of him again. He was coming from her house and heading down the road toward the bus stop. It seemed like he was in a big hurry, because he was walking really fast. I met him on the road and got a good look at him. He was stylish, very nicely dressed. He was no slacker by any means."

"He was about thirty, you said?"

"Well, maybe a little younger or a little older than that. It's hard to tell."

Johan could feel his pulse quicken. This old lady might actually have seen the killer.

"Do you know whether he had a car?"

"Yes, there's been a car that I didn't recognize parked out here a couple of times. A Saab. Quite old. I don't know what model it was, but it looked like it had at least ten years under its belt."

After Johan was done with the interview, he and Peter went back to their car to drive to police headquarters, where the press conference was going to be held. He got hold of the reporter for national news, Robert Wiklander, who had already arrived. *Aktuellt* was going to broadcast live. There weren't any outside broadcast vans on Gotland that had the technical equipment needed for a live transmission, but a van from Stockholm was due to arrive in time for the nine o'clock news. That meant that Johan and Peter could go over to the editorial offices to put together their material for the later broadcasts that night.

Until then, they were free. Regional wouldn't be doing a report on Midsummer Eve. Robert and his cameraman would take over for the rest of the evening. Johan had been promised Midsummer Day off, too. Robert had worked on Gotland before and knew the setup. He promised to call Johan the next day only if it was absolutely necessary.

Mamma, help. It's so dark. Mamma, help me. So dark.

He was crying with his open mouth pressed against the soft down pillow. Repeating the same words over and over. Snot was running from his nose. He squeezed his eyes shut so hard that he saw creepy figures wriggling around in the darkness. On the inside of his eyelids squirmed bright worms, snakes with giant heads, and monsters swaying from side to side. He was lying on his side with his knees drawn up and his arms wrapped around the pillow, a hard ball of pain in his stomach. Now and then he rocked back and forth as he lay there. The pillowcase was wet with tears and snot.

It was four in the afternoon. His sister was out in the barn, and his parents wouldn't be home until six.

It had turned out to be a terrible day. They grabbed him on the way home from school. He had actually been feeling happy. That hadn't happened in such a long time that he'd almost forgotten what it felt like—a tingle of joy in his stomach, mixed with a touch of hope that his situation might be about to change. He hadn't been subjected to any teasing or malicious remarks all day long, and at recess a boy from another class had even talked to him. They had agreed to bring their hockey pictures on the following day. When he hurried off, as usual, after the last class and ran across the playground, they were already there, the hated demons.

They blocked his way. He tried to escape, but they were faster. They grabbed hold of him and dragged him down the stairs outside the gym. Between the entrance to the gym and the stairwell, there was a broom closet that was never used. That's where they took him. Panic flung him into a fog. Hard, dry, unrelenting hands were clamped over his mouth. He tasted the salt of his own tears as they ran between the fingers and onto his lips. Two of them were holding his arms and covering his mouth while the others punched him. They beat him all over his body, clawing and biting him. It got worse and worse. When one of them started unbuttoning his pants, he thought he was going to die. Strong arms took hold of him and forced him down on the floor.

They whipped his backside with a jumprope. Stinging, persistent lashes. *They took turns, one after the other. Everyone wanted a chance. He squeezed his eyes shut and tried to think about something else. Sunshine, a bath, an ice cream cone. The fishing trips with his grandfather. The beating continued without stopping as they hurled insults at him. Their voices were filled with contempt. You disgusting piece of blubber. You pig.*

After a while he started having trouble breathing. The hands were pressed so hard over his mouth that he couldn't get any air. He screamed, but not a sound came out. The scream would sit inside his body for the rest of his life.

He felt something warm running between his legs.

"Shit, how disgusting. He's pissed himself," said a voice.

"Let's get out of here," said someone else. The beating stopped, the grip loosened, and they were gone from the broom closet. He collapsed onto the cement floor. He didn't know how long he lay there. Finally he managed to get to his feet, straighten his clothes, and leave. When he reached home, he went up to his room, closed the door, and alternated between crying and screaming. He curled up on his bed. His backside stung and had started to bleed. They never hit him in the face. He thought it was because they didn't want any marks to show. In the midst of his despair, he felt ashamed. What a loser he was, to be subjected to such abuse. He didn't dare tell anyone.

"Mamma!" he shrieked into the pillow. "Mamma!"

At the same time, he knew that when she came home he would act perfectly normal. By then he would have dried his tears and washed his face. He would also drink several glasses of water to calm himself down. Like so many times before, she wouldn't notice a thing. And he hated her for that.

For the press conference the Visby police had chosen the largest hall available at headquarters. Every last seat in the room was taken. Now the media from the rest of Scandinavia had become interested in this case of the mysterious serial killer who was eluding the Swedish police.

Knutas expressly asked the journalists not to disclose the identity of the victim. All members of her family had not yet been notified. The police had not been able to contact her brother, who was out sailing along the Swedish west coast.

No mention was made of the asthma inhaler.

Knutas had never felt under such great pressure before. He was dead tired, and furious at being cheated out of his Midsummer party. Furious that a new murder had been committed. Furious that they weren't any closer to solving the case. Several times he looked to his colleagues for assistance in answering the journalists' questions—in particular to Karin Jacobsson, but also to Martin Kihlgård, who turned out to be a rock in this kind of situation.

In spite of their failure to catch the murderer, which had proved deadly once again, Knutas was forced to defend the enormous amount of work that had already been accomplished. His words sounded hollow, even to his own ears. The image of the dead Gunilla Olsson had become permanently etched onto his retina, and there it remained during the entire press conference.

All the reporters in attendance did everything they could to refute the police argument and attack the work that had been done so far. Sometimes Knutas wondered how journalists could stand to do their job: their endlessly critical attitude, their eternal search for some type of conflict, and their constant focus on the negative. How could they live with themselves? What did they talk about at the dinner table at home? The war in the Middle East? The situation in Northern Ireland? The monetary union? Prime Minister Persson's tax policies?

He was suddenly overwhelmed by an enormous sense of fatigue. The questions were buzzing through the air like angry hornets. He was losing his concentration. He downed a whole glass of water and managed to pull himself together.

Afterward, the reporters buttonholed him for individual interviews.

Two hours later it was finally over. He told his colleagues that he didn't want to be disturbed, and he shut himself up in his office. When he sank down on the chair at his desk, he felt close to tears. Good Lord, he was a grown man—but he was dead tired and starving, and he realized that he'd had nothing to eat since breakfast except for a sandwich, since his Midsummer dinner had been so cruelly interrupted. No wonder hunger was gnawing at his stomach. He called his wife at their summer house in Lickershamn.

"Come home, sweetheart. The guests left a long time ago. The party never really got going. There's lots of food left over. I'm going to put together a real Midsummer plate for you, and we have cold beer. Doesn't that sound good? Why don't you leave right now?"

Her soft voice made him feel warm and vulnerable.

Johan honored the request from the police not to make public the name or photo of the latest murder victim. He didn't even say that she was a potter.

When Johan and Peter were finally done with their work, they decided to go out, even though it was past midnight and they were dog tired. It was still Midsummer Eve, as Peter pointed out.

Johan agreed. For several days he had called and sent text messages to Emma's cell phone without getting any reply. She was undoubtedly out in some summer meadow celebrating Midsummer with her entire dear family. It was no use to keep yearning for her. It would never work out. Still, he ached with longing, and the only thing that helped was to drown it in alcohol. He wanted to forget about Emma, about the murders, about his depressed mother, about the whole fucking lot of it.

They went to an inn down by the harbor. Everyone there was having a good time and seemed not to know about the latest homicide. *Most people probably have other things to do on Midsummer Eve than watch the news,* thought Johan. For the time being they were blissfully ignorant.

They both ordered beer.

"How's it going with Emma?" asked Peter.

"Oh, I think it's hopeless. It'll never work out."

"But how do you feel about her?"

"I feel too much. That's the trouble. I just don't know. We've known each other such a short time, but I've never met anyone like her. She's a real pain in the neck," said Johan, and then he grinned.

"What are you going to do?"

"I don't know. I guess the only thing to do is to say to hell with her, pure and simple. I don't feel like talking about it right now. This day has just been too much to take."

"Okay. Happy Midsummer," said Peter. "Cheers." He drank the rest of his beer in one gulp.

A couple of giggling young girls with long hair, dressed in tight tops with bare midriffs, elbowed their way toward the men to try to order something at the bar. Glossy lips and laughing eyes. Peter seized the opportunity at once.

"It's on me, girls. What'll you have?"

The girls exchanged knowing glances. They looked up at Johan and Peter, blinking thick lashes that had been carefully curled.

"A glass of wine, thanks," they said in unison.

For Peter the night turned out to be more fun than he had expected. Johan made an effort to be drawn into the party mood, but without success. He made the mistake of drinking too much. As Midsummer Day dawned, he was bent over the toilet in his hotel room, throwing up over and over.

SATURDAY, JUNE 23

Emma called on the following day.

"Hi. It's me."

"Hi," croaked Johan sleepily.

"I'm sorry I haven't called before, but we've been away for Midsummer. And I needed to think about things," she added in a low voice.

His drowsy state was replaced with a gradually increasing sense of hope.

"How are you?" she went on. "You sound really tired. Did you just wake up?"

"Uh-huh."

"It's two in the afternoon."

"Is it that late?"

"I want to see you. We've had a fight. I told Olle that I needed to get away for a while. At least for a few days. He's staying with the children at his brother's house in Burgsvik. I need to see you."

She was almost transparent, gray-faced and hunched over, as if she had shrunk since they had last seen each other. She just stood there, with a red nose and swollen eyes. He pulled her into the room.

"What's happened?"

"Nothing's happened. I'm just completely worn out. I have no idea what to do."

"Sit down."

Emma was sniffling. Johan brought her some toilet paper. They sat down on the bed.

"The holiday was awful," she said. "We went out to visit Olle's brother and his family. I knew I had to get away from you, to feel like things were normal and get some distance. We went swimming and played games and barbecued in the evenings. The kids were having a great time, of course, with their cousins and grandparents and all. It was tremendously difficult. Occasionally I felt completely empty. It was incredibly annoying that everyone acted as if nothing had happened. They just went on with all the usual things, you know. Barbecued the steaks and made coffee. Played kubb. It's a Viking log-throwing game," she explained when he looked puzzled. "Mowed the lawn. The more chaotic I feel inside, the harder it is to deal with all the normal things in daily life. Can you understand that?"

She went on without waiting for a reply.

"Olle is going to stay out there with the kids for a while. I said that I needed to go home. To be alone. Olle thinks this is about everything that has been happening, that I'm going through some kind of shock. He thinks it's a crisis that will pass. He called up a therapist that he wants me to see. But I don't think that's the only thing going on. It doesn't feel like it. It's as if I don't have anything to say to Olle anymore. As if we don't have anything in common."

She blew her nose hard several times.

"I have no idea what I'm going to do. This isn't just about you and me. We've only seen each other a few times. It's crazy. I don't know what's come over me. I must have a screw loose."

"I've never met anyone like you before, but I don't want to make trouble for you or your family," said Johan.

"It's not all your fault. I jumped into this situation with my eyes open. And why did I do that? It must be because Olle and I simply have nothing left. There's nothing between us anymore. It's over. Deep inside I don't think it would have made any difference if you and I hadn't met. Olle and I would still have split up, sooner or later."

Tears spilled out.

Johan put his arms around her. "Maybe we should take a break from each other. Is that what you want?"

"No, I don't."

They were both silent for a while. Johan stroked Emma's hair. Held her close. Felt the warmth of her body.

"I need a cigarette," said Emma, and got up to get one. She sat down in the armchair next to the window. "Do you have anything to drink?"

"Sure, what would you like?"

"A Coke. Is there any chocolate?"

Johan opened the minibar and took out two sodas and a chocolate cookie.

"So what do you know about the latest murder?" Emma asked. "It's such a nightmare. Pretty soon I won't even dare go outside. Who was she? Do you know?"

"She was a potter. Her name is Gunilla Olsson. Thirty-five years old. Apparently she's been living abroad until recently. She lived alone. She's from Ljugarn. Did you know her?"

"No, I don't think so. What is it that made him kill those girls? They don't seem to have anything in common. One was married and had children, another lived with her boyfriend, and the third lived alone. One lived in Stockholm, one in Visby, and one way out in the countryside."

She drank some of her Coke and lit the cigarette. "One worked with computers, one was a hairdresser, and then the third was a potter. It makes you wonder whether they all belonged to some strange sect or some chat room on the Internet. Were they living double lives? Haven't you been able to find out anything?"

"No," he had to confess, feeling ashamed. "I haven't been able to dig up much in this case." How much digging had he done, in fact? Not much. Of course he had contact with his source and several others at police headquarters, but he hadn't invested a lot of effort in finding out any answers himself. And that wasn't like him. It was Emma's fault, he thought.

"I guess I've been thinking too much about you."

"And I think too much about you," she said. "I think about you all the time. Nonstop."

She crept into his arms. Together they formed one body.

"I love you," he said, his lips against her hair. For the first time he actually loved a woman. "I dream about you. I want to live with you. Have a house here on Gotland. Take care of your children and ours. Grow my own potatoes."

He laughed and held her face between his hands. "Just think, that's something I've always wanted. To have my own potato patch and be able to go out and pull up my own potatoes to eat with grilled salmon in the summertime. That's what we did out in the country when I was little."

As Emma drove home, she realized that she was in love. Head over heels in love.

Karin Jacobsson turned out to be right. A third murder committed within the course of a few weeks had scared both the Gotlanders and the tourists. Many women no longer dared go out alone. The high season on Gotland always started in earnest around Midsummer and lasted for almost two months, up until the annual Medieval Festival, which fell during the second week of August. Shortly after that, summer vacation would be over for all the schoolchildren, and then the tourists went back to the mainland.

In late August, life usually returned to normal, except for a few stragglers still enjoying a Gotland vacation. Right now it was the end of June, and the high season was just beginning, but cancellations were starting to pour in at the tourist bureau, the hotels, and the campgrounds.

The Visby police were feeling the pressure from all sides. On the morning of Midsummer Day, Knutas received calls from the county police chief, the head of tourism, the director of trade and industry, the chairman of the municipal executive board, and the county governor. Not to mention the conversation he had with the national police commissioner. What was required was quite simple and crystal clear. They had to catch the murderer.

The members of the investigative team had quickly returned to police headquarters in Visby, and now they were all sitting in the conference room of the criminal department. It was eleven o'clock in the morning.

Knutas began the meeting. He was grateful that the media had chosen not to divulge Gunilla Olsson's identity. Almost twenty-four hours after the body had been discovered, the police still hadn't been able to reach her brother.

"Welcome back," he greeted everyone. "I'm glad that you could all be here. The latest victim is Gunilla Olsson, thirty-five, who was presumably murdered on the night before Midsummer Eve. She made her living as a potter, quite successfully, and she lived alone on a farm out in Närr. No children. We'll start with a few pictures."

The lights were turned off, and since the curtains had been drawn in front of the windows, it was almost completely dark. The pictures clicked into view as Knutas talked. Most of those present had a hard time keeping their eyes on the images, occasionally having to turn away in revulsion.

"According to the preliminary statement from the ME, she received a greater number of blows than the other two women. The wounds are also of a different nature than on the previous victims. In this case, the killer acted with even greater ferocity. He wildly hacked at the whole body. It's difficult to say what type of axe was used. The wounds are ragged, and some of them penetrated quite deeply. None of the blows were aimed at the sexual organs. There is nothing to indicate that she was raped. Just like the other victims, she had a pair of panties in her mouth. The murder weapon was not found, but we did find something on site that may have come from the killer."

Pictures of the asthma inhaler appeared on the screen.

"This is an inhaler used by asthmatics," said Knutas. "It was found in the yard, outside the pottery workshop. The victim did not suffer from asthma, nor did her friend. Of course it could have come from someone else, a neighbor or an acquaintance. We're continuing to knock on doors in the vicinity. There are fingerprints on it, which we're in the process of analyzing, to see if we can find a match in police records. So far nothing else of interest has been found at the crime scene. As for the victim's background, she was originally from Visby. Twenty years ago her family moved to Ljugarn. For the past ten years Gunilla Olsson lived in Hawaii, on the island of Maui, to be more precise. She came back here just last January and bought that farm in När, presumably using the money that her parents left her. They died in a car accident six years ago. You may remember the incident. Outside Lärbro a minibus collided with a sedan, and five people were killed. It was winter and very slippery. Two of the fatalities were children."

The local officers murmured as they recalled the accident.

"Well, at any rate, Gunilla Olsson's parents were in the passenger car," Knutas went on. "Her parents' name was Broström. Gunilla changed her last name to Olsson when she came of age. That was her mother's maiden name. Evidently she and her parents did not get along. Any questions?"

"Do we know that she was killed inside the workshop?" asked Wittberg.

"Yes. All indications are that the workshop was the scene of the murder."

"Do we have anything new about a possible connection between the previous victims?" asked Norrby.

"Well, let's see. Kihlgård?" Knutas gave his colleague an inquiring look.

"Hmm. The group that's been in Stockholm has come up with quite a bit. Both of them lived in Stockholm. Frida lived there all her life, and Helena for the past twenty-two years. The latest address for both of them in Stockholm was in Södermalm. They actually lived only a stone's throw from each other. Helena Hillerström shared an apartment with her boyfriend, Per Bergdal, on Hornsgatan, and Frida Lindh and her family lived on Brännkyrkagatan. They had no friends in common, but there is one point of connection. Both were registered members of a Friskis & Svettis gym. There's a branch in Horns-tull where both of them worked out. Helena Hillerström used to go there on Thursdays and Saturdays, while Frida Lindh usually went on Mondays and Wednesdays, and occasionally on Saturdays. They might have met each other there. We've talked to people at the club and shown them pictures of the victims. Both of them were recognized. We've interviewed all the Friskis managers, both male and female. Nothing out of the ordinary has turned up so far. None of them has any contact with Gotland, except that most of them have been here on vacation, of course."

"Well, that's not much to go on," Sohlman said dryly.

"We still think the killer may be in Stockholm, and that's where a connection can be found," Kihlgård continued, unperturbed. "Gunilla Olsson also went to Stockholm several times this spring. A shop in Gamla Stan sold her work."

"I agree that it's possible the killer could live in Stockholm," said Jacobsson. "If that's the case, the question is: Why did he murder them here on Gotland?"

"No matter what," said Knutas, "we have to do some more digging into this. I'm thinking of going to Stockholm tomorrow. The NCP and the Stockholm police are working on the case, of course, but I want to go over there myself, at least for a couple of days. I suggest that you come with me, Karin."

"Sure," she nodded.

"Good. Kihlgård, you're in charge for the time being. Someone has to check up on what Jan Hagman and Kristian Nordström were doing during the Midsummer holiday. How much of their background have we checked? And what's their connection to Stockholm? We need to dig deeper into all of it, and right away. Norrby and Wittberg can work on that. I don't trust that Hagman in the slightest. I also want to take another look at the circumstances surrounding his wife's death. There's something fishy about it. Right now it's a matter of working around the clock. We can't let the killer strike again."

SUNDAY, JUNE 24

By the next day, Knutas and Jacobsson were in Stockholm. They grabbed a cab to take them from the airport to police headquarters on Kungsholmen. The sun was scorching. It was almost eighty-six degrees, and as they approached Norrtull the traffic got much worse. The air was shimmering with heat and exhaust fumes. Knutas was always fascinated by the incredible snarl of traffic every time he came to the capital. Even on a Sunday in the middle of summer, the cars were just creeping along.

They drove across Sankt Eriksbron, passed Fridhemsplan, choked with traffic with its countless red lights, and turned down Hantverkargatan to head toward Kungsholmtorg.

He had always thought there was something very imposing about Kungsholmen, with the county council building, the city hall, and the courthouse all in one place. He recalled that someone had once told him that the courthouse was built by the architect who was the runner-up in the competition to see who would build Stockholm's city hall at the beginning of the twentieth century. The winner was Ragnar Östberg, but in second place was Carl Westman. He was the one who designed the courthouse on Scheelegatan. In Knutas's eyes it was just as splendid as city hall. Behind it stood police headquarters. They were supposed to have a meeting in the old building, a handsome yellow structure surrounded by a lush park.

What a difference from our sheet-metal box, thought Knutas as they huffed and puffed their way up the grand stone staircase in the heat. They had taken off their jackets. Knutas glanced with envy at Jacobsson's bare legs. She was wearing a skirt for a change.

It was calm inside police headquarters on this Sunday after Midsummer. A few people were scattered around in offices, working. It was evident that vacation time had started.

In a room that had a view of the park, they met with the police chief and a group from the NCP.

Right after the meeting they had lunch in a nice restaurant across from the courthouse. Then they went with Detective Superintendent Kurt Fogestam to the residential area in Södermalm where Helena had lived. The house stood almost at the end of Hornsgatan, very close to the water and venerable Liljeholmsbadet, with its floating bathhouse, built on pontoons out in the water. There had been frequent threats to tear it down, but so far it was still standing.

On the corner of Hornsgatan and Långholmsgatan stood the Friskis & Svettis gym. *That's where she went to work out,* thought Knutas. *Maybe that's where she met the killer.*

The apartment was on the top floor. There wasn't room for all of them in the rickety elevator. Much to the relief of the stockier men, Jacobsson offered to take the stairs. It was a run-down building. Through one door they could hear pop music, through another the faint clinking of a piano. *What are people doing indoors on a brilliantly sunny summer day?* thought Karin.

Per Bergdal, still on sick leave from his job, opened the door after a couple of rings. They hardly recognized him. He was suntanned and looking healthy. His hair was cut short, and he had shaved.

He greeted them solemnly. "Come in."

The interior of the apartment was in sharp contrast to the shabby entryway. It was big and bright with high ceilings and beautiful parquet floors that shone in the sunlight. If you leaned to one side to look out the window, you could see the glittering waters of Årstaviken. Extending out from the living room was a big modern kitchen with a refrigerator-freezer and stove hood made of stainless steel. Decorative tiles arranged in a pattern covered the walls. Knutas noticed a fancy blender. A long counter with bar stools on both sides separated the kitchen from the living room, which was furnished with sheepskin chairs and a table topped with a colorful mosaic. An elegant top-of-the-line stereo system took up one wall. The opposite wall was covered with CDs in an attractive birch rack. Bergdal apparently had very expensive tastes.

"I'll get right to the point," said Knutas. "As I'm sure you know, three women have now been murdered on Gotland. In each case the method used was the same. We believe the same perpetrator was responsible for all three deaths. We're here to look for some connection between Helena and the second victim, Frida Lindh. Frida lived here in Södermalm. To be more precise, she lived on Brännkyrkagatan until a year ago, when she and her family moved to Visby. Her husband is from Gotland. Both Frida and Helena worked out at the Friskis & Svettis gym here. We wonder if they might have met each other there, or whether it was at the gym that they met the killer."

Knutas paused and studied Bergdal's face intently. He looked shocked.

"So you think the murderer is here in Stockholm?" Bergdal asked.

"Yes, that's a possibility. Do you know any of the people that Helena met when she worked out?"

"Not really," he said hesitantly. "She usually went over there with a couple of her friends who live in the neighborhood. I don't know if she used to meet anyone else there. I can't remember anything special. Of course she sometimes mentioned the people she met. Someone she happened to talk to. Occasionally she would run into an old colleague from work, but I don't think there was anyone she was seeing more often. You could ask her friends who worked out with her. They might know."

"Okay. We'll get in touch with them. Do you recognize the name of Frida Lindh from before?"

"No."

"Was there anything else that happened prior to Helena's death? Something that may have come to mind since then?"

"I've hardly done a thing except think about Helena and who could have killed her, but I can't come up with anything. I just want you to catch him, so this horrible nightmare will be over."

"We're doing everything we can," said Knutas.

"There's one thing I should show you that I found up in the attic yesterday. Wait here a minute," said Bergdal, and stood up.

He came right back with a cardboard box. He opened the lid and took out a bundle of papers.

"I don't know whether it's of any importance to you anymore, but I was absolutely right about this." He handed the bundle to Knutas.

Knutas glanced through the papers. They were love letters and notes, and e-mails that Helena had printed out and saved.

"The box was hidden at the very back of the attic. Inside an old cabinet. That's why I didn't find it earlier. My brother just moved into a big house, and he wants to have the cabinet. I opened it to see if there was anything inside. That's when I found those."

The e-mails were four years old. They were written over a month's time, in October. *An autumn romance novel,* thought Knutas, *and a steamy one.* The sender was Kristian Nordström.

So that was how things stood. The question was why Nordström had so stubbornly refused to admit that there was anything between him and Helena, in spite of repeated queries when he was interviewed. It was incomprehensible.

Knutas phoned Kihlgård and asked him to call Nordström in for another round of questioning at once. He cursed himself for not staying in Visby. He would have given a great deal to conduct that interview himself.

That wasn't possible, though. They were in Stockholm, and they might as well continue with what they had come here to do. It wasn't certain that the affair with Nordström would have any significance in the investigation.

They took the box of letters with them.

After getting the names and phone numbers of Helena's workout friends, they went over to the Friskis & Svettis gym. In spite of the summer heat and the fact that it was only three in the afternoon, the place was crowded with people. They entered the bright, airy reception area, going past benches with a large number of shoes placed underneath. Through a glass window they could see into a room where thirty or more tanned individuals were jumping around to Latin music, led by a muscular girl without an ounce of fat, wearing a tight leotard.

They walked over to the receptionist, a blond woman in her forties. She looked very healthy in a white T-shirt with the company's logo printed on the front. Knutas introduced Jacobsson and himself and then asked to speak to the boss.

"I'm the boss," said the blonde.

"Then you know that we're looking for someone who can tell us something about two women who came here to work out," said Knutas. "Do you recognize either of them?" he asked as he took an envelope out of his inside pocket. He pulled out two photographs. "This is Helena Hillerström. She was the first one murdered."

The woman behind the counter cast a brief glance at the photo. She shook her head. "No, I don't know her. I've already seen that picture. So many people come through here. It depends when she worked out. She might not have come here when I was working."

Knutas showed her the picture of Frida Lindh.

The woman's expression changed. "Yes, this one I know. Frida. Frida Lindh. She came here to work out for several years."

"Did she come here alone?"

"Yes, I think so. Almost always."

"Did you know her well?"

"No, I don't think you could say that. We used to chat a bit sometimes when she was here, but that was about it."

"Do you know whether she was friends with anyone else here?"

"No, I don't know. She usually came alone, but once in a while she would bring a friend along."

"Male or female?"

"Just girlfriends, as far as I remember."

"Thank you," said Knutas.

None of the other employees had anything new to add. Most of them recognized the two murdered women, but they couldn't come up with anything special to say about them.

An hour later the detectives left the gym with Ricky Martin's "She Bangs" echoing in their ears.

Nordergravar, part of medieval Visby's defenses, was located on the other side of the main road, as seen from the school, completely outside the northern part of the ring wall.

Today was Friday, and he skipped out of the so-called rest hour, saying he had a dentist appointment but had forgotten his note from home. It gave him the chance to leave school earlier than everyone else. His teacher had believed him and let him go. He thought it was incredible that she hadn't noticed anything. Didn't she know what the others did to him? Or was she just pretending not to notice? He wasn't sure.

As he left the school behind on this Friday afternoon, he felt lighthearted. Almost happy. It wouldn't be long before summer vacation started, and then all his classmates would disperse. He would be starting middle school on the other side of town, and then he would be rid of his tormentors. Right now he was thinking of celebrating by giving himself a reward. He had found a ten-krona bill lying on the floor under a dresser at home. He took it with him. Now he was going to buy some candy—and not just some ordinary candy. He was on his way to the candy store on Hästgatan, near Stora Torget. It was an old-fashioned shop with big lumps of rock candy hanging in the window. Going there was one of his favorite things to do. When he and his sister were little, they often went there on Saturdays with their father. Nowadays that seldom happened. His father had withdrawn from them more and more, growing increasingly silent and surly as the children got older.

The candy store was like a dream, and he jogged across Nordergravar. He had chosen that route because he thought it was exciting. He used to imagine medieval battles between the Swedes and the Danes, and how the wars were waged right here, down to the very last drop of blood. As he ran, all alone, up and down among the hills, he completely forgot about his horrible daily life.

He picked up a long stick and began jabbing it in the air. Pre-

tending that he was one of the soldiers fighting for the Swedish king against Denmark's King Valdemar Atterdag, who conquered Greenland and claimed the island as a Danish province in the fourteenth century. He was so immersed in his game that he didn't notice the four kids standing at the top of the hill, watching him. With a sudden bellow, they bounded down the slope and threw themselves on him. Since there were four of them, it was easy to wrestle him to the ground. He didn't have a chance. He was totally taken by surprise and couldn't even make a sound.

"Now you're really scared, aren't you, little fatty," hooted the worst of them, the leader. The others snickered spitefully as they held his hands in an iron grip.

"You're not thinking of pissing yourself this time, are you? No, we'll see to it that you don't wet your pants so that Mamma gets mad. Uh-uh, you don't have to do that," she taunted him. And to his surprise, she took hold of his belt and unfastened it.

When she started unbuttoning his pants, he got hysterical. This was just about the worst thing that could happen. He tried to struggle as best he could, kicking and screaming. He didn't have a chance. Triumphantly the leader pulled off his pants. He was ashamed when his stomach and legs were uncovered. He tried to bite the hands that were holding him.

"Look, what a fat little pig. It's about time you went on a diet, don't you think?"

Then the leader seized hold of his underpants and took them off, too.

"What a tiny dick!" she shouted, and the others laughed loudly. The humiliation burned like fire, and he was panic-stricken. He closed his eyes and screamed as loud as he could until he felt something soft being stuffed in his mouth and smelled his own underpants. The leader and one of the other hated demons were pressing the cloth into his mouth.

"Now you're going to shut your trap, goddamn it," snarled the leader, and her hard hands clamped onto his mouth to keep the underpants inside.

He thought he was going to suffocate. He couldn't get any air, and he was struggling desperately under their hands. Everything went black before his eyes. From far away he could hear one of the voices.

"Stop it. Let him go. He can't breathe."

The hands released him, and he heard them leave.

He lay there for a while, keeping his eyes closed in case they changed their minds and came back. When he finally dared get up, he didn't know how long he had been lying in that hollow. His underpants were on the ground next to him. Quickly he got dressed.

When he stuck his hand in his pants pocket, he discovered that the ten-krona bill was gone.

Helena Hillerström's parents lived in the well-to-do neighborhood of Stocksund just north of Stockholm. Jacobsson and Knutas had decided to go out there themselves to talk to the parents. Hans and Agneta Hillerström were home, and the father had said on the phone that they were welcome to come over.

Neither of them had ever been out to Stocksund before, and they were impressed by the big houses with the generous yards. They passed Värtan, with its glittering water. The well-dressed inhabitants of Danderyd were out, strolling along the shoreline promenade. The turn-of-the-century house belonging to the Hillerströms stood on a hill with an enormous plot of land around it. They could glimpse parts of it through the huge lilac hedge.

Helena's father opened the door. He was a tall, lanky man with thinning hair, a fresh complexion, and plenty of wrinkles on his suntanned but solemn face. "Good day," he greeted them with a certain formality. "Please come in."

They stepped inside the hallway, which had an impressively high ceiling. Round columns framed the grand wooden staircase that led up to the second floor.

Jacobsson sighed to herself. What a magnificent house.

From the hall they caught a glimpse of the living room and several sitting rooms with a row of big windows facing the yard. Agneta

Hillerström appeared at once. She, too, was tall and slender, with steel gray hair cut in an attractive page-boy style.

They sat down on a soft, comfortable sofa group in the living room. Dainty coffee cups and a plate of cookies were on the table. *Coconut balls*, Knutas observed, and put one in his mouth. How strange. Somehow that type of cookie didn't really fit in with the rest of the setting. That's what he and the twins usually baked for their birthday. His kids loved them.

"We know that you've talked to the police several times before, but I wanted to meet you in person," he said. "I'm in charge of the investigation on Gotland. At the present time, we do not have a suspect, but a good deal of information has come to light during the investigation, and I'd like to talk to you about some of it. Is that all right?"

"Of course," they said in unison, giving him an inquisitive look.

Knutas cleared his throat. "To get right to the point. It has come to our attention that your daughter had a relationship with one of her high school teachers. A PE teacher by the name of Jan Hagman. Did you know about this?"

The husband was the one who answered. He spoke in a resigned tone of voice. "Yes, we knew about it. Helena told us after it had been going on for a while. She ended up getting pregnant by that scumbag. She was only seventeen." Hans Hillerström's expression grew tense, and he began wringing his hands.

"She was pregnant?" Knutas raised his eyebrows. They didn't know about this.

"The whole thing was hushed up. She had an abortion, of course. We forbade her to see him ever again. We talked to the principal, and Hagman was asked to leave. He got a job at another school, someplace down south in Sudret. The man was married and had two children. That swine even had the nerve to call us here at home. He said that he loved Helena. What a fool. He was more than twice her age. He said he was ready to leave his family and take care of Helena and the child. I threatened to kill him if he ever tried to get in touch with her again."

"How did Helena take all of this?" asked Jacobsson.

"She was deeply depressed at first. She had fallen in love with that idiot, and she was mad at us for not letting her see him anymore. She didn't think we understood. The abortion wasn't a nice experience, either. She was sad for a long time afterward. We took a trip to the West Indies so that she could get away from the whole thing. In the fall, she started her third year in school as planned. Things didn't go well at first, but she recovered quite quickly. Helena has always had lots of friends, and I think that was really important," he said thoughtfully.

A brief silence followed. Both Knutas and Jacobsson felt rather low-spirited. It was a sad story. On the wall hung a big portrait of Helena in a gold frame, a photograph from her graduation. She was smiling, and her long dark hair framed her face. Knutas felt a pang as he looked at it. It was terrible that her life should end the way it had.

He broke the silence. "How was your relationship with your daughter?"

"Not without its problems, I suppose," replied Hans Hillerström. "As she got older she stopped talking to us about anything important. She became more reserved. Not with other people, just with us. We didn't understand why."

"Did you try to find out what the reason was?"

"Well, not directly. We thought that with time it would pass."

"From what I understand, you continued to go out to the cabin in the summertime, and you still have family on Gotland. Do you know whether Helena ever saw Jan Hagman again?"

"Not as far as we know," replied the father. "We never discussed the matter."

Now the mother spoke for the first time. "I tried to talk to her about it a few times. Tried to find out how she felt and how she was doing. She said that she had gotten over it. She realized that it was impossible for them to continue the relationship. As for the baby, she said that she thought it was the right thing to do, to have an abortion. She couldn't have taken care of a child on her own. She didn't want to, either. She viewed it mostly as something bad that had to be gotten rid of. Like an illness." She pressed her lips together.

"How were things between her and Per?" asked Jacobsson.

"Things were good. They were together for a long time, and in my view he seemed to be very much in love with her. The fact that he was at first suspected of committing the murder was really hard on us. I think she was everything to him. I'm sure they would have gotten married. If all this hadn't happened," said the mother, and her voice faded away.

"Do you know whether she ever met anyone else while she was with Per? Whether she had any kind of crisis for a period of time? They were together for many years, after all."

"No, I don't know about anything like that. Things always seemed so good when we asked. Weren't they?" Agneta Hillerström gave her husband a questioning look.

"I never heard anything, either, about there being any problems," he concurred.

"We've found some new connections between Helena and the second victim, Frida Lindh," said Knutas. "For one thing, they both worked out at the Friskis & Svettis gym in Hornstull. Have you ever heard mention of anyone she might have met there?"

Both Hillerströms shook their heads.

"Why didn't you say anything about the Jan Hagman story before?" asked Knutas.

"We didn't think it was important," said the father. "It happened so long ago. Do you think that Hagman murdered Helena?"

"We can't rule out anything, and everything that has to do with Helena is of importance to the police. Is there anything else in Helena's past that you haven't told us?"

"No," said Hans Hillerström. "I don't think so."

"Nothing that happened recently, either?"

"No."

Knutas wondered how the previous interviews with the couple had proceeded. How could it be that none of this had come out right from the beginning? He decided to discuss it with Karin later on. *If all the interviews are equally incomplete, we're going to have to do them over, every last one of them,* he thought grimly.

His stomach was growling. It was time to leave. "Well, I think we're done for now. Did Helena still have her own room in the house?"

"Yes, upstairs."

"Could we take a look at it?"

"Yes, sure. The police have already gone over the room, but of course you can look at it if you like."

Hans Hillerström led the way up the impressive staircase. The second floor had ceilings just as high as the rooms downstairs. They walked along a big, bright hallway and then through a sitting room where Knutas caught sight of a balcony and a flash of water. There were fireplaces everywhere.

Helena's room was quite large. High mullioned windows faced out on the yard. It looked as if the room had not been used in a long time. An old-fashioned wooden bed with tall bedposts stood in one corner. Next to it was a white nightstand. Near one of the windows stood a writing desk, an old easy chair, and several bookshelves filled with books.

Hans Hillerström left them alone, closing the door behind him. They searched through the drawers, the shelves, and the closet without finding anything of interest. Suddenly Jacobsson gave a whistle. Behind a photograph of the summer house on Gotland, a slit had been made in the wallpaper. A photo had been slipped inside the rip.

"Look at this," she said.

It showed a man on a big boat, a passenger ferry—presumably the Gotland Ferry. He was standing on deck with the wind blowing through his hair and the blue sky behind him. He was smiling happily at the photographer, and he had one hand in his pants pocket. It was without a doubt Jan Hagman, almost twenty years younger and forty pounds lighter than when they last saw him.

"Look," said Jacobsson. "He has that silly look of delight on his face that only someone newly in love ever has. It must be Helena who took the picture."

"We'll take this with us," said Knutas. "Come on, let's go."

It was a relief to leave that melancholy house and get out into the green of summer. The flower beds were dazzling, children were playing on the street outside the house, and in a yard a short distance away the neighbors were having a barbecue.

"We need to look into this story with Hagman a lot more closely. We have to check out his alibi again. He didn't say a word about the abortion. Why was he keeping that a secret? But why would he want to kill Helena? From what I can see, he loved her. And why so many years later? Could he have been jealous? Did he see her with her new boyfriend and become seized by madness?"

"That seems highly improbable," Jacobsson said. "And it's been twenty years since they had that affair. Why would he kill his wife now? Why didn't he do it back *then*, in that case?"

"That's a good question. And how does this all fit together with the death of Frida Lindh? And Gunilla Olsson?"

"It may not have anything at all to do with Hagman," said Jacobsson. "Maybe we're on the wrong track. All the victims have ties to Stockholm. The murderer could just as well be over here somewhere."

"You could be right," said Knutas. "But it's past seven, and my stomach is screaming. We'll go see Frida Lindh's parents tomorrow, and then we'll check out the shop in Gamla Stan where Gunilla Olsson's pottery was sold. Right now I want a strong drink and a proper meal. What about you?"

"That sounds wonderful," said Jacobsson, giving him a pat on the shoulder.

Wittberg knocked on the door of Kihlgård's office and stepped inside, out of breath.

"We've collated the answers to the question about who has asthma among all the people close to the victims. Look at this," he said, placing the paper on Kihlgård's desk. "These are the names of the people who either have asthma or suffer from some other respiratory allergy."

Kihlgård read through the list, which consisted of about twenty names. Both Kristian Nordström and Jan Hagman were on it.

"Hmmm," he murmured, and looked up at Wittberg. "I see that Nordström is an asthmatic. I've just heard from Knutas that he had a sexual relationship with Helena Hillerström after all."

"No shit. Recently?"

"No, it was a few years ago. I want two officers to go out to see Hagman and two to see Nordström. Don't call them ahead of time. I want to surprise them. Bring both of them in for questioning, and see that you bring back an inhaler from both of them, too."

They were sitting facing each other at the kitchen table with cups of coffee in front of them. The children were still out in the country visiting their cousins. Olle had come home to Roma to talk to Emma. He seemed nervous as he looked at his wife across the table. At the same time, he couldn't hide his frustration.

"What's going on with you?" he began.

"I don't know."

He raised his voice. "You've been completely unreachable for several weeks now. Ever since Helena died. What's wrong?"

"I don't know," she repeated tonelessly.

"Goddamn it, you can't just keep saying you don't know," he flared up. "You don't want me to hug you or touch you. We haven't had sex in I don't know how long. I try to help you by talking about Helena, but you don't want that. You don't give a shit about me or the kids, and every five minutes you're going off to town and leaving my mother behind as a babysitter. What's going on? Have you met someone else?"

"No," she said quickly, hiding her face in her hands.

"Well, what the hell am I supposed to think?" he shouted. "You're not the only one suffering, you know. I knew Helena, too. I also think it was horrible, what happened. I'm in shock, too, but you only think of yourself."

Suddenly she exploded.

"All right!" she screamed. "Then to hell it with all. Let's just get divorced. We don't have anything in common anymore anyway!" She jumped up and dashed into the bathroom, slamming the door.

"Nothing in common!" he bellowed. "We have two children in common, for God's sake. Two *young* children. Don't you give a damn about them, either? Don't they mean anything to you?"

Emma sat down on the lid of the toilet and turned on the faucets full blast so she wouldn't have to hear Olle's shouting. She pressed her fingers against her ears. She was totally at a loss. What should she do? It was unthinkable to tell him about Johan. Not now. She just couldn't. At the same time that she was mad at Olle, she was plagued by a guilty conscience. She felt trapped. After a while she turned off the water and sat down on the toilet lid again. Just sat there for a very long time. Her life was in chaos. Someone had killed her best friend. It might even be someone she knew. The thought had crossed her mind, but it was just too awful to be true.

What did she know about the people around her? What dark secrets were hidden behind the closed doors in people's homes? The murderer had shattered all sense of security in her life. What did she have to fall back on?

Then she started thinking further. There was one person in the world she trusted completely, and that was Olle. If there was anyone who had ever stood by her, it was him. He always had time to listen; he got up in the middle of the night to make her tea if she was having nightmares; he took care of her when she was pregnant. He cleaned up her vomit when she had the stomach flu, and he wiped her brow when she gave birth to their children. He loved her when she cried, when her nose was running, when she was sick with chicken pox or had her period. Olle. What on earth did she think she was doing?

Resolutely she stood up and rinsed off her face. There was total silence on the other side of the door. Cautiously she opened it.

He wasn't there. She went into the living room. He wasn't there, either. It was dead silent in the house. Emma went upstairs and peeked into the bedroom. There he was, lying on his stomach on the bed, hugging a pillow. His eyes were closed, as if he were asleep. She lay down next to him and moved close. He didn't answer right away. Then he put his arms around her and kissed her all over her face.

"I love you," she murmured. "It's just the two of us."

Handwritten pieces of paper lay in a big pile on the desk in front of him. Some of them had numbers on them. Johan had written down everything he knew about the three murders. Then he started putting the puzzle together. First Helena. The party. The fight. The murder on the beach. The axe. The people at the party. Kristian. The boyfriend, Per.

He continued in the same way with the other two. When he was done, he put the pieces of paper into three piles. *What is it that connects all three?* he thought.

Frida Lindh met a man on the night she was out with her girl-friends. Why hadn't he come forward? It could mean that he was in-volved in the murders. If he wasn't out of the country, that is.

On a piece of paper he wrote *Frida+a man, 30–35*. Afterward the man goes up in smoke. Gone.

The neighbor woman Johan had talked to told him about a man in Gunilla Olsson's house. He was also between thirty and thirty-five and attractive. On another paper he wrote *Gunilla+man, 30–35*.

When it came to Helena, she had flirted with Kristian at the party on the night before she was killed. He was thirty-five and good-looking.

On a piece of paper he wrote *Helena+man, 35=Kristian*.

Kristian had been questioned by the police several times, and he un-doubtedly had an alibi for the night of the murder; otherwise they would have taken him in. Still he was the most obvious suspect. Was he the one who showed up at the Monk's Cellar on the evening Frida Lindh was murdered? If so, why didn't any of the employees or anyone among the guests remember him? They ought to know him. Kristian Nordström worked abroad a good deal, but even so. He could have dis-guised himself, of course. But what could be Kristian's motive?

He got up, crossed the editing room, and put on what must be his third pot of coffee that night. It was a quarter to midnight. He yawned, making an effort to think along new lines. What if he dropped Kristian? Then what was left? The police investigation in Stockholm. What did that mean? They were most likely following up on some new lead that he didn't know about. He had tried to pump Knutas before they left, but without results.

Emma couldn't think of anything else about Helena, either. Yet they had known each other since school.

A sense of longing came over him.

Emma. The image of her when they last met. The light in her hair as she sat there in the chair by the window, her face pale. Her very being enchanted him. Her power terrified and enticed him. He wanted to call her but realized that it was much too late.

He laid his head down on the pile of papers and fell asleep.

The young people left the party at its height. The Strand Restaurant in Nisseviken had been rented out for the evening, and the dance floor was packed with festively dressed teenagers. The music was turned up to the absolute maximum. In the bar, glasses were being filled, one after the other. The mood was one of wild exhilaration. It was the last night of the Midsummer holiday, and it was high time for a party, even though it was a Sunday evening.

Carolina giggled at Petter, who was holding her hand in his, leading her down toward the beach. "You dope, what are you doing?"

He headed past the beach huts that were rented out to tourists as cabins during the summer season.

"Come on, come here," he said, kissing her on the throat.

Both of them were drunk. Happy, too. In just a few days they would have to part. Carolina was going to the States to study, while Petter's eleven-month military service way up north in Boden was awaiting him. It was a matter of enjoying the time they had left.

They romped around on the beach, with Petter shoving Carolina ahead of him at the same time he kissed the back of her neck. His hand fumbled inside her clothes as their entwined bodies moved forward, away from the beach and any people.

It was close to three in the morning, almost daylight. Since several other couples would certainly be coming down to the beach, they wanted to find an out-of-the-way spot. When they came farther out on the point, they discovered a solitary fishing shack a short distance away.

"That's where we'll go," said Petter.

"You're crazy. It's too late to go out there now," protested Carolina. "Someone might be out there."

"Let's check!"

He took Carolina by the hand, and they ran across the stones at the edge of the shore.

They could see that the shack was deserted. It didn't look as if it had been used in a long time.

"Perfect. Let's go in," said Petter.

A rusty lock was the only thing blocking their way.

"Do you have a hairpin?"

"Should we really do this?"

"Why not? We can stay here as long as we want without anyone bothering us."

"What if someone comes?"

"Uh-uh. You can see that it's all locked up. I don't think anybody's been here in years," said Petter as he worked to open the lock with the hairpin. Carolina stood on her toes and tried to peek in through the single window at the back. A dark blue curtain hung in front of it, blocking the view. *This is great for us,* she thought, elated. Petter's enthusiasm was contagious. This was really exciting. Making love in an old, abandoned fishing shack.

"Okay, I got it."

With a creak, the door opened. They peeked inside. The shack consisted of only one room. There was a wooden bench, a rickety table, and a chair. The walls were a filthy yellow and cold. An old calendar from the ICA supermarket hung askew on a hook. It smelled damp and stuffy.

Delighted, Petter spread out his hoodie on the floor.

They had been asleep for several hours when Carolina woke up because she needed to pee. At first she had no idea where she was. Then she remembered. *Oh, that's right. The party. The shack.* She untangled herself from Petter's arms and with some effort managed to get to her feet. She felt sick.

She tottered out of the shack and squatted down to pee. Afterward she washed herself in the clear, cold water of the sea.

She should wake Petter up. How were they going to get home? They were way out in the sticks. Shivering, she walked back to the shack. Petter lay stretched out on the floor with an old blanket over him.

The table was covered with a red oilcloth with coffee stains on it. A thermos stood on the floor. Even though the shack seemed to have been abandoned, Carolina had a feeling that someone had been here recently.

She was freezing after her hasty bath. The blanket covering Petter looked awfully thin. At the same time, she felt like lying down for a while longer. She would try to sleep a little, and maybe the nausea would pass. She looked around for something else to use as a cover and noticed that the bench had a lid that could be opened. She lifted it up. Inside was a bundle of clothes, or rather several bundles.

She took out one of the pieces of clothing and held it up. It was a shirt, and it had big patches of what looked like dried blood on it. Cautiously she began rummaging among the clothes. A dress, a top, a pair of bloody jeans, a torn bra, a dog leash. Her head started to spin. She shook Petter awake.

"Look, look inside the bench!" she urged him.

Petter got up, groggy with sleep, and looked at the clothes. "What the hell?"

He let the lid fall shut with a bang, took out his cell phone, and called the police.

MONDAY, JUNE 25

Gamla Stan in Stockholm looked a good deal like Visby. Knutas was always struck by that thought whenever he visited the capital. He enjoyed the atmosphere. Many of the beautiful buildings with masonry anchors on the facades and sculptures above the entrances were from the 1600s, when Sweden was a major European power and Stockholm was expanding rapidly. The buildings stood close together, a reminder of how densely populated the city once had been.

The narrow cobblestone streets branched out from the city's historic midpoint, Stortorget, like the arms of an octopus. Nowadays Gamla Stan was filled with restaurants, cafés, and small shops that sold antiques, handicrafts, and of course tons of knickknacks.

Gamla Stan and Visby had many things in common. The German influence was strong in both cities during the Middle Ages. German merchants had dominated both Stockholm and Visby and set their mark on the buildings and street names. In the past, Gamla Stan had also been encircled by a defensive wall. It was torn down in the seventeenth century to make room for the numerous stately houses that were built along the shore. Beyond the facades facing the street in the stone city, you could find little green oases and flowering gardens, just like in Visby.

Knutas and Jacobsson were plodding toward Österlånggatan, which appealed to Knutas more than the commercial street of Västerlånggatan. On the eastern street there were more galleries, handicraft shops, and restaurants.

That was also the location of the shop where Gunilla Olsson's pottery was sold. In the shop window facing the street, various ceramic objects were on display. A bell rang as they opened the door.

There were no customers in the shop. The owner was a stylish woman in her sixties.

Knutas introduced himself and his colleague, explaining why they were there.

The woman's face took on a worried expression. "It's so horrible, all those murders. Completely incomprehensible."

"Yes," Knutas agreed. "As I understand it, you sold Gunilla's pottery in your shop. How long have you been doing that?"

"Only a few months. Things were going well for her. I saw her work at a show on Gotland this past winter, and I fell for it at once. She was talented. My customers thought so, too. I would sell out of her work almost as soon as the pieces were delivered. These bowls are especially popular," she said, pointing to a tall, wide bowl with lots of small hollows in it. The bowl was enthroned on its own shelf.

"Did Gunilla talk much about her personal life?" asked Jacobsson.

"No. She was very reserved. We didn't have much personal contact. Usually we talked on the phone. Somebody else took care of the deliveries. She came to visit my shop once in the spring, and I was over on Gotland and saw her just a few weeks ago."

"What did the two of you do?"

"Well, I was staying at a hotel in Visby. There were several artists that I wanted to visit. One day I went out to her farm, and it was quite pleasant. We had lunch and looked at her workshop."

"You didn't notice anything out of the ordinary?"

"No, not at all."

"Did she tell you about any new people she had met, maybe a boyfriend?"

"No, but there was actually a young man who stopped by. We were just having lunch, and he didn't want to disturb her when she had visitors. He greeted me very politely at any rate, and we talked for a bit before he left."

"Do you remember his name?"

"His name was Henrik. I remember it well because that's my brother's name."

"What about his last name?"

"He didn't say."

"Did they seem to be close friends?"

"Well, that's hard to say. He just stopped by very briefly. I had the feeling that he lived nearby, that maybe he was a neighbor."

"How would you describe him?" asked Knutas.

"He was about her age. Tall and well built. Thick ash-blond hair. And he had especially beautiful eyes. I think they were green."

It's great how artists have such a keen sense of observation, thought Knutas. "Was there anything else you noticed?"

"Yes. Even though I had the feeling that he was a neighbor, he couldn't have come from När originally because he had a real Stockholm accent. I wouldn't bet five öre that he was from Gotland."

Knutas's cell phone rang. He heard Kihlgård's agitated voice saying that the clothing of the murdered women had been found by some young people in a fishing shack in Nisseviken.

Knutas quickly cut short the conversation, thanking the woman for her help. Then he and Jacobsson went back out to the street.

He told her about the clothes. "We might as well go back home," he said. "We've done just about everything we can here, and he's on Gotland. That much is clear."

A couple of hours later they were sitting on a plane, on their way back to Visby.

Emma hadn't slept well. She had the feeling that it was very early when she awoke. She glanced at the clock. Only five thirty.

Olle lay next to her. He seemed to be sound asleep. His mouth was wide open, and with every exhalation she could smell his bad breath. She got up and went into the bathroom. As she sat down to pee, the thought of Johan flitted past, but in the next second she pushed it aside. Everything was going to be fine between her and Olle now. She turned on the shower and enjoyed the feeling of the water washing over her body. She wrapped a bath towel around herself and went back to lie down beside Olle and put her head right next to his. *Of course I love him,* she thought at the same time as a tiny bit of doubt intruded. *He's my Olle, after all.*

How tired she was of herself! All this vacillating back and forth. Why couldn't she make up her mind about how she felt?

She sat up and looked at him. He was lying there, unaware that she was studying him, naked and as vulnerable as a child. Maybe she didn't love him anymore. Maybe it was over. The thought made her dizzy. The father of her children. But wasn't the whole point to be in love and cherish someone? She had given him her promise for life. To love him in sickness and in health. What about if she no longer felt attracted to him?

Her gaze slid over his forehead and eyelids. She wondered what was hidden inside, what his thoughts were.

What about the children? Their two wonderful children. As parents they had a responsibility that was as big as the universe.

And what about herself? What sort of person was she, to be willing to give up everything so hastily and risk her whole way of life? It was so perilous. How did she dare? It wasn't just a matter of her and Olle. This had to do with the future of her entire family. The children's future.

At the same time, the fact that she had fallen in love with Johan was making her rise and fall like a ship on a stormy sea.

She got up, went out to the kitchen, and lit a cigarette, even though it was only six fifteen. She didn't worry about the fact that she was smoking indoors. There would be time enough to air it out before the children came home.

Her thoughts shifted with each new puff. Maybe she should just wait. Accept her inner turmoil. She didn't have to make a decision right now. Better just to wait for a while. See how things went.

She didn't want to spend any more energy on thinking about her chaotic emotional life.

Suddenly her cell phone rang. She took it out of her purse and punched the button for text messages.

CAN'T SLEEP. CAN YOU? / JOHAN.

She went out on the steps and called him.

He answered at once. "Yes?"

A red flame spread from her head to her stomach and out into her arms to the very tips of her fingers.

"Hi. It's me. Emma."

"Hi. I miss you."

"I miss you, too."

"When can we meet?"

"I don't know. Olle is home right now. We had a talk. He's going back to be with the children today. They're at Olle's brother's house in Burgsvik. His parents are there, too."

"So we can meet, can't we?"

"I don't know. How?"

"If your husband is going to be away, you'll be alone. I can come out to see you."

"Here? No, that's impossible, you must realize that. We can't meet here at my house."

"Then you could come here."

"I can't keep sneaking around, scared to death that somebody will see me."

An idea popped into Emma's head. It was crazy, of course, but what the hell.

"I just remembered that I have to go out to my parents' house on Fårö one of these days. No one's there. They're away on a long vacation, and I promised to keep an eye on the house for them. I was thinking of taking along my friend Viveka and staying for a few days. You could come with me instead. I'd like to get out of here today. I'm going crazy here at home. I really need to get away. The house is right on the sea. It's an amazing place."

"What about your friend?"

"That's no problem. I'm sure that Viveka can come later. I'll talk to her. She actually knows about you."

"She does?" He felt his cheeks burning and couldn't help feeling flattered.

"That sounds great, but I can't stay for several days. I've got work to do, what with the latest murder and all. But one night should be all right, and I can start work a little later tomorrow. I won't be ready to leave until about six this evening, though."

"That doesn't matter. I'll go out there first."

Emma went back inside the house. The feeling of doom in her body was mixed with anticipation and a dose of guilt.

When Olle woke up, she served him breakfast in bed.

"I've come to a decision," she said. "I need time to think. I have to have some space. So much has been happening lately. I really don't know what to make of it all. I don't know what I want anymore."

"But last night you said . . ." He sounded disappointed.

"I know, but I'm still not sure," she apologized. "About us. I don't know what we have left anymore. Or maybe it's just everything with Helena and these murders. I need to get away."

"I understand," he said sympathetically. "I know this has been really rough on you. What are you going to do?"

"Well, first of all, I'm going out to my parents' house. I promised to keep an eye on it anyway. I'm going there today."

"Alone?"

"No. Viveka said she'd go with me. I've already talked to her." She felt a pang in her heart. Yet another lie. It was scary to see how easy it was to lie.

"I was hoping you'd come with me today, you know. What should I tell the kids?"

"Tell them the truth. That I have to go out and take care of their grandparents' house for a few days."

"Okay," said Olle. "I'm sure they'll understand, and you'll have a lot of time to spend together the rest of the summer."

She felt guilty that he was being so understanding. *It would almost be easier if he got mad,* she thought. A feeling of irritation rose inside her.

"Thanks, sweetheart," was all she said, giving him a quick hug.

Knutas had asked Kihlgård to call everyone in for a meeting at police headquarters that afternoon, after he and Jacobsson got back to Gotland. Knutas started the meeting.

"So we've found what we think are the clothes of the victims inside a fishing shack in Nisseviken. They're being analyzed right now by our techs before they're sent on to SCL. The shack has been cordoned off, and we're in the process of investigating who the owner is. It was apparently abandoned and hasn't been used in years. Family members are on their way here to identify the items of clothing. This discovery proves that the killer is probably here on Gotland, so we need to focus all our investigative work here from now on. In the meantime, what else have we found out that's new?"

"We received an answer today regarding the fingerprints on the asthma inhaler that was found on Gunilla Olsson's property," said Kihlgård. "There was no match with any prints in police records. We've checked to see who among the victims' circle of friends had asthma or some similar kind of respiratory allergy. It turns out that both Jan Hagman and Kristian Nordström suffer from asthma. Later today their inhalers will be compared with the one found at Gunilla Olsson's home."

"Good," said Knutas. "What did your interviews with them turn up?"

"Regarding the interview with Jan Hagman, we confronted him with the question of why he didn't tell us about the abortion when we were out at his place earlier. He gave us a reasonably credible explanation. He didn't think the abortion was of any importance to us. Also, his children don't know about his relationship with Helena Hillerström, so he didn't want to go into too many details. During the time we were there, he seemed terrified that his son might hear what we were talking about."

"I can understand that," said Knutas. "We should have asked him to come here instead. What about Nordström?"

"It seemed incomprehensible that he kept on stubbornly insisting that he never had any relations with Helena. When we told him about the letters, he caved in and admitted it at once. On the other hand, he couldn't explain why he had previously denied it. He just said that he didn't want to be considered a suspect."

"What else?"

"Witnesses have told us that a strange man was seen at Gunilla Olsson's house during the past few weeks. He was seen at her property both in the morning and in the evening, so it's not unlikely that we're talking about a boyfriend," Kihlgård continued. "The witnesses describe him as tall and good-looking, and about the same age as Gunilla."

"Have the witnesses had a look at any photographs? Of Kristian Nordström or Jan Hagman, for instance?"

"No, they haven't," Kihlgård admitted, a bit shamefaced.

"Why is that?"

"To be quite honest, I don't have a good answer for that. Does anyone else?" Kihlgård looked around at his colleagues.

"We just have to acknowledge that it's something we failed to do. It simply fell through the cracks," said Wittberg.

"See that it's done. Right after the meeting," said Knutas sternly. "What about the alibis for Nordström and Hagman? Have they been checked out again?"

"Yes," replied Sohlman, "and they seem to hold up."

"Seem to?"

"Hagman's alibi is based on statements from his son and a neighbor. The neighbor confirms that they were out emptying nets when the first murder was committed. When Frida Lindh was killed, Hagman's son was visiting him. Both claim to have been asleep at the time of the murder, since it happened in the middle of the night. When the last murder occurred, he was out fishing with the same neighbor who had been emptying nets with him before. That was on the night before Midsummer. After that they celebrated at the neighbor's house, and Hagman passed out on the couch."

"What about Nordström?"

"Apparently he has no alibi for the first murder," Sohlman went on. "He was at the party at Helena Hillerström's summer house until close to three in the morning. Then he shared a cab as far as Visby with

Beata and John Dunmar. Afterward, he continued on to his house. He arrived home just before four in the morning. He lives in Brissund. The taxi driver confirms that he got out of the cab at his house and that he was very drunk. It seems highly unlikely, to put it mildly, that he would then go back forty miles to the Hillerström cabin and wait on the beach to kill Helena. Besides, he flew to Copenhagen that very same day. He took a flight from Visby to Stockholm in the afternoon. And when the other two murders were committed, he wasn't even on Gotland. When Frida Lindh was killed, he was in Paris, and when Gunilla Olsson died, he was in Stockholm. No one saw Kristian Nordström in the Monk's Cellar on the night that Frida Lindh was killed. They should have recognized him. He could have waited for her on the way home. That's a possibility. On the other hand, the man that Frida was talking to at the bar still hasn't come forward, and that puts him at the top of the list of suspects. He was Swedish, and no one could have avoided hearing all the appeals for him to notify the police."

"Well, there could be other reasons why he hasn't come forward. Maybe he has something to hide that has nothing to do with all this," said Jacobsson.

"Sure, that's always possible," Sohlman admitted.

"The woman who sells Gunilla Olsson's pottery told us that she met a man about thirty-five years old at Gunilla's house. He was tall and good-looking," said Knutas. "He introduced himself as Henrik. He didn't have a Gotland accent. She said he sounded like a Stockholmer. Frida Lindh's women friends reported that the man Frida met at the Monk's Cellar was named Henrik. The bartender said that the man sitting with her at the bar spoke with a Stockholm accent. That doesn't necessarily mean that he's not from here. He could be from Gotland but moved to the mainland long ago. Maybe one of his parents is from the mainland. That could explain why he doesn't have a Gotland accent, or he may have disguised his accent so as not to be recognized. Of course it's also possible that he's from the mainland but knows the island well and is living over here at the moment. I'm leaning more toward the idea that we need to be looking for someone who's from the island. If we at least start with that idea, what do we know about the killer? His name may be Henrik. He's tall, and he wears a size 11½ shoe. He's between thirty and forty years old, and he suffers from asthma. There are only about fifty-eight thousand of us living here on the island. There can't be many who fit that description. By now we also have so much information from witnesses about this man that we should be able to create a sketch of him. Maybe it's time we did that."

"I disagree," said Kihlgård. "It would only start a panic."

A murmur of agreement was heard from several of those sitting around the table.

"Does anyone have a better suggestion?" asked Knutas, throwing out his arms. "All indications are that the murderer is here on the island. A serial killer, who might strike again at any time. We've found the clothing, but what else do we really have? We can't come up with any connection between the victims that seems to have any significance for the investigation. There are no witnesses to any of the murders. He struck when the victims were alone, and no one was nearby. In each instance, he disappeared fast as lightning. Nobody heard anything, nobody saw anything. At the same time, plenty of people must have seen him. He's been all over the island, for God's sake. Fröjel, Visby, När, Nisseviken. He's been to an inn and out at the beach; he's been walking around town and out at När. A sketch of him might make it possible for us to catch him quickly."

"That seems to be the only alternative," agreed Sohlman. "We have to do something extreme. He could kill again at any time. There was only a week between the last two murders. Maybe now it will be only a few days before he strikes again. We're running out of time."

"That's fucking crazy," thundered Kihlgård. "What do you think will happen when people see that sketch? They'll associate it with practically everyone they know. We'll be completely flooded with tips. It'll be sheer hysteria, I can promise you that. Then we'll be the ones responsible. And how are we going to find time to deal with it all? We already have our hands full trying to nail down this lunatic."

"What would we base the sketch on?" Jacobsson asked. "We have two witnesses who have seen a person who might be the perpetrator: the woman who sold Gunilla Olsson's pottery and the neighbor who noticed a man near her house. Then we have Frida Lindh's women friends, of course, who saw the man at the bar, but we still don't know if he could be the perp. That's just a suspicion. How much do their accounts coincide? And what happens if they're wrong? There are two big risks with using a sketch. First, the witnesses may have remembered things wrong, so we'll be putting out a picture that doesn't gibe with reality. Second, it's possible that they didn't see the killer at all. They may have seen someone else instead. I think the risks are too great to use a sketch. It seems stupid to resort to something so drastic right now."

"Drastic?" Knutas repeated, his voice filled with sarcasm. "Is it so strange that we need to resort to drastic measures in this case? We have three homicides on our hands. An entire island paralyzed with fear. Women who don't even dare stick their noses outside at the height of the summer heat, while practically the whole country is breathing down our necks. The prime minister is going to be calling us up next! We need to solve this thing. I want the killer caught within a week, whatever the cost. We're going to bring in a police artist right now and get him to put together a sketch. I want it publicized as soon as possible. I also want to bring in Hagman and Nordström immediately for more questioning. And I personally want to talk to everyone who was at the party at the Hillerström home. Every single one of them. The same goes for Frida Lindh's friends. How's it going with outlining the victims' lives? Have we gotten anywhere?"

Björn Hansson from the National Criminal Police was the one who answered. "We're working hard on that. Helena Hillerström moved to Stockholm when she was twenty, and it looks as if she never met Frida Lindh. Helena and Gunilla Olsson went to different high schools and middle schools and don't seem to have had any interests in common. We haven't been able to link Gunilla and Frida together, either. As everyone knows, Frida Lindh lived in Stockholm. Her real name was Anni-Frid, and her birth name was Persson. These things take time, and it's not easy now that it's summer. Every other person seems to be on vacation."

"I know, I know," said Knutas impatiently. "Keep digging into things and ratchet up the pace as much as possible. There's no time to lose."

After the meeting Knutas retreated to his office. He was furious at everyone and everything. He sat down at his desk. His shirt was sticking to him. Big patches of sweat had spread under his arms. He hated feeling so grubby. The heat they had all been longing for was already making him miserable. It made it hard to think, almost impossible to concentrate. More than anything, he would have liked to go home and take a long, cool shower and drink a couple of quarts of ice water. He stood up and pulled down the blinds. Police headquarters had no air-conditioning. It was considered too expensive to install, since it was needed on only a few days of the year. He was looking forward to the remodeling that was scheduled for the fall. He hoped they would have the good sense to install air-conditioning then. A person needed to be able to think, for God's sake, in order to solve a difficult homicide case.

Finding the clothing was at least a step forward. He would go out to see the shack later on. Right now it was best to let the techs do their work undisturbed. He began leafing through the folders containing transcripts of the interviews. Three folders: one for Helena Hillerström, one for Frida Lindh, and one for Gunilla Olsson. He had an uneasy feeling that various things in the investigation had simply passed him by. His visit to Stockholm had proved as much: the interview with Helena Hillerström's parents, the abortion that no one had mentioned before. What about the other interviews? He decided to go through all of the transcripts one more time, starting with the parents.

Gunilla Olsson didn't have any, and they still hadn't been able to reach her brother. He opened Frida Lindh's folder. Gösta and Majvor Persson. Gullvivegränd 38 in Jakobsberg. He had planned to see them in Stockholm, but the discovery of the clothing prevented him from doing so. He started reading. The interview seemed to be in order, but Knutas still wanted to talk to the parents himself.

The phone was picked up after four rings. A faint female voice could be heard on the other end. "The Persson residence."

He introduced himself.

"You'll have to speak to my husband," said the woman. Her voice was even fainter, bordering on inaudible. "He's out in the yard. Just a minute."

A moment later the husband picked up the phone. "Yes, hello?"

"This is Detective Superintendent Anders Knutas from Visby. I'm in charge of the investigation into the murder of your daughter. I know that you've been interviewed by the police, but I'd like to ask you a few more questions."

"Yes?"

"When did you last see your daughter?"

A brief pause.

The father replied in a toneless voice. "It was a long time ago. We didn't see each other very often, unfortunately. Our contact with her could have been better. We last saw each other when they were moving. The children wanted to see us."

Another pause that lasted a little longer.

Then the father spoke again. "But I spoke to her on the phone last week, when Linneas turned five. A man should be allowed to talk to his grandchildren on their birthdays at least."

"How did Frida seem at the time?"

"She sounded happy, for a change. She said that she was starting to like living on Gotland. It was hard for her at first. She didn't really want to move there at all. She did it for Stefan's sake. Typical that she should end up meeting a Gotlander. She hated Gotland. Never wanted to talk about the time when we lived there."

Knutas was speechless. He had a hard time taking in what the man on the other end had just said.

"Hello?" said the father after a few seconds.

"What did you say? You used to live on Gotland?" Knutas gasped.

"Yes, we moved over there to try it out, but we stayed only a few months."

"What were you doing here?"

"I worked for the military and was transferred to the P18 regiment. That was a long time ago. In the seventies. We rented out our house here in Jakobsberg, but we didn't like it there. Frida was especially unhappy. She kept skipping school and seemed completely changed at home. Impossible to deal with."

"Why didn't you mention this during the first police interview?" asked Knutas indignantly. He was having a difficult time checking his impatience.

"I don't know. It was for such a short time, and so long ago."

"What year did you live in Visby?"

"Let me see . . . Well, it must have been '78. It was unfortunate for Frida. She had to change schools in the middle of the semester in sixth grade. We moved at Easter time."

"How long did you live here?"

"We were planning to stay at least a year, but my wife developed cancer, and we wanted to move back to Stockholm to be near her family. We moved back home at the beginning of summer."

"Where did you live?"

"Hm, what was the name of the street? It was a short distance outside the wall, at any rate. Iris something. Irisdalsgatan. That's it."

"So Frida went to Norrbacka School?"

"That's right. That was the name of it."

After he hung up, Knutas grabbed his cell phone and called Kihlgård, who told him that he was just about to enjoy some lamb chops at the Lindgården Restaurant.

"Frida Lindh lived in Visby as a child."

"What did you say?"

"That's right. She lived here for a few months when she was in the sixth grade. Her father was in the military, and he was stationed in Visby."

"When was this?"

"It was in 1978. In the spring. She went to Norrbacka School, and they lived on Irisdalsgatan. That's in the same neighborhood as

Rutegatan, where Helena Hillerström lived. This could be the break-through we've been looking for."

"You're right. I'm leaving now."

"Good."

It didn't take long before the police determined that Gunilla Olsson had attended the same school. Frida Lindh was a year younger than the others, but she had started school at the age of six instead of seven. The police soon found the common denominator. The three murdered women had all been in the same sixth-grade class.

The weather seemed to be turning out the way the meteorologists had predicted. The sky was a threatening grayish black, and moving in from the west was a dark cloud cover that looked as if it held plenty of rain. Emma was standing at the bow of the car ferry, watching the island of Fårö come closer. The ride across the sound took only a few minutes, but she wanted to breathe in the sea air and enjoy the view. Fårö was her favorite place. She wasn't the only one drawn to this wild, bare island with its limestone sea stacks and long, sandy beaches. In the summer it was swarming with tourists.

Ten years ago, her parents had enormous luck when they bought the stone house up by Norsta Auren, a beach that stretched for several miles. A family friend knew the woman who wanted to sell the place. She would sell it only to someone from Gotland. Usually the few houses that were up for sale went to affluent Stockholmers. Many celebrities escaped to the island to find some seclusion—actors, artists, and politicians, not to mention Ingmar Bergman, who lived here year round. Without hesitation, her parents had moved out here from Visby. They had never regretted it for a second.

Emma stopped at the Konsum supermarket on the way to pick up some last-minute provisions. She glanced at the headlines for the evening papers as she went inside the store. Both of them had a big picture of the latest murder victim. The photo showed a woman about her own age with long dark hair in braids. Now they were publishing her name and a picture, too. Emma bought both papers. In the car she scanned the articles. A woman viciously murdered, just like the others. A sense of uneasiness filled her stomach. When she reached the house, she would read the papers in peace and quiet. She drove fast, taking the road to the northern part of Fårö. At the four-way stop near Sudersand, she turned left. She pulled in at the local bakery, where she always stopped when she was going to visit her parents. She chatted with the girls behind the counter. She knew everyone here.

The sky was growing darker.

When she turned off onto the last bumpy section of road and headed toward the sea where the house stood, she discovered a red Saab behind her. A lone man was at the wheel. A pair of binoculars lay on the dashboard. *Must be a birdwatcher,* she thought. The point near her parents' house was a popular haunt for ornithologists. When she parked outside the house, she saw the man turn around and drive back the way he had come. *So that's it, a birdwatcher with no sense of direction,* she thought.

Emma had just shut the door behind her when it started to rain. As she put down the grocery bags in the hallway, she saw a flash of lightning outside the window. Thunder rumbled, and the rain began pounding on the tin roof. Because of the storm, it was very dark inside.

The house smelled stuffy. Her parents had already been away for a week. She went out to the kitchen and cautiously tried to open a window, but the strong wind made it impossible. She set the bags on the kitchen bench and started filling up the cupboards. Good thing she had brought food, since there wasn't much in the house. Her parents were planning to be away for a long time. They would be traveling through China and India for three more weeks. After they both retired several years ago, they had taken one long trip each year.

Emma unpacked. First she would put all the food away in the kitchen, then put clean sheets on the double bed in her parents' room.

She was looking forward to Johan arriving. To spending a whole evening and a whole night with him. Eating dinner and breakfast together.

Her emotional life had been a roller coaster over the past few days. One minute she wanted to continue her secure life with Olle; the next she was ready to leave everything for Johan. It was true that she was in love with Johan, but what did she really know about him?

It was easy to fall in love in the summer, and the fact that they had to meet in secret undoubtedly added some spice to it. He didn't have to take any responsibility. He lived alone, had no children, and only had himself to think about. Of course it was easy for him. She had a whole family to consider, especially the children. Was she really prepared to destroy their whole life just because she was in love with someone else? How long would that love last?

Emma pushed these thoughts aside. She turned on the radio for a little music and then went upstairs to make the bed. She felt heat wash over her as she thought about what they would be doing in that bed later on.

Rain was pelting against the panes, but she couldn't resist opening the window to let in some fresh air. Up here it was better. The bedroom window faced the woods.

When she was through arranging things, she made some coffee, sat down at the kitchen table with a cigarette, and looked out.

A low stone wall surrounded the house. Looking over it, she had a clear view of the sea, which surged up and down in the wind. Here the beach was quite narrow. It grew wider the farther out you went on the point. At the very end, where the beach was widest, people often sunbathed in the nude. Many times she herself had run naked out into the sea, shrieking with joy, her voice drowned out by the roar of the waves.

Maybe we can go skinny-dipping tomorrow morning, she thought, *before Johan has to go to work.* If only the weather would improve.

Viveka had promised to come for lunch the next day. Emma didn't want to be alone.

She stood up and roamed through the house. It had been a long time since she had visited her parents. She didn't really have much contact with them. There had always been a certain distance between them, even when she was little. She had always felt as if she needed to achieve something to make them happy, and of course they had been pleased whenever she made a nice drawing, got all the answers right on a test, or performed well at a gymnastics tournament. The distance between Emma and her parents had not diminished any over the years, though, and by now it was impossible to bridge. She found it so difficult to act natural in their company. She usually felt guilty because she didn't call or visit them enough. At the same time, she thought that since they were retired and had oceans of time, they could show a greater interest in coming to visit her. They could help out with the children, maybe take them on an outing or go to Pippi Longstocking Land, which the kids loved. She and Olle seldom had time for that. Whenever her parents finally did come to visit, they would sit glued to the sofa and expect to be waited on. They would often make comments about how messy things were in the house or say that the children needed haircuts. It was exhausting, but she couldn't see any way to change the situation. Her parents wouldn't stand for any criticism, and if she ever challenged them, they just became defensive. It always ended with her father getting mad.

The living room looked the way it always did. A sofa with floral upholstery and an antique table from one of the countless auctions that her parents loved to go to. The fireplace probably hadn't been used in a while. It had been neatly swept clean. She was pleased to find firewood in a basket next to the hearth.

The wooden stairs up to the second floor creaked. She went into the guest room, which she and her sister, Julia, counted as their own. This was where they always slept when they visited their parents, staying among the things that they had left behind when they moved out.

She sat down on the bed. It smelled even more stuffy in here, and dustballs had collected in the corners.

The bookshelves that covered one wall were filled with books. Her gaze swept over the spines. *Kitty, The Five of Us, Children 312,* the horse books about Britta and Silver, *Kulla-Gulla,* and her mother's old childhood books. She pulled one off the shelf and giggled at the language and the cover. It was a drawing of a slender young woman with red lips and a kerchief just about to hop into a sports car with a dark, Ken-doll kind of man at the wheel. *Obstacles to Love* was the sensational title.

That might very well apply to me, she observed dryly.

She found a thick stack of well-thumbed issues of *Starlet* and *The Story of My Life.* Emma smiled to herself when she recalled how she and her sister had devoured them, discussing the gripping fates that befell these young girls. On another shelf stood a row of old photo albums. For a long time she sat looking at pictures from her childhood. Birthdays, riding camp, last days of school. With her friends at the beach, at a barbecue on a summer evening, and with her mother and father and Julia at Gröna Lund amusement park in Stockholm. Helena was in a lot of the pictures, too.

There they were: as thin eleven-year-olds at the beach; when they were thirteen at a class party, wearing far too much eyeliner; and then in the choir, neatly lined up. Happy girls who loved horses and went to riding school. Dressed in white for confirmation. Ladylike and glittering in long dresses for their senior prom.

Her eye fell on a stack of old school yearbooks. She pulled one out and looked up the class that she and Helena had belonged to.

CLASS 6A it said at the top. Below was a photo of the school, the principal, and their teacher, then photographs of their classmates, each with a name underneath. *How young we were,* she thought. Some were childish-looking, with round, rosy cheeks. Others were pale, with bored expressions. A few had the early traces of a teenager's complexion. Some of the girls wore makeup, and the downy upper lips of some of the boys bulged faintly from the snuff they used. She looked at herself, at the very bottom of the page, since her maiden name, Östberg, came last in the alphabet. And Helena. So sweet, with her dark hair hiding half her face. She was staring straight into the camera with a solemn expression.

She moved her index finger from one picture to the next. Ewa

Ahlberg, Fredrik Andersson, Gunilla Broström. Her finger stopped on the blond girl with a shawl around her neck, peering at the photographer from under her bangs.

Gunilla Broström. She had just seen that face on a grown-up. It was the woman in the newspapers. The same Gunilla who had been murdered. Emma dashed down to the kitchen to get the evening papers. It was definitely her. Back then she had blond hair, but it was the same face. She had forgotten about Gunilla. They hadn't been especially good friends.

Both Gunilla and Helena had fallen victim to the same killer.

In the next second, when it became clear to her what they had in common, she felt as if she had been struck on the head.

Anni. *Where is Anni-Frid? She must be Frida . . .* It couldn't be true. Her eyes searched through the faces . . . Why wasn't Anni there? *Oh, that's right, she didn't arrive until the spring. From Stockholm. Then they moved back. We called her Anni, even though her name was Anni-Frid,* thought Emma. She realized that it must be the same person.

All three in the same class. Now she was the only gang member left.

The girls who belonged to the gang weren't all friends. She and Helena were best friends, of course, but then that oddball Gunilla joined in along with the newcomer, Anni. Something made the four of them decide to gang up together and torment him. It didn't go on for very long, maybe a few months. It started rather innocently, just a little teasing and some shoving. Then it got worse and worse. They egged each other on. Everyone took part, but Helena was the one who took the lead. It was really the only thing they had in common: persecuting him. Maybe Gunilla and Anni saw the harassment as a way of being friends with her and Helena, who were considered the tough girls at school. Maybe it was their way of being included in the gang.

That wasn't what happened. Summer vacation arrived, and they all scattered. Anni moved back to Stockholm, and Emma never saw her again. Only Emma and Helena ended up in the same class in middle school. For them, the harassment didn't mean a thing. After that summer, all four of the girls had presumably forgotten all about it.

He apparently had not.

Her hands were shaking as she turned the pages in the yearbook. A couple of pages farther on. Class 6C. She scanned the faces. There he was. The fifth picture from the left.

His round face was pale and solemn, with the hint of a double chin. Short, cropped hair. It was him. He was the common denominator.

A great wave of nausea welled up inside her. She hardly had time to react before she threw up violently on the floor.

Just then the phone rang. The ringing echoed stubbornly through the house.

Instead of answering, she went into the bathroom to clean herself up. She felt so dizzy that she was weak in the knees. He had killed them, one after another. Now she was the only one left.

The phone rang again. She stumbled down the stairs.

It was Johan.

"Hi. It's me. I got done early. I'm leaving now."

Emma couldn't get a word out.

"What is it? What's wrong?"

She sank down onto the floor with the receiver pressed to her cheek. She whispered the words.

"I figured out the connection between the victims. All of them were in the same class in sixth grade. In my class . . . We were in a girl gang that harassed a boy in one of the other classes. He must be the murderer. One time we stuffed his underpants in his mouth. Just like he did to the others. He killed them all except for me. Do you understand? I'm next in line. What if he's here? I might be overreacting, but there was a car driving behind me on the last part of the road out to the house. Then it just turned around. There was a man driving it."

"What kind of car was it?"

"An old Saab. I think it was red, and—"
That was as far as she got. The line went dead.

The shower had just started spraying cold water over his shampooed hair when his cell phone rang. Knutas had taken a break and gone home to eat. He was taking a cold shower to try to clear his mind. Now he heard his wife answering his phone.

It took only twenty seconds before she was pounding on the bathroom door.

"Anders, Anders, come out here! You have to take this. It's urgent!"

He turned off the shower, tore open the door, and reached for the phone. His wife grabbed a towel and helped dry him off while he listened. There was an agitated voice on the other end.

"This is Johan Berg from Regional News. Send cars and people over to Fårö. Right now! Emma Winarve is over there all alone at her parents' house, and she thinks the murderer is after her. That he might be there right now. She figured out the connection. All the victims were in the same sixth-grade class. They were in a gang that tormented a boy in another class. He's killed all of them except her."

"What the hell are you saying?"

"Emma is positive that it's the boy they tormented. He's the killer. They once stuffed his underpants in his mouth."

"What's his name?"

"I don't know. She didn't have time to tell me. We got cut off. But she thinks he's out there right now. A car was following her all the way up to the house. Then it disappeared. It was an old Saab. It was red. You have to go out there right now. I'm on my way myself."

"Where on Fårö?"

Johan read off the directions that Emma had given him. "You drive past Ekeviken and the sign for Skär. Then you come to an abandoned ice cream stand. Turn left onto the forest road leading out to the sea. Drive until the road ends. That's where the house is."

"Wait for us," said Knutas calmly. "Don't go out there ahead of us."

"Like hell I will. Get out there, and do it fast." Johan hung up.

Knutas punched in the number for the duty officer.

"Send three cars to Fårö. Now! The killer we've been looking for is probably out there. Notify the local police in Fårösund and tell them to go up to Norsta Auren and take along weapons and bulletproof vests. The suspect is believed to be driving an older-model red Saab. Tell them to leave immediately. I'll have further instructions later. Block off the ferry, at least on the Fårö side, until we get there. No one leaves the island. Understood? I'll call Jacobsson. You get hold of Wittberg and Norrby. Tell them to contact me. I want them over on Fårö, too. And someone needs to get hold of Olle Winarve. Tell him to call me."

Knutas hung up and then punched in the number for Jacobsson's cell phone.

"Anders here. Where are you?"

"Shopping at Hemköp."

"Leave your groceries and go out and wait on Norra Hansegatan. On the same side as police headquarters. I'll pick you up."

"What's going on?"

"I'll tell you later."

Knutas pulled on his underwear and pants. His wife didn't ask any questions. She just held out his bulletproof vest and his service pistol. He didn't need to say anything, and he was grateful for that.

A minute later he was sitting in his car with the blue light on, the siren wailing, and shampoo in his hair.

Carefully he washed his hands. Rubbing them over and over with the soap. He wanted to feel totally clean when it was time. He had taken a long, hot shower, washed his hair, and shaved. Really squandered the hot water that his parents were always so stingy about. Then he took out a shirt, pants, and tie and dressed with care.

His mother had given him the tie for Christmas. It was perfect for the occasion. He was alone in the house. His father was out fishing with a neighbor. His mother had gone out shopping, but she would be back soon.

He heard the gravel crunching as the car turned into the yard. He was totally calm. He had prepared carefully. Everything he needed was in the box. Neat and tidy.

He looked in the mirror, pleased with what he saw. A man in his prime who is finally taking control of his own life, *he thought before he closed the bathroom door and went downstairs to meet his mother.*

She had her arms full of bags.

"Why didn't you come out to the car and help me?" she said reproachfully. "Didn't you hear me drive up? You must have known I'd have a lot to carry."

She didn't even look at him as she spoke. She didn't notice all the trouble he'd taken to look nice. She just took off her shoes, hung up her ugly old coat on the hook in the hallway, and started carrying in the bags. Her usual reproachful martyr voice, full of self-pity. He just stood there, staring at her in silence. He always disappointed her. It had been that way ever since he could remember. Her expectations never matched up with reality. She always demanded something more from him. A little extra. He had never felt that his mother was completely satisfied with anything he did. On the other hand, she had always favored his sister. His little sister. Everything always went so well for her. She never quarreled, never caused any trouble. She got good grades in school, had lots of friends, and never whined or complained. All these years he had longed for a warm hug and unconditional love. A mother who placed no demands on him, who was simply there. That was something he had never had. Instead, she had shut him out and constantly looked for faults. He had made great efforts, he had tried, but things never really worked out. She had no idea that he was harassed and tormented. He had shut it all inside and felt ashamed, and he bore all of it alone. He had never felt that he could confide in anyone.

His mother blamed him for her own shortcomings. It was because of him that she hadn't been able to fulfill her dream of becoming a nurse.

He had to suffer because his mother was unhappy with her own life. Because she couldn't get a good job. Because she didn't love her husband. She had shriveled up into a bitter, dried-up woman, full of self-pity.

Had she ever taken responsibility for anything? For her own life? For her children? For him?

Hatred welled up inside him, blocking out all thoughts as she muttered and unpacked the groceries.

What a wretched person she was. Now he couldn't wait any longer. He took three long strides toward her and grabbed her from behind.

"What are you doing?" she cried as he held her as if in a vise.

He pulled out a piece of rope that he had in his pocket and tied her hands behind her back. Then he dragged her out into the hall, used his elbow to press down the door handle, and lugged her across the yard and into the barn. She was kicking and screaming. She bit his hand so hard that he started to bleed. He didn't notice the pain. He didn't say a word. Now he was in control. He held on to her as he picked up the thick rope that he had prepared that morning. It was already tied into a noose and firmly attached to one of the beams in the roof. He gripped her wrists hard and forced her to spread out her fingers and touch the chair before he hauled her up onto it. He climbed onto a ladder next to the chair and made her touch the beam and the rope with the noose, knots and all.

When that was done, she just stood there, staring at him with a look of astonishment on her face, the noose around her neck. She had fallen silent, and her lower lip was quivering. How ugly she is, he observed coldly, and then checked the noose one last time.

Then he positioned himself right in front of her and looked at her. His eyes were filled with contempt. He felt a peace inside that he had never felt before. A total sense of calm that filled him like warm milk.

Without hesitating, he kicked away the chair.

The line was dead. Why had they been cut off? True, the phone service had gone down before in bad weather. Or had the wire been cut? That thought terrified Emma. She had to get hold of her cell phone.

It was out in the kitchen. She dashed out there and punched in Johan's number without getting through. The reception was poor out here, of course. Damn it. What if the killer was nearby? He couldn't have come inside the house; she would have heard him. It would take Johan more than an hour to get here. Maybe an hour and a half.

She remembered that she had opened a window in the bedroom, and she ran upstairs to close it. When she leaned out to grab hold of the window latch, she saw him. He was standing on the other side of the wall, just outside the yard. She knew it was him even though she didn't recognize him. He looked up at her. She had time to notice that he was wearing dark clothing before she swiftly drew back behind the curtains.

She wouldn't have a chance against him. Quickly she went out of the bedroom to look around for something she could use as a weapon.

Johan must have called the police, she thought. *I just need to fend him off until they get here.* But how the hell was she going to do that?

He was undoubtedly on his way in, now that he had seen her. The greatest chance of finding some kind of weapon would be in the kitchen. At least there were knives. She had just made up her mind to venture downstairs when she heard the front door open.

It occurred to her that she had forgotten to lock it. How could she not have locked the door? She cursed herself.

Her eyes fell on her sister's baseball bat that stood leaning against the wall in a corner of the guest room. Julia had brought it home with her after spending a year as an exchange student in the United States. It had never been used before, but right now it might come in handy.

Tingstäde, Lärbro, and then full speed ahead for Fårösund. Knutas glanced again at the clock on the instrument panel. The minutes were ticking away at the speed of a rocket. He had spoken to the two local police officers from Fårösund, who were much too slow for his liking. They were now up by the four-way stop at Sudersand and had just turned off for Ekeviken and Skär. The fact that the rain was coming down like a wall in front of the car and obscuring his view didn't make the driving any easier. It was six fifteen in the evening, and as luck would have it, there were very few cars on the road. Jacobsson was sitting next to him with her cell phone pressed to her ear, busy filling Kihlgård in on the latest developments.

They had tried many times to get in touch with Emma on the cell phone. A recorded voice kept stubbornly repeating that it was not possible to reach the desired number at the present time. Please try later. The phone at the house was dead as a doornail.

Knutas drove fast, his eyes fixed on the main road that led to Fårösund. They had to reach Emma Winarve in time. He floored the accelerator and stared hard through the rain curtain on the windshield, taking the curves as fast as he could.

Jacobsson ended her phone conversation.

"Kihlgård is on his way with several others from the team. They're right behind us. This is horrible," she said, looking at him.

"How many are on their way to the house?"

"The two local officers, who should be there soon, and then the two of us and three other cars. About ten in all. Everyone has a bulletproof vest except me."

"You'll have to stay outside and keep watch," said Knutas. "If only he doesn't get there before us. But we need more manpower. We might have to set up a roadblock. Call and ask for more backup. Tell them to bring the dogs, too. And then there's that crazy TV journalist, who's on his way out there. I tried to stop him, but now he's not answering his phone, either. If only he doesn't make a mess of the whole thing."

The Bunge Museum appeared on the right-hand side, and right after that they reached Fårösund.

At the ferry dock they found the area cordoned off by police tape and guarded by several part-time firemen at the request of the local police. Knutas gratefully greeted them. Immediately afterward the ferry, which had been waiting for them, was on its way across the sound.

The thunder and rain were gone. Emma was standing behind the door to the guest room. She couldn't think of any other place to hide. She could hear the faint sound of music coming from the radio down-stairs. She wished she could just slip inside the wall and disappear. Her muscles were tensed, and she was concentrating on trying to hold her breath. The faces of her children flitted past her mind's eye. She wanted to cry but controlled herself.

Suddenly she heard the familiar creaking of the stairs. Cautiously she peeked out at the hall through the slit in the door. Her heart was pounding so hard that she thought it must be audible. She saw his hand. It was gripping a shaft of wood. An axe. A trembling sob escaped her. She bit her own hand to make herself keep still. The man went into her parents' bedroom. In a flash she made up her mind. Out into the hall and two big leaps down the stairs before he was after her. She stumbled and fell headlong onto the living room floor. He grabbed her ankle when she tried to stand up. With a howl she turned over and managed to land a direct hit on his hand with the baseball bat. He screamed and released his grip long enough for her to get to her feet.

Sobbing, she stumbled out to the hall and headed for the front door. She grabbed the door handle, but the door was locked, and she couldn't get it open before he was on her. He grabbed her by the hair and dragged her backward into the kitchen.

"You fucking slut," he snarled. "You bitch, you fucking bitch. Now I'm going to make you beg. You disgusting whore."

He shoved her into a sitting position, keeping one hand in a tight grip on her throat.

"Now it's your turn, you little slut. Now it's your turn, goddamn it."

His face, only a few inches away from hers, was dark with rage. His breath smelled of mint, which reminded her of something. Her paternal grandfather. He smelled the same way. Throat lozenges. Big, white, and transparent, the kind that you could suck on forever. They came in a brown paper bag. Grandfather was always offering them to everyone.

Just as he raised the axe in the air and took aim, he loosened his grip on her throat slightly. Somehow she summoned up great strength. With a bellow she used both hands to tear his hand away from her throat and at the same time slammed him down to the floor. She landed on top of him and bit his cheek so hard that she could taste blood in her mouth. This time she managed to get the door open and flee outside.

She ran toward the stone wall and threw herself over it. Now she was down on the beach. She cursed the light and kept going. The sand was hard packed, which made it easy to run. And she was used to running. She had gone out jogging here hundreds of times before. When she had gone some distance, she couldn't help looking back to see how close he was. To her surprise she discovered that he wasn't there at all. She stopped and looked around in bewilderment. Not a soul as far as the eye could see.

He must have been more hurt than I thought, she told herself. Relieved, she kept on running toward the lighthouse. There were usually people around there. If only she could reach it, she would be safe. It wasn't yet in sight. First she had to round the point of the shore, and that was still a good distance away. She was now running at a more even pace. It was almost ghostly on the beach. Completely deserted. All she heard was the panting of her own breath and the gentle thudding of her own feet.

On the last stretch of shoreline the sand was replaced by stones. She almost fell but kept her balance. When she reached the other end of the beach, she was completely exhausted. Sweat was running down her back. No one seemed to be there, but soon she'd be up on the road, and then safety wouldn't be far away.

On the path to the lighthouse she allowed herself to take a little breather. The small cluster of houses near the lighthouse looked deserted. She continued running toward the parking lot and discovered a car parked at the edge of the woods.

When she got closer, she saw that it was a red Saab.

All her running had been in vain.

She managed to think that he must have gotten in the car and driven to the lighthouse, and then the blow struck her on the back of the head.

Two police officers were standing outside the house when Johan finally reached it. Emma was nowhere in sight. He parked his car outside the wall and went into the yard.

"My name is Johan Berg. I'm a journalist," he said, and showed them his press card. "I'm a friend of Emma Winarve. Where is she?"

"We don't know. The house is empty, and we're waiting for reinforcements. You'll have to leave the area immediately, sir."

"Where's Emma?"

"I told you, we don't know," said one of the officers sternly.

Johan turned on his heel and ran around the wall of the house, heading down toward the shore.

He ignored the police, who were shouting after him. As soon as he reached the beach, he saw tracks in the sand. Very visible footprints.

He ran in Emma's tracks, rounded the point, and saw the lighthouse. The footprints continued. With relief he observed that the tracks were still from only one person. She must have gone to the lighthouse to seek help. But where was the killer?

He looked up at the raised grassy berm that ran along the beach before the woods took hold. He might have been following her from up there. He would have a good view from there, too.

Exhausted and out of breath, Johan reached the lighthouse and headed up the path toward the parking lot.

"Emma," he shouted.

No answer. No cars in the parking lot, and he couldn't see any people, either. Where had she gone?

He tried to make out any tracks in the grass, but there was nothing distinct. Instead, he continued along the deserted asphalt road. Silent and desolate, with woods on both sides. He looked at the nearby houses. No sign of life. The sound of an engine suddenly came closer, and he turned around.

A police car stopped with screeching brakes, and out climbed Knutas and Jacobsson.

"Have you seen or heard anything?" Knutas demanded.

"No, but I saw some tracks in the sand, and I think they're Emma's. They led this way."

Knutas's cell phone rang. The conversation was brief.

"Jens Hagman is probably the murderer," he reported after hanging up. "Jan Hagman's son. They found him in the school records. He's the same age as the victims. He was in another sixth-grade class. His father, Jan Hagman, owns a red 1987 Saab. And it's missing."

Jacobsson stared at him in surprise. "It was the son?" she exclaimed. "Why didn't we figure that out earlier!"

"Not now," snapped Knutas. "We'll have time for self-reproaches later on. Right now we've got to catch him."

The main road that led to the ferry dock was blocked off at several places. The police set up a temporary base at the Sudersand campgrounds. A search party of officers with dogs started combing the wooded area between Skärsände and the lighthouse. Olle Winarve arrived.

After talking to Grenfors back in Stockholm, Johan called Peter. Of course they had to report on what was happening. At the same time, his concern for Emma was practically tearing him apart.

It was when he found the letter that he decided to kill Helena. He was sitting in his mother's bedroom. His parents had had separate rooms for years. He didn't see anything strange about that. He had never seen them hug or give each other any other sign of affection. His mother was hanging out there in the barn. It would be a while before his father came home. He had several hours to go through things in her room before he would have to call the police and report that he had found his mother dead. He pulled open the drawers in her dresser and systematically went through them. Old pieces of paper with almost illegible notes, receipts, photographs of that stupid cat that his mother had loved. She loved the cat more than us, *he thought bitterly. A few ugly pieces of jewelry, a thimble, ballpoint pens with ink that had dried up.* How long ago was it that she went through these drawers herself? *he thought with annoyance.*

Then he found something that caught his interest. At the very bottom of one of the drawers lay a crumpled envelope, yellow with age. He read what it said on the front: To Gunvor.

It was his father's handwriting. He frowned and opened the envelope. It was only a one-page letter. There was no date.

Gunvor

I've been up all night, thinking, and now I'm prepared to tell you what's been going on with me lately. I know that you've been wondering what has happened, even though, as usual, you haven't said a word.

The truth is that I've met someone else. I think this is the first time in my life that I've understood what real love is. It's not something that I planned. It just happened, and there was nothing I could do to prevent it.

We've been seeing each other for six months. I thought that it might just be something fleeting that wouldn't last, but it's turned out to be just the opposite. I love her with all my heart, and I've decided that I want to share my life with her. She's also pregnant. I want to take care of her and our child.

We both know that you've never loved me. So many times I've been surprised and frightened by your coldness. Both toward me and toward the children. It's over now. I've found someone that I love. She's one of my students. Her name is Helena Hillerström. By the time you find this letter, I'll be living in an apartment in town. I'll call you later.

Jan

He crumpled up the letter as the tears streamed from his eyes. Helena Hillerström, of all people. It was easy for him to make up his mind.

Emma woke up because she was freezing. It was dark, and the air was dripping with moisture. She was lying on something hard and cold. It took a few minutes for her eyes to grow accustomed to the darkness. A narrow strip of light was seeping in through an opening higher up on one wall. She was inside what seemed to be an underground room. The floor and walls were cement, and the room was bare except for two benches attached on either side. She was lying on one of them. She estimated that the room was about eight feet square. The sloping ceiling was low and made the space seem even more cramped. It was no more than seven feet to the highest point. There was no door. Instead, there was an iron hatch in the ceiling. A rusty iron ladder was fastened to the wall and led up the hatch. She realized that she must be imprisoned inside one of the old defense bunkers. There were a number of them on Gotland and Fårö. She and her friends used to play in them when they were kids.

Her throat was dry, and she had a sour taste of vomit in her mouth. She also had a throbbing ache at the back of her head. She wanted to touch it to see if it was bleeding, but that turned out to be impossible. Her hands and feet were tied tight with rope. Her eyes swept over the damp gray walls. The hatch in the ceiling was the only way out, and it was closed. Probably locked on the outside. What was she doing here? Where was Hagman? And why hadn't he killed her at once? The fact that she was still alive made her think that maybe there was still hope. The rope was chafing her skin. She had no idea what time it was or how long she had been lying here. Her body felt stiff and tender. With some effort she managed to sit up. She raised herself up, trying to look out the small opening, but she couldn't do it. She tried to twist her hands around, but the rope made that almost impossible. She could move her feet only a few inches.

Emma listened for any noise, but no sounds seemed to penetrate from outside. The room was almost completely silent. Leaves rustled on the floor. A brown-spotted frog had slipped inside the bunker. Then she noticed another one. Several moths were up on the ceiling, asleep. The air was musty and raw.

She lay down again and closed her eyes, hoping the aching would stop. She needed to be able to think clearly.

Suddenly there was a rattling noise. The hatch in the ceiling was lifted away. A pair of legs became visible, and a man climbed down into the bunker. It was Jens Hagman.

He gave her a cold stare as he held a bottle of water to her lips.

With his help she greedily took several big swallows without daring to look up at him. Afterward, she sat there without uttering a word. She didn't know what to do, but she was determined to be on guard, to see how he would react.

He sat down on the bench across from her. He had closed the hatch, and the room was once again almost totally dark. She could hear him breathing in the dim light. Finally she broke the silence.

"What are you planning to do?"

"Shut up. You have no right to talk."

He leaned back against the wall and closed his eyes.

"I need to pee," she whispered.

"What the hell do I care?"

"Please. I'm going to pee my pants."

Reluctantly he got up and loosened the rope. She had to squat down and pee as he looked on. When she was done, he tied her up again. He glared at her and then climbed back up the ladder and was gone.

The hours passed. She lay on her side on the bench, slipping in and out of sleep. Dreams mixed with thoughts. She couldn't distinguish one thing from another. Occasionally a thick blanket of apathy settled over her. She was in his hands. There was nothing she could do. She might as well just lie down and die. Finish out her days in this bunker on Fårö. Then images of her children would flash past, like bits of crystal. Sara and Filip. The last time she had seen them was out at the home of Olle's brother in Burgsvik. She pictured the children waving to her at the gate as she drove away. Would that be the last time they ever saw each other?

Her joints ached, and her hands were prickling. They were about to go numb. She held them up toward the narrow strip of light. The tight rope had turned her wrists red. She decided to try thinking constructively and sat up again. What options did she have? Could she try to overpower him when he opened the hatch next time? Hardly. He was much bigger than she was, and there was nothing she could use as a weapon. She wondered where this bunker was located. Presumably far from the nearest house, although at this time of the summer there were always people around—people taking walks and hiking through the woods and the fields, taking advantage of Sweden's legal right of access to private land. She looked up at the narrow slit in the wall. Should she try screaming? Hagman might be right outside. She guessed that he must be staying in his car. What did she have to lose if he heard her? She was probably still alive because he needed her to make his escape from here. That meant the police were out there, searching for her. As long as they stayed on Fårö, he couldn't kill her.

Her legs were tied as tightly as they had been before. It was hard for her to move, but she managed. She succeeded in reaching the opposite wall. She stretched up as close to the opening as she could and began screaming for help at the top of her lungs. She kept on shouting until she was worn out. Then she sat down on the bench and waited, her eyes stubbornly fixed on the opening. The minutes ticked by. Not a sign from Hagman or anyone else. She repeated the process until she couldn't do it anymore.

She lay down again. Maybe it was better to try some sort of strategy. To talk to him. Ask him to forgive her. Convince him that she was sorry.

Yes, that's what she should do.

TUESDAY, JUNE 26

Anders Knutas was sitting in the barrackslike building that served as a cafeteria and store for the Sudersand campgrounds. He had a cup of coffee and a cheese sandwich in front of him.

It was six thirty in the morning, and Emma Winarve was still missing. The police had arrested the father, Jan Hagman, at his home and taken him to headquarters. They didn't know whether he was involved in the murders or not, but they didn't want to take any chances.

Worry was gnawing at Knutas. Was Emma still alive? Hagman ought to be somewhere on Fårö. Travel by ferryboat had been halted at an early stage, and the main road to the ferry was blocked off. He couldn't possibly have left the island, except by means of his own boat. Knutas considered that possibility most unlikely. The police had been combing Fårö's coast. Which way could he have gone? There was no archipelago and no islands close by where he might have found refuge. He couldn't have made it to Gotska Sandön or the mainland without being discovered. The only possibility was that he might have traveled in his own boat and gone ashore somewhere along the Gotland coast. No, that seemed preposterous.

So we have to assume he's still here on the island, thought Knutas, sucking on a sugar cube as he poured coffee into the saucer. Whenever he was alone, he drank from the saucer, just like his father. He slurped up the coffee with the sugar cube between his teeth.

As far as they knew, Jens Hagman had no friends or relatives on the island. According to his father, the family didn't know anyone on Fårö, although they had spent a lot of time there when the children were growing up. Several summers they had rented a cabin in

Ekeviken. *That means that Hagman knows the area well,* thought Knutas.

In the northern section of the island, a search had been made of all the houses, barns, cabins, cottages, tents, and camping trailers. The process was still going on.

Could he be hiding somewhere else? Of course it was possible that he was hiding outdoors, but that was unlikely. The risk of being discovered was too great. Could he have an accomplice? Certainly, although that, too, seemed unlikely. He had killed three women in a matter of a few weeks. Who would want to help him? He was a madman who might do anything at all.

She had worked out several alternative plans by the time the hatch was opened once again. Hagman was carrying a knife.

"Please, don't hurt me," she begged as he climbed down to the floor to stand in front of her.

He was holding the knife in his hand. The blade gleamed in the dim light.

Hagman looked at her with an inscrutable expression on his face. "Why shouldn't I hurt you?"

"I understand why you killed the others. It was terrible, what we did to you."

"You don't understand a thing," he snarled, and his eyes blazed with anger.

The only weapon she had was her power of persuasion. She went on. "I know that it was unforgivable, and I've thought of contacting you so many times. I wanted to ask you to forgive me. I'm so sorry. But we were just kids."

"Just kids," he snorted with contempt. "That's easy for you to say. My life has been hell because of what all of you did to me. I've always been so damned afraid. Because of you, I could never meet any girls, I never dared have any kind of contact with people, and I've been so fucking lonely. *Just kids,*" he repeated, his voice filled with scorn. "You knew what you were doing. My whole life was destroyed because of you. Now it's your turn to pay."

Emma desperately tried to think of something more to talk about, to win time, but she was also terrified that she might provoke him.

"So why did you decide not to kill me?" she asked.

"Don't think it's just some lucky coincidence. I've planned out everything very carefully."

"What do you mean?"

"I wanted to take out everybody who ever tormented me, one by one, starting with the worst of the lot. After I did that, it was time to go after Helena."

"What?"

For a moment her terror subsided slightly and was replaced by surprise.

He looked at her in the dark. "My so-called mother. Everyone thinks she took her own life."

He laughed mirthlessly.

"The police are such fools. They swallowed the whole scenario. But I did it. I killed her, and I enjoyed doing it. She had no right to live. A mother who gives birth to children she doesn't care about at all. What kind of mother is that?" Jens Hagman's voice had grown more shrill. He was practically screaming. It felt as if the air in the bunker might give out.

"So she didn't care about you?" Emma whispered, in an attempt to calm him down.

"I'm a botched abortion just walking around. That's what I've always been. Unwanted," he said harshly. "But that bitch ended up paying for it. She certainly did," he said triumphantly as he stared at her.

She couldn't help seeing the madness in his eyes.

The thought struck her with all its force. There was no way out. She was never going to see her children again. She made the utmost effort not to start crying, not to lose control.

At that moment, the faint sound of a helicopter was heard. Hagman gave a start and listened intently.

"Don't move, or I'll kill you instantly," he snarled. "And keep quiet."

The helicopter seemed to be circling right overhead. Suddenly Knutas's voice sounded through a megaphone.

"Jens Hagman! This is the police. We know you're down there. You might as well give yourself up. We've got you surrounded, and we've taken your car. You don't have a chance. The best thing you can do is surrender. Come out with your hands over your head!"

Hagman dragged Emma off the bench with such force that she almost fell over. He was holding the knife to her throat as he backed up toward the opening in the wall. He peered out. Emma caught a glimpse of the sea. It was clear that he was confused. He was cornered, and that made him even more dangerous. She wished he would ease up his hold on her throat.

For a moment there was silence.

Then the voice shouted through the megaphone again.

"Hagman! This is the police speaking. You don't have a chance. Come out with your hands over your head!"

Jens Hagman acted fast and decisively. He cut the rope off Emma's ankles, pushed up the hatch, and shoved her up the ladder ahead of him. He was right behind her. Warm air greeted her at the top. Emma saw her chance to escape. She would exit before he did. The ladder was so narrow and the bunker's opening so small that it would be impossible for both of them to emerge at the same time. When she was almost above ground and about to take the last step up and out of the bunker, she kicked with all her might at Hagman below her on the ladder. The kick struck him in the face, and he started swearing. The next moment she felt his hand around one of her ankles, and she tumbled to the ground outside.

Her attempt to escape was over even before it began.

Hagman snarled into her ear, "Try another trick like that and you're dead. Just so you know."

She squinted up at the morning light and let her gaze take in as much as it could from her trapped position. They were at the edge of the woods, with the sea on one side and green-clad hills on the other, surrounded by police officers with weapons drawn. On a slope a short distance away stood Anders Knutas with the megaphone in his hand.

Hagman held her in front of him like a shield.

"Everybody, get away! Otherwise I'm going to kill her, right here and now. I only want the superintendent to stay. I want a car with a full tank of gas and a hundred thousand kronor in a bag in the car. Plus food and water, enough for three days. If you don't do as I say, I'll slit her throat. Do you understand? And it has to be fast! If I don't get the car within two hours, I'll kill her."

Knutas lowered the hand holding the megaphone. A minute passed. Then, "We'll do what you ask," he shouted back.

He turned to a colleague standing next to him, and they exchanged a few words. Five minutes later all the officers were gone. Hagman hadn't moved from his position. Emma saw the sea and some gulls flying over the water, poppies in bloom, blueweed, almond blossoms, and chicory. It was all so beautiful that it hurt. Again she thought about her children. Their summer vacation had begun, but here she stood. Only an inch from death.

Knutas was talking on his cell phone. When he finished the conversation, he began shouting toward them. "We have a problem with securing the money so quickly. We need more time."

The hold on Emma's throat tightened.

"I don't give a shit about your problems. Get the money here. You have exactly one hour and fifty minutes left. Or else she dies!"

As if to emphasize his words, he nicked Emma's throat so the blood ran. She didn't even feel the pain.

Almost two hours later a green Audi drove up onto the road a hundred yards away from where they stood. An officer climbed out.

Knutas shouted to Hagman. "The car has a full tank of gas. The keys are in the ignition."

The officer lifted out a suitcase, which he opened to show them the contents. He held up some bundles of bills.

"And inside the suitcase is a hundred thousand kronor in hundred-krona bills," shouted Knutas. "Along with food and water. Just like you wanted."

"Good," screamed Hagman in reply. "Move at least two hundred yards away from the car. I want safe passage to the ferry. It's going to take us across to Fårösund. Otherwise she dies," he repeated.

"Understood," shouted Knutas.

Jens Hagman shoved Emma in front of him toward the car. He kept his eyes moving constantly in all directions.

The engine howled. Then the Audi swung around, and the next instant they were out on the road heading for Fårösund.

Thoughts were racing through Emma's mind. She had to do something. As soon as they shook off the police, he was going to kill her. She was certain of that. They were already approaching the ferry. She could tell by the markings on the asphalt of the road.

Hagman slowed down. There was the ferry, waiting. She could see the captain up in the wheelhouse. A sailor stood on deck to cast off.

Then everything started happening at breakneck speed.

Police cars came rushing from all directions. Jens Hagman reacted with lightning speed and steered around them. Officers tried to yank open the doors but were knocked away as Hagman sharply turned the Audi. A short distance up the hill, he ran into more police cars. He drove off the road and continued cross-country, weaving among the juniper bushes and boulders. He lost control of the car, and Emma managed to scream before they smashed right into a pine tree. The sound of the crash was tremendous. She was flung into the windshield, which shattered. An explosion of glass rained down on her. She managed to see Hagman getting out and taking off. Thick clouds of smoke billowed up around her. She opened the car door with her foot, threw herself out, and collapsed onto the ground.

Karin Jacobsson saw the car from far away. Then she could make out Emma lying on the ground next to the car. Hagman was running away from it. She pulled her pistol out of the holster and snapped off the safety.

"Hagman!" she yelled to the other officers. "There he is!"

At the same moment, Jens Hagman saw her. He started running for the woods. Behind her, Jacobsson could hear voices shouting to each other. She held her gun up and aimed at Hagman's legs, racing after him.

"Halt!" she commanded.

Instead, he disappeared behind an old windmill.

Jacobsson slowed down. She knew that he was armed. He might easily overpower her if she wasn't prepared.

Cautiously she slipped around the side of the windmill. She heard a sound and turned around. Suddenly Hagman was on her. They rolled around on the ground. The crack of the shot that went off was deafening. The body on top of hers went limp.

When Emma woke up in Visby Hospital, it took a moment before she remembered what had happened. Then the images came back, one by one. The bunker. Knutas with the megaphone. Hagman holding the knife to her throat. Then the crash.

She opened her eyes. Blinked. Two blurry figures were standing next to the bed. Someone was sitting on a chair farther away.

"Mamma," said a small voice.

It was Filip. Now she could see him clearly. His face was thin and pale, his eyes shiny. A second later he was in her arms, and Sara was right behind him.

"My dear sweet children. Everything's going to be fine now," Emma comforted them. Out of the corner of her eye she saw her husband get up from his chair and come toward her.

He sat down on the edge of the bed and took her hands in his. It was over. Finally over.

A nurse came in and explained that they would have to come back tomorrow. They hugged her one more time.

Emma realized how tired she was. She had to sleep. She would just get up to pee. Her whole world had been turned upside down. The time she had spent imprisoned in the bunker with Hagman felt like an eternity. That was what she thought as she listened to the stream of urine splashing into the toilet. She washed up, drank a glass of water, and went back to her room.

Next to the bed stood a vase with daisies and cornflowers. A card was attached to one of the stems. She smiled as she read what it said. It was from Knutas. He told her to get well soon and said he would call her the following day.

She crawled into bed and straightened her pillow. Her body was black and blue, and she had a headache. Right now all she wanted was to go to sleep.

As she was about to turn off the light on the nightstand, her eyes fell on a vase of yellow roses that stood on the windowsill.

With an effort, she got out of bed and found an envelope stuck in the bouquet. The card was from Johan. It said, "Do you want to have a potato patch with me?"

Knutas took a long puff on his pipe, which gave him a terrible coughing fit. Normally he hardly ever smoked. He spent most of the time just fussing with his pipe, filling it and sucking on the stem, but not lighting it. A very effective way to avoid lung cancer. Over the past few days, though, he had started smoking like never before. In half an hour the investigative team was going to meet to go over the dramatic events that had shaken all of Gotland this summer.

Knutas reviewed them in his mind.

As he was sitting in the barracks at the Sudersand campgrounds, his colleague Lars Norrby had called from Visby. He reported that one of Gunilla Olsson's neighbors had identified Jens Hagman as the man who was seen at Gunilla's house during the weeks before the murder. *So that's how cold-blooded he was,* thought Knutas. He had made a point of getting to know Gunilla before he killed her.

It was Knutas himself who came up with the idea that Jens Hagman might be hiding in one of the old defense bunkers on Fårö. There were lots of them on the island. When the police began searching the northwest section of Fårö, it didn't take long before they found Hagman's car in the woods. The Saab was scantily covered with juniper branches, but it was so sheltered that it was hard to see from the air.

Knutas blamed himself for the fact that the drama ended with Hagman being fatally shot.

Karin Jacobsson went into shock and had to spend several days in the hospital. She had never even wounded anyone before. Now she was at risk of being accused of dereliction of duty and possibly manslaughter. The investigation, which would be carried out by the internal affairs division of the police, would have to prove it. Actually Knutas was entirely to blame. He was in charge of the operation. Maybe things would have turned out differently if they hadn't agreed to Hagman's demands. If they had called in a negotiator. Or if they had stormed the bunker.

He gave a big sigh. It was impossible to say.

He had thought a lot about Hagman. His whole life had been colored by hatred, which had developed so strongly during his childhood. It turned out to have affected all his dealings with women. He had never managed to have any sort of long-term relationship. He lived alone and had a hard time establishing social contacts. He had quit his studies at the university and worked as a ticket collector in Stockholm's subway system. Even his relationship with his sister was strained. They had never been good friends, in spite of the fact that the age difference between them was only a few years.

Their parents had done nothing to see to it that the sister and brother maintained any kind of contact. The mother had always favored the daughter. The father, Jan Hagman, had cared less and less about his family as time went on. He had retreated into himself. Just like the mother. Neither of them had noticed what was happening with their son—the torments he was subjected to, his loneliness, or the anxiety he felt. The result was devastating.

The children had been like two isolated islands floating through life, without support or help from anyone. Both had to deal with their own problems and their own emotions. There was no sense of unity, no family solidarity.

In some ways, Knutas could understand Jens Hagman. A person

didn't necessarily have to be mentally ill to commit murder. It was sometimes enough to be seriously abused.

The issue of poor parental contact was woven like a red thread through the entire murder investigation. It was the same with the victims. Helena Hillerström, Frida Lindh, and Gunilla Olsson had all had strained relationships with their parents. Knutas had a feeling that it was the same with Emma Winarve. It was one thing that both the victims and the perpetrator had in common. He wondered what the turning point was that pushed him over the edge.

Knutas got up and looked out across the sun-drenched parking lot. A ladybug was crawling along the windowsill. He let it climb onto his finger and opened the window.

It spread its wings and flew away.

ACKNOWLEDGMENTS

This story is entirely fiction. Any similarities between the characters in this novel and real individuals are coincidental. The settings described in the book are as they appear in real life, with a few exceptions. Occasionally I have taken the liberty of changing things for the sake of the story. For instance, I closed the local TV newsroom on Gotland and moved the coverage from Gotland to Stockholm. The only reason for this is that it provided a better way for me to tell the story. I am a great admirer of Swedish Television's regional news program, Östnytt's Gotland coverage, and their local team on Gotland, which does exist in reality. Any errors that may have slipped in are my own.

First and foremost, I want to thank my husband, journalist Cenneth Niklasson, for his critiques, ideas, and inspiration while I was working on this book. He is my greatest and most constant supporter.

My thanks also to Gösta Svensson, a former detective superintendent of police in Visby, for his invaluable assistance with the police work; Anna-Maja Persson, a journalist at Swedish Television, for her continual encouragement and pep talks; Martin Csatlos of the forensic medicine division in Solna; Johan Gardelius, a crime technician with the Visby police; Mats Wihlborg, district prosecutor in Visby; Claes Kullberg and Peter Sandström, in Gotland County; Berit Nicklasson, my mother-in-law, in Sanda; and Conny Niklasson, in Visby, for photographic assistance.

Thanks to my teachers for their valuable input: Lena Allerstam, Lilian Andersson, and Bosse and Kerstin Jungstedt.

Thanks to my Swedish editor, Ulrika Åkerlund, for all her help with this book, and to my publisher at Bonniers, Jonas Axelsson, who believed in me.

Last but not least, I thank my children, Rebecka and Sebastian, for their great patience with their mother's writing.

Mari Jungstedt
Älta, April 2003